The Life

Charlotte Bronte

Volume 2

Elizabeth Cleghorn Gaskell

CHAPTER I.

During this summer of 1846, while her literary hopes were waning, an anxiety of another kind was increasing. Her father's eyesight had become seriously impaired by the progress of the cataract which was forming. He was nearly blind. He could grope his way about, and recognise the figures of those he knew well, when they were placed against a strong light; but he could no longer see to read; and thus his eager appetite for knowledge and information of all kinds was severely balked. He continued to preach. I have heard that he was led up into the pulpit, and that his sermons were never so effective as when he stood there, a grey sightless old man, his blind eyes looking out straight before him, while the words that came from his lips had all the vigour and force of his best days. Another fact has been mentioned to me, curious as showing the accurateness of his sensation of time. His sermons had always lasted exactly half an hour. With the clock right before him, and with his ready flow of words, this had been no difficult matter as long as he could see. But it was the same when he was blind; as the minute-hand came to the point, marking the expiration of the thirty minutes, he concluded his sermon.

Under his great sorrow he was always patient. As in times of far greater affliction, he enforced a quiet endurance of his woe upon himself. But so many interests were quenched by this blindness that he was driven inwards, and must have dwelt much on what was painful and distressing in regard to his only son. No wonder that his spirits gave way, and were depressed. For some time before this autumn, his daughters had been collecting all the information they could respecting the probable success of operations for cataract performed on a person of their father's age. About the end of July, Emily and Charlotte had made a journey to Manchester for the purpose of searching out an operator; and there they heard of the fame of the late Mr. Wilson as an oculist. They went to him at once, but he could not tell, from description, whether the eyes were ready for being operated upon or not. It therefore became necessary for Mr. Brontë to visit him; and towards the end of August, Charlotte brought her father to him. He determined at once to undertake the operation, and recommended them to comfortable lodgings, kept by an old servant of his. These were in one of numerous similar streets of small monotonous-looking houses, in a suburb of the town. From thence the following letter is dated, on August 21st, 1846:---

"I just scribble a line to you to let you know where I am, in order that you may write to me here, for it seems to me that a letter from you would relieve me from the feeling of strangeness I have in this big town. Papa and I came here on Wednesday; we saw Mr. Wilson, the oculist, the same day; he pronounced papa's eyes quite ready for an operation, and has fixed next Monday for the performance of it. Think of us on that day! We got into our lodgings yesterday. I think we shall be comfortable; at least our rooms are very good, but there is no mistress of the house (she is very ill, and gone out into the country), and I am somewhat puzzled in managing about provisions; we board ourselves. I find myself excessively ignorant. I can't tell what to order in the way of meat. For ourselves I could contrive, papa's diet is so very simple; but there will be a nurse coming in a day or two, and I am afraid of not having things good enough for her. Papa requires nothing, you know, but plain beef and mutton, tea and bread and butter; but a nurse will probably expect to live much better; give me some hints if you can. Mr. Wilson says we shall have to stay here for a month at least. I wonder how

Emily and Anne will get on at home with Branwell. They, too, will have their troubles. What would I not give to have you here! One is forced, step by step, to get experience in the world; but the learning is so disagreeable. One cheerful feature in the business is, that Mr. Wilson thinks most favourably of the case."

"August 26th, 1846.

"The operation is over; it took place yesterday Mr. Wilson performed it; two other surgeons assisted. Mr. Wilson says, he considers it quite successful; but papa cannot yet see anything. The affair lasted precisely a quarter of an hour; it was not the simple operation of couching Mr. C. described, but the more complicated one of extracting the cataract. Mr. Wilson entirely disapproves of couching. Papa displayed extraordinary patience and firmness; the surgeons seemed surprised. I was in the room all the time; as it was his wish that I should be there; of course, I neither spoke nor moved till the thing was done, and then I felt that the less I said, either to papa or the surgeons, the better. Papa is now confined to his bed in a dark room, and is not to be stirred for four days; he is to speak and be spoken to as little as possible. I am greatly obliged to you for your letter, and your kind advice, which gave me extreme satisfaction, because I found I had arranged most things in accordance with it, and, as your theory coincides with my practice, I feel assured the latter is right. I hope Mr. Wilson will soon allow me to dispense with the nurse; she is well enough, no doubt, but somewhat too obsequious; and not, I should think, to be much trusted; yet I was obliged to trust her in some things. . . .

"Greatly was I amused by your account of ------'s flirtations; and yet something saddened also. I think Nature intended him for something better than to fritter away his time in making a set of poor, unoccupied spinsters unhappy. The girls, unfortunately, are forced to care for him, and such as him, because, while their minds are mostly unemployed, their sensations are all unworn, and, consequently, fresh and green; and he, on the contrary, has had his fill of pleasure, and can with impunity make a mere pastime of other people's torments. This is an unfair state of things; the match is not equal. I only wish I had the power to infuse into the souls of the persecuted a little of the quiet strength of pride---of the supporting consciousness of superiority (for they are superior to him because purer)---of the fortifying resolve of firmness to bear the present, and wait the end. Could all the virgin population of ------ receive and retain these sentiments, he would continually have to veil his crest before them. Perhaps, luckily, their feelings are not so acute as one would think, and the gentleman's shafts consequently don't wound so deeply as he might desire. I hope it is so."

A few days later, she writes thus: "Papa is still lying in bed, in a dark room, with his eyes bandaged. No inflammation ensued, but still it appears the greatest care, perfect quiet, and utter privation of light are necessary to ensure a good result from the operation. He is very patient, but, of course, depressed and weary. He was allowed to try his sight for the first time yesterday. He could see dimly. Mr. Wilson seemed perfectly satisfied, and said all was right. I have had bad nights from the toothache since I came to Manchester."

All this time, notwithstanding the domestic anxieties which were harassing them--- notwithstanding the ill-success of their poems---the three sisters were trying that other literary venture, to which Charlotte made allusion in one of her letters to the Messrs. Aylott. Each of them had written a prose tale, hoping that the three might be published together. "Wuthering Heights" and "Agnes Grey" are before the world. The third---Charlotte's contribution---is yet in manuscript, but will be published shortly after the appearance of this memoir. The plot in itself is of no great interest; but it is a poor kind of interest that depends upon startling incidents rather than upon dramatic development of character; and Charlotte Brontë never excelled one or two sketches of portraits which she had given in "The Professor", nor, in grace of womanhood, ever surpassed one of the female characters there described. By the time she wrote this tale, her taste and judgment had revolted against the exaggerated idealisms of her early girlhood, and she went to the extreme of reality, closely depicting characters as they had shown themselves to her in actual life: if there they were strong even to coarseness,---as was the case with some that she had met with in flesh and blood existence,---she "wrote them down an ass;" if the scenery of such life as she saw was for the most part wild and grotesque, instead of pleasant or picturesque, she described it line for line. The grace of the one or two scenes and characters, which are drawn rather from her own imagination than from absolute fact stand out in exquisite relief from the deep shadows and wayward lines of others, which call to mind some of the portraits of Rembrandt.

The three tales had tried their fate in vain together, at length they were sent forth separately, and for many months with still-continued ill success. I have mentioned this here, because, among the dispiriting circumstances connected with her anxious visit to Manchester, Charlotte told me that her tale came back upon her hands, curtly rejected by some publisher, on the very day when her father was to submit to his operation. But she had the heart of Robert Bruce within her, and failure upon failure daunted her no more than him. Not only did "The Professor" return again to try his chance among the London publishers, but she began, in this time of care and depressing inquietude, in those grey, weary, uniform streets; where all faces, save that of her kind doctor, were strange and untouched with sunlight to her,---there and then, did the brave genius begin "Jane Eyre". Read what she herself says:---"Currer Bell's book found acceptance nowhere, nor any acknowledgment of merit, so that something like the chill of despair began to invade his heart." And, remember it was not the heart of a person who, disappointed in one hope, can turn with redoubled affection to the many certain blessings that remain. Think of her home, and the black shadow of remorse lying over one in it, till his very brain was mazed, and his gifts and his life were lost;---think of her father's sight hanging on a thread;---of her sister's delicate health, and dependence on her care;---and then admire as it deserves to be admired, the steady courage which could work away at "Jane Eyre", all the time "that the one-volume tale was plodding its weary round in London."

I believe I have already mentioned that some of her surviving friends consider that an incident which she heard, when at school at Miss Wooler's, was the germ of the story of Jane Eyre. But of this nothing can be known, except by conjecture. Those to whom she spoke upon the subject of her writings are dead and silent; and the reader may probably have noticed, that in the correspondence from which I have quoted, there has been no allusion whatever to the publication of her poems, nor is there the least hint of the intention of the sisters to publish any tales. I remember, however, many little particulars which Miss Brontë gave me, in answer to my inquiries respecting her mode of composition, etc. She said, that it was not every day, that she could write. Sometimes weeks or even months elapsed before she felt that she had anything to add to that portion of her story which was already written. Then, some morning, she would waken up, and the progress of her tale lay clear and bright before her, in distinct vision, when this was the case, all her care was to discharge her household and filial duties, so as to obtain leisure to sit down and write out the incidents and consequent thoughts, which were, in fact, more present to her mind at such times than her actual life itself. Yet notwithstanding this "possession" (as it were), those who survive, of her daily and household companions, are clear in their testimony, that never was the claim of any duty, never was the call of another for help, neglected for an instant. It had become necessary to give Tabby---now nearly eighty years of age---the assistance of a girl. Tabby relinquished any of her work with jealous reluctance, and could not bear to be reminded, though ever so delicately, that the acuteness of her senses was dulled by age. The other servant might not interfere with what she chose to consider her exclusive work. Among other things, she reserved to herself the right of peeling the potatoes for dinner; but as she was growing blind, she often left in those black specks, which we in the North call the "eyes" of the potato. Miss Brontë was too dainty a housekeeper to put up with this; yet she could not bear to hurt the faithful old servant, by bidding the younger maiden go over the potatoes again, and so reminding Tabby that her work was less effectual than formerly. Accordingly she would steal into the kitchen, and quietly carry off the bowl of vegetables, without Tabby's being aware, and breaking off in the full flow of interest and inspiration in her writing, carefully cut out the specks in the potatoes, and noiselessly carry them back to their place. This little proceeding may show how orderly and fully she accomplished her duties, even at those times when the "possession" was upon her.

Any one who has studied her writings,---whether in print or in her letters; any one who has enjoyed the rare privilege of listening to her talk, must have noticed her singular felicity in the choice of words. She herself, in writing her books, was solicitous on this point. One set of words was the truthful mirror of her thoughts; no others, however apparently identical in meaning, would do. She had that strong practical regard for the simple holy truth of expression, which Mr. Trench has enforced, as a duty too often neglected. She would wait patiently searching for the right term, until it presented itself to her. It might be provincial, it might be derived from the Latin; so that it accurately represented her idea, she did not mind whence it came; but this care makes her style present the finish of a piece of mosaic. Each component part, however small, has been dropped into the right place. She never wrote down a sentence until she clearly understood what she wanted to say, had deliberately chosen the words, and arranged them in their right order. Hence it comes that, in the scraps of paper covered with her pencil writing which I have seen, there will occasionally be a sentence scored out, but seldom, if ever, a word or an expression. She wrote on these bits of paper in a minute hand, holding each against a piece of board, such as is used in binding books, for a desk. This plan was necessary for one so short-sighted as she was; and, besides, it enabled her to use pencil and paper, as she sat near the fire in the twilight hours, or if (as was too often the case) she was wakeful for hours in the night. Her finished manuscripts were copied from these pencil scraps, in clear, legible, delicate traced writing, almost as easy to read as print.

The sisters retained the old habit, which was begun in their aunt's life-time, of putting away their work at nine o'clock, and beginning their study, pacing up and down the sitting room. At this time, they talked over the stories they were engaged upon, and described their plots. Once or twice a week, each read to the others what she had written, and heard what they had to say about it. Charlotte told me, that the remarks made had seldom any effect in inducing her to alter her work, so possessed was she with the feeling that she had described reality; but the readings were of great and stirring interest to all, taking them out of the gnawing pressure of

6

daily-recurring cares, and setting them in a free place. It was on one of these occasions, that Charlotte determined to make her heroine plain, small, and unattractive, in defiance of the accepted canon.

The writer of the beautiful obituary article on "the death of Currer Bell" most likely learnt from herself what is there stated, and which I will take the liberty of quoting, about Jane Eyre. "She once told her sisters that they were wrong---even morally wrong---in making their heroines beautiful as a matter of course. They replied that it was impossible to make a heroine interesting on any other terms. Her answer was, 'I will prove to you that you are wrong; I will show you a heroine as plain and as small as myself, who shall be as interesting as any of yours.' Hence 'Jane Eyre,' said she in telling the anecdote: 'but she is not myself, any further than that.' As the work went on, the interest deepened to the writer. When she came to 'Thornfield' she could not stop. Being short-sighted to excess, she wrote in little square paper-books, held close to her eyes, and (the first copy) in pencil. On she went, writing incessantly for three weeks; by which time she had carried her heroine away from Thornfield, and was herself in a fever which compelled her to pause."

This is all, I believe, which can now be told respecting the conception and composition of this wonderful book, which was, however, only at its commencement when Miss Brontë returned with her father to Haworth, after their anxious expedition to Manchester.

They arrived at home about the end of September. Mr. Brontë was daily gaining strength, but he was still forbidden to exercise his sight much. Things had gone on more comfortably while she was away than Charlotte had dared to hope, and she expresses herself thankful for the good ensured and the evil spared during her absence.

Soon after this some proposal, of which I have not been able to gain a clear account, was again mooted for Miss Brontë's opening a school at some place distant from Haworth. It elicited the following fragment of a characteristic reply:---

"Leave home!---I shall neither be able to find place nor employment, perhaps, too, I shall be quite past the prime of life, my faculties will be rusted, and my few acquirements in a great measure forgotten. These ideas sting me keenly sometimes; but, whenever I consult my conscience, it affirms that I am doing right in staying at home, and bitter are its upbraidings when I yield to an eager desire for release. I could hardly expect success if I were to err against such warnings. I should like to hear from you again soon. Bring ------ to the point, and make him give you a clear, not a vague, account of what pupils he really could promise; people often think they can do great things in that way till they have tried; but getting pupils is unlike getting any other sort of goods."

Whatever might be the nature and extent of this negotiation, the end of it was that Charlotte adhered to the decision of her conscience, which bade her remain at home, as long as her presence could cheer or comfort those who were in distress, or had the slightest influence over him who was the cause of it. The next extract gives us a glimpse into the cares of that home. It is from a letter dated December 15th.

"I hope you are not frozen up; the cold here is dreadful. I do not remember such a series of North-Pole days. England might really have taken a slide up into the Arctic Zone; the sky looks like ice; the earth is frozen; the wind is as keen as a two-edged blade. We have all had severe colds and coughs in consequence of the weather. Poor Anne has suffered greatly from asthma, but is now, we are glad to say, rather better. She had two nights last week when her cough and difficulty of breathing were painful indeed to hear and witness, and must have been most distressing to suffer; she bore it, as she bears all affliction, without one complaint, only sighing now and then when nearly worn out. She has an extraordinary heroism of endurance. I admire, but I certainly could not imitate her." . . . "You say I am to 'tell you plenty.' What would you have me say? Nothing happens at Haworth; nothing, at least, of a pleasant kind. One little incident occurred about a week ago, to sting us to life; but if it gives no more pleasure for you to hear, than it did for us to witness, you will scarcely thank me for adverting to it. It was merely the arrival of a Sheriff's officer on a visit to B., inviting him either to pay his debts or take a trip to York. Of course his debts had to be paid. It is not agreeable to lose money, time after time, in this way; but where is the use of dwelling on such subjects? It will make him no better."

"December 28th.

"I feel as if it was almost a farce to sit down and write to you now, with nothing to say worth listening to; and, indeed, if it were not for two reasons, I should put off the business at least a fortnight hence. The first reason is, I want another letter from you, for your letters are interesting, they have something in them; some results of experience and observation; one receives them with pleasure, and reads them with relish; and these letters I cannot expect to get, unless I reply to them. I wish the correspondence could be managed so as to be all on one side. The second reason is derived from a remark in your last, that you felt lonely, something as I was at Brussels, and that consequently you had a peculiar desire to hear from old acquaintance. I can understand and sympathise with this. I remember the shortest note was a treat to me, when I was at the above-named place; therefore I write. I have also a third reason: it is a haunting terror lest you should imagine I forget you---that my regard cools with absence. It is not in my nature to forget your nature; though, I dare say, I should spit fire and explode sometimes if we lived together continually; and you, too, would get angry, and then we should get reconciled and jog on as before. Do you ever get dissatisfied with your own temper when you are long fixed to one place, in one scene, subject to one monotonous species of annoyance? I do: I am now in that unenviable frame of mind; my humour, I think, is too soon over-thrown, too sore, too demonstrative and vehement. I almost long for some of the uniform serenity you describe in Mrs. ------'s disposition; or, at least, I would fain have her power of self-control and concealment; but I would not take her artificial habits and ideas along with her composure. After all I should prefer being as I am. . . You do right not to be annoyed at any maxims of conventionality you meet with. Regard all new ways in the light of fresh experience for you: if you see any honey gather it." . . . "I don't, after all, consider that we ought to despise everything we see in the world, merely because it is not what we are accustomed to. I suspect, on the contrary, that there are not unfrequently substantial reasons underneath for customs that appear to us absurd; and if I were ever again to find myself amongst strangers, I should be solicitous to examine before I condemned. Indiscriminating irony and faultfinding are just sumphishness, and that is all. Anne is now much better, but papa has been for near a fortnight far from well with the influenza; he has at times a most distressing cough, and his spirits are much depressed."

So ended the year 1846.

CHAPTER II.

The next year opened with a spell of cold dreary weather, which told severely on a constitution already tried by anxiety and care. Miss Brontë describes herself as having utterly lost her appetite, and as looking "grey, old, worn and sunk," from her sufferings during the inclement season. The cold brought on severe toothache; toothache was the cause of a succession of restless miserable nights; and long wakefulness told acutely upon her nerves, making them feel with redoubled sensitiveness all the harass of her oppressive life. Yet she would not allow herself to lay her bad health to the charge of an uneasy mind; "for after all," said she at this time, "I have many, many things to be thankful for." But the real state of things may be gathered from the following extracts from her letters.

"March 1st.

"Even at the risk of appearing very exacting, I can't help saying that I should like a letter as long as your last, every time you write. Short notes give one the feeling of a very small piece of a very good thing to eat,---they set the appetite on edge, and don't satisfy it,---a letter leaves you more contented; and yet, after all, I am very glad to get notes; so don't think, when you are pinched for time and materials, that it is useless to write a few lines; be assured, a few lines are very acceptable as far as they go; and though I like long letters, I would by no means have you to make a task of writing them. . . . I really should like you to come to Haworth, before I again go to B------. And it is natural and right that I should have this wish. To keep friendship in proper order, the balance of good offices must be preserved, otherwise a disquieting and anxious feeling creeps in, and destroys mutual comfort. In summer and in fine weather, your visit here might be much better managed than in winter. We could go out more, be more independent of the house and of our room. Branwell has been conducting himself very badly lately. I expect, from the extravagance of his behaviour, and from mysterious hints he drops (for he never will speak out plainly), that we shall be hearing news of fresh debts contracted by him soon. My health is better: I lay the blame of its feebleness on the cold weather, more than on an uneasy mind."

"March 24th, 1847.

"It is at Haworth, if all be well, that we must next see each other again. I owe you a grudge for giving Miss M------ some very exaggerated account about my not being well, and setting her on to urge my leaving home as quite a duty. I'll take care not to tell you next time, when I think I am looking specially old and ugly; as if people could not have that privilege, without being supposed to be at the last gasp! I shall be thirty-one next birthday. My youth is gone like a dream; and very little use have I ever made of it. What have I done these last thirty years? Precious little."

The quiet, sad year stole on. The sisters were contemplating near at hand, and for a long time, the terrible effects of talents misused and faculties abused in the person of that brother, once their fond darling and dearest pride. They had to cheer the poor old father, into whose heart all trials sank the deeper, because of the silent stoicism of his endurance. They had to watch over his health, of which, whatever was its state, he seldom complained. They had to save, as much as they could, the precious remnants of his sight. They had to order the frugal household with increased care, so as to supply wants and expenditure utterly foreign to their self-denying natures. Though they shrank from overmuch contact with their fellow-beings, for all whom they met they had kind words, if few; and when kind actions were needed, they were not spared, if the sisters at the parsonage could render them. They visited the parish-schools duly; and often were Charlotte's rare and brief holidays of a visit from home shortened by her sense of the necessity of being in her place at the Sunday-school.

In the intervals of such a life as this, "Jane Eyre" was making progress. "The Professor" was passing slowly and heavily from publisher to publisher. "Wuthering Heights" and "Agnes Grey" had been accepted by another publisher, "on terms somewhat impoverishing to the two authors;" a bargain to be alluded to more fully hereafter. It was lying in his hands, awaiting his pleasure for its passage through the press, during all the months of early summer.

The piece of external brightness to which the sisters looked during these same summer months, was the hope that the friend to whom so many of Charlotte's letters are addressed, and who was her chosen companion, whenever circumstances permitted them to be together, as well as a favourite with Emily and Anne, would be able to pay them a visit at Haworth. Fine weather had come in May, Charlotte writes, and they hoped to make their visitor decently comfortable. Their brother was tolerably well, having got to the end of a considerable sum of money which he became possessed of in the spring, and therefore under the wholesome restriction of poverty. But Charlotte warns her friend that she must expect to find a change in his appearance, and that he is broken in mind; and ends her note of entreating invitation by saying, "I pray for fine weather, that we may get out while you stay."

At length the day was fixed.

"Friday will suit us very well. I DO trust nothing will now arise to prevent your coming. I shall be anxious about the weather on that day; if it rains, I shall cry. Don't expect me to meet you; where would be the good of it? I neither like to meet, nor to be met. Unless, indeed, you had a box or a basket for me to carry; then there would be some sense in it. Come in black, blue, pink, white, or scarlet, as you like. Come shabby or smart, neither the colour nor the condition signifies; provided only the dress contain E------, all will be right."

But there came the first of a series of disappointments to be borne. One feels how sharp it must have been to have wrung out the following words.

"May 20th.

"Your letter of yesterday did indeed give me a cruel chill of disappointment. I cannot blame you, for I know it was not your fault. I do not altogether exempt ------ from reproach. . . . This is bitter, but I feel bitter. As to going to B------, I will not go near the place till you have been to Haworth. My respects to all and sundry, accompanied with a large amount of wormwood and gall, from the effusion of which you and your mother are alone excepted.---C. B.

"You are quite at liberty to tell what I think, if you judge proper. Though it is true I may be somewhat unjust, for I am deeply annoyed. I thought I had arranged your visit tolerably comfortable for you this time. I may find it more difficult on another occasion."

I must give one sentence from a letter written about this time, as it shows distinctly the clear strong sense of the writer.

"I was amused by what she says respecting her wish that, when she marries, her husband will, at least, have a will of his own, even should he be a tyrant. Tell her, when she forms that aspiration again, she must make it conditional if her husband has a strong will, he must also have strong sense, a kind heart, and a thoroughly correct notion of justice; because a man with a WEAK BRAIN and a STRONG WILL, is merely an intractable brute; you can have no hold of him; you can never lead him right. A TYRANT under any circumstances is a curse."

Meanwhile, "The Professor" had met with many refusals from different publishers; some, I have reason to believe, not over-courteously worded in writing to an unknown author, and none alleging any distinct reasons for its rejection. Courtesy is always due; but it is, perhaps, hardly to be expected that, in the press of business in a great publishing house, they should find time to explain why they decline particular works. Yet, though one course of action is not to be wondered at, the opposite may fall upon a grieved and disappointed mind with all the graciousness of dew; and I can well sympathise with the published account which "Currer Bell" gives, of the feelings experienced on reading Messrs. Smith and Elder's letter containing the rejection of "The Professor".

"As a forlorn hope, we tried one publishing house more. Ere long, in a much shorter space than that on which experience had taught him to calculate, there came a letter, which he opened in the dreary anticipation of finding two hard hopeless lines, intimating that 'Messrs. Smith and Elder were not disposed to publish the MS.,' and, instead, he took out of the envelope a letter of two pages. He read it trembling. It declined, indeed, to publish that tale, for business reasons, but it discussed its merits and demerits, so courteously, so considerately, in a spirit so rational, with a discrimination so enlightened, that this very refusal cheered the author better than a vulgarly-expressed acceptance would have done. It was added, that a work in three volumes would meet with careful attention."

Mr. Smith has told me a little circumstance connected with the reception of this manuscript, which seems to me indicative of no ordinary character. It came (accompanied by the note given below) in a brown paper parcel, to 65 Cornhill. Besides the address to Messrs. Smith and Co., there were on it those of other publishers to whom the tale had been sent, not obliterated, but simply scored through, so that Messrs. Smith at once perceived the names of some of the houses in the trade to which the unlucky parcel had gone, without success.

To MESSRS. SMITH AND ELDER.

"July 15th, 1847.

"Gentlemen---I beg to submit to your consideration the accompanying manuscript. I should be glad to learn whether it be such as you approve, and would undertake to publish at as early a period as possible. Address, Mr. Currer Bell, under cover to Miss Brontë, Haworth, Bradford, Yorkshire."

Some time elapsed before an answer was returned.

A little circumstance may be mentioned here, though it belongs to a somewhat earlier period, as showing Miss Brontë's inexperience of the ways of the world, and willing deference to the opinion of others. She had written to a publisher about one of her manuscripts, which she had sent him, and, not receiving any reply, she consulted her brother as to what could be the reason for the prolonged silence. He at once set it down to her not having enclosed a postage-stamp in her letter. She accordingly wrote again, to repair her former omission, and apologise for it.

To MESSRS. SMITH AND ELDER.

"August 2nd, 1847.

"Gentlemen,---About three weeks since, I sent for your consideration a MS. entitled "The Professor", a tale by Currer Bell. I should be glad to know whether it reached your hands safely, and likewise to learn, at your earliest convenience, whether it be such as you can undertake to publish.---I am, gentlemen, yours respectfully,

"CURRER BELL.

"I enclose a directed cover for your reply."

This time her note met with a prompt answer; for, four days later, she writes (in reply to the letter which she afterwards characterised in the Preface to the second edition of "Wuthering Heights", as containing a refusal so delicate, reasonable, and courteous, as to be more cheering than some acceptances):

"Your objection to the want of varied interest in the tale is, I am aware, not without grounds; yet it appears to me that it might be published without serious risk, if its appearance were speedily followed up by another work from the same pen, of a more striking and exciting character. The first work might serve as an introduction, and accustom the public to the author's the success of the second might thereby be rendered more probable. I have a second narrative in three volumes, now in progress, and nearly completed, to which I have endeavoured to impart a more vivid interest than belongs to "The Professor". In about a month I hope to finish it, so that if a publisher were found for "The Professor", the second narrative might follow as soon as was deemed advisable; and thus the interest of the public (if any interest was aroused) might not be suffered to cool. Will you be kind enough to favour me with your judgment on this plan?"

While the minds of the three sisters were in this state of suspense, their long-expected friend came to pay her promised visit. She was with them at the beginning of the glowing August of that year. They were out on the moors for the greater part of the day basking in the golden sunshine, which was bringing on an unusual plenteousness of harvest, for which, somewhat later, Charlotte expressed her earnest desire that there should be a thanksgiving service in all the churches. August was the season of glory for the neighbourhood of Haworth. Even the smoke, lying in the valley between that village and Keighley, took beauty from the radiant colours on the moors above, the rich purple of the heather bloom calling out an harmonious contrast in the tawny golden light that, in the full heat of summer evenings, comes stealing everywhere through the dun atmosphere of the hollows. And up, on the moors, turning away from all habitations of men, the royal ground on which they stood would expand into long swells of amethyst-tinted hills, melting away into aerial tints; and the fresh and fragrant scent of the heather, and the "murmur of innumerable bees," would lend a poignancy to the relish with which they welcomed their friend to their own true home on the wild and open hills.

There, too, they could escape from the Shadow in the house below.

Throughout this time---during all these confidences---not a word was uttered to their friend of the three tales in London; two accepted and in the press---one trembling in the balance of a publisher's judgment; nor did she hear of that other story "nearly completed," lying in manuscript in the grey old parsonage down below. She might have her suspicions that they all wrote with an intention of publication some time; but she knew the bounds which they set to themselves in their communications; nor could she, nor can any one else, wonder at their reticence, when remembering how scheme after scheme had failed, just as it seemed close upon accomplishment.

Mr. Brontë, too, had his suspicions of something going on; but, never being spoken to, he did not speak on the subject, and consequently his ideas were vague and uncertain, only just prophetic enough to keep him from being actually stunned when, later on, he heard of the success of "Jane Eyre"; to the progress of which we must now return.

To MESSRS. SMITH AND ELDER.

"August 24th.

"I now send you per rail a MS. entitled 'Jane Eyre,' a novel in three volumes, by Currer Bell. I find I cannot prepay the carriage of the parcel, as money for that purpose is not received at the small station-house where it is left. If, when you acknowledge the receipt of the MS., you would have the goodness to mention the amount charged on delivery, I will immediately transmit it in postage stamps. It is better in future to address Mr. Currer Bell, under cover to Miss Brontë, Haworth, Bradford, Yorkshire, as there is a risk of letters otherwise directed not reaching me at present. To save trouble, I enclose an envelope."

"Jane Eyre" was accepted, and printed and published by October 16th.

While it was in the press, Miss Brontë went to pay a short visit to her friend at B------. The proofs were forwarded to her there, and she occasionally sat at the same table with her friend, correcting them; but they did not exchange a word on the subject.

Immediately on her return to the Parsonage, she wrote:

"September.

"I had a very wet, windy walk home from Keighley; but my fatigue quite disappeared when I reached home, and found all well. Thank God for it.

"My boxes came safe this morning. I have distributed the presents. Papa says I am to remember him most kindly to you. The screen will be very useful, and he thanks you for it. Tabby was charmed with her cap. She said, 'she never thought o' naught o' t' sort as Miss sending her aught, and, she is sure, she can never thank her enough for it.' I was infuriated on finding a jar in my trunk. At first, I hoped it was empty, but when I found it heavy and replete, I could have hurled it all the way back to B------. However, the inscription A. B. softened me much. It was at once kind and villainous in you to send it. You ought first to be tenderly kissed, and then afterwards as tenderly whipped. Emily is just now on the floor of the bed-room where I am writing, looking at her apples. She smiled when I gave the collar to her as your present, with an expression at once well-pleased and slightly surprised. All send their love.---Yours, in a mixture of anger and love."

When the manuscript of "Jane Eyre" had been received by the future publishers of that remarkable novel, it fell to the share of a gentleman connected with the firm to read it first. He was so powerfully struck by the character of the tale, that he reported his impression in very strong terms to Mr. Smith, who appears to have been much amused by the admiration excited. "You seem to have been so enchanted, that I do not know how to believe you," he laughingly said. But when a second reader, in the person of a clear-headed Scotchman, not given to enthusiasm, had taken the MS. home in the evening, and became so deeply interested in it, as to sit up half the night to finish it, Mr. Smith's curiosity was sufficiently excited to prompt him to read it for himself; and great as were the praises which had been bestowed upon it, he found that they had not exceeded the truth.

On its publication, copies were presented to a few private literary friends. Their discernment had been rightly reckoned upon. They were of considerable standing in the world of letters; and one and all returned expressions of high praise along with their thanks for the book. Among them was the great writer of fiction for whom Miss Brontë felt so strong an admiration; he immediately appreciated, and, in a characteristic note to the publishers, acknowledged its extraordinary merits.

The Reviews were more tardy, or more cautious. The Athenaeum and the Spectator gave short notices, containing qualified admissions of the power of the author. The Literary Gazette was uncertain as to whether it was safe to praise an unknown author. The Daily News declined accepting the copy which had been sent, on the score of a rule "never to review novels;" but a little later on, there appeared a notice of the Bachelor of the Albany in that paper; and Messrs. Smith and Elder again forwarded a copy of "Jane Eyre" to the Editor, with a request for a notice. This time the work was accepted; but I am not aware what was the character of the article upon it.

The Examiner came forward to the rescue, as far as the opinions of professional critics were concerned. The literary articles in that paper were always remarkable for their genial and generous appreciation of merit nor was the notice of "Jane Eyre" an exception; it was full of hearty, yet delicate and discriminating praise. Otherwise, the press in general did little to promote the sale of the novel; the demand for it among librarians had begun before the appearance of the review in the Examiner; the power of fascination of the tale itself made its merits known to the public, without the kindly finger-posts of professional criticism; and, early in December, the rush began for copies.

I will insert two or three of Miss Brontë's letters to her publishers, in order to show how timidly the idea of success was received by one so unaccustomed to adopt a sanguine view of any subject in which she was individually concerned. The occasions on which these notes were written, will explain themselves.

"Oct. 19th, 1847.

"Gentlemen,---The six copies of "Jane Eyre" reached me this morning. You have given the work every advantage which good paper, clear type, and a seemly outside can supply;---if it fails, the fault will lie with the author,---you are exempt.

"I now await the judgment of the press and the public.---I am, Gentlemen, yours respectfully,

C. BELL."

MESSRS. SMITH, ELDER, AND CO.

"Oct. 26th, 1847.

"Gentlemen,---I have received the newspapers. They speak quite as favourably of "Jane Eyre" as I expected them to do. The notice in the Literary Gazette seems certainly to have been indited in rather a flat mood, and the Athenaeum has a style of its own, which I respect, but cannot exactly relish; still when one considers that journals of that standing have a dignity to maintain which would be deranged by a too cordial recognition of the claims of an obscure author, I suppose there is every reason to be satisfied.

"Meantime a brisk sale would be effectual support under the hauteur of lofty critics.---I am, Gentlemen, yours respectfully,

"C. BELL."

MESSRS. SMITH, ELDER, AND CO.

"Nov. 13th, 1847.

"Gentlemen,---I have to acknowledge the receipt of yours of the 11th inst., and to thank you for the information it communicates. The notice from the People's Journal also duly reached me, and this morning I received the Spectator. The critique in the Spectator gives that view of the book which will naturally be taken by a certain class of minds; I shall expect it to be followed by other notices of a similar nature. The way to detraction has been pointed out, and will probably be pursued. Most future notices will in all likelihood have a reflection of the Spectator in them. I fear this turn of opinion will not improve the demand for the book---but time will show. If "Jane Eyre" has any solid worth in it, it ought to weather a gust of unfavourable wind.---I am, Gentlemen, yours respectfully,

"C. BELL."

MESSRS. SMITH, ELDER, AND CO.

"Nov. 30th, 1847.

"Gentlemen,---I have received the Economist, but not the Examiner; from some cause that paper has missed, as the Spectator did on a former occasion; I am glad, however, to learn through your letter, that its notice of "Jane Eyre" was favourable, and also that the prospects of the work appear to improve.

"I am obliged to you for the information respecting "Wuthering Heights".---I am, Gentlemen, yours respectfully,

"C. BELL."

To MESSRS. SMITH, ELDER, AND CO.

"Dec. 1st, 1847.

"Gentlemen,---The Examiner reached me to-day; it had been missent on account of the direction, which was to Currer Bell, care of Miss Brontë. Allow me to intimate that it would be better in future not to put the name of Currer Bell on the outside of communications; if directed simply to Miss Brontë they will be more likely to reach their destination safely. Currer Bell is not known in the district, and I have no wish that he should become known. The notice in the Examiner gratified me very much; it appears to be from the pen of an able man who has understood what he undertakes to criticise; of course, approbation from such a quarter is encouraging to an author, and I trust it will prove beneficial to the work.---I am, Gentlemen, yours respectfully,

C. BELL.

"I received likewise seven other notices from provincial papers enclosed in an envelope. I thank you very sincerely for so punctually sending me all the various criticisms on "Jane Eyre"."

TO MESSRS. SMITH, ELDER, AND CO.

"Dec. 10th, 1847.

"Gentlemen,---I beg to acknowledge the receipt of your letter inclosing a bank post bill, for which I thank you. Having already expressed my sense of your kind and upright conduct, I can now only say that I trust you will always have reason to be as well content with me as I am with you. If the result of any future exertions I may be able to make should prove agreeable and advantageous to you, I shall be well satisfied; and it would be a serious source of regret to me if I thought you ever had reason to repent being my publishers.

"You need not apologise, Gentlemen, for having written to me so seldom; of course I am always glad to hear from you, but I am truly glad to hear from Mr. Williams likewise; he was my first favourable critic; he first gave me encouragement to persevere as an author, consequently I naturally respect him and feel grateful to him.

"Excuse the informality of my letter, and believe me, Gentlemen, yours respectfully,

CURRER BELL."

There is little record remaining of the manner in which the first news of its wonderful success reached and affected the one heart of the three sisters. I once asked Charlotte---we were talking about the description of Lowood school, and she was saying that she was not sure whether she should have written it, if she had been aware how instantaneously it would have been identified with Cowan Bridge---whether the popularity to which the novel attained had taken her by surprise. She hesitated a little, and then said: "I believed that what had impressed me so forcibly when I wrote it, must make a strong impression on any one who read it. I was not surprised at those who read "Jane Eyre" being deeply interested in it; but I hardly expected that a book by an unknown author could find readers."

The sisters had kept the knowledge of their literary ventures from their father, fearing to increase their own anxieties and disappointment by witnessing his; for he took an acute interest in all that befell his children, and his own tendency had been towards literature in the days when he was young and hopeful. It was true he did not much manifest his feelings in words; he would have thought that he was prepared for disappointment as the lot of man, and that he could have met it with stoicism; but words are poor and tardy interpreters of feelings to those who love one another, and his daughters knew how he would have borne ill-success worse for them than for himself. So they did not tell him what they were undertaking. He says now that he suspected it all along, but his suspicions could take no exact form, as all he was certain of was, that his children were perpetually writing---and not writing letters. We have seen how the communications from their publishers were received "under cover to Miss Brontë." Once, Charlotte told me, they overheard the postman meeting Mr. Brontë, as the latter was leaving the house, and inquiring from the parson where one Currer Bell could be living, to which Mr. Brontë replied that there was no such person in the parish. This must have been the misadventure to which Miss Brontë alludes in the beginning of her correspondence with Mr. Aylott.

Now, however, when the demand for the work had assured success to "Jane Eyre," her sisters urged Charlotte to tell their father of its publication. She accordingly went into his study one afternoon after his early dinner, carrying with her a copy of the book, and one or two reviews, taking care to include a notice adverse to it.

She informed me that something like the following conversation took place between her and him. (I wrote down her words the day after I heard them; and I am pretty sure they are quite accurate.)

"Papa, I've been writing a book."

"Have you, my dear?"

"Yes, and I want you to read it."

"I am afraid it will try my eyes too much."

"But it is not in manuscript: it is printed."

"My dear! you've never thought of the expense it will be! It will be almost sure to be a loss, for how can you get a book sold? No one knows you or your name."

"But, papa, I don't think it will be a loss; no more will you, if you will just let me read you a review or two, and tell you more about it."

So she sate down and read some of the reviews to her father; and then, giving him the copy of "Jane Eyre" that she intended for him, she left him to read it. When he came in to tea, he said, "Girls, do you know Charlotte has been writing a book, and it is much better than likely?"

But while the existence of Currer Bell, the author, was like a piece of a dream to the quiet inhabitants of Haworth Parsonage, who went on with their uniform household life,---their cares for their brother being its only variety,---the whole reading-world of England was in a ferment to discover the unknown author. Even the publishers of "Jane Eyre" were ignorant whether Currer Bell was a real or an assumed name,---whether it belonged to a man or a woman. In every town people sought out the list of their friends and acquaintances, and turned away in disappointment. No one they knew had genius enough to be the author. Every little incident mentioned in the book was turned this way and that to answer, if possible, the much-vexed question of sex. All in vain. People were content to relax their exertions to satisfy their curiosity, and simply to sit down and greatly admire.

I am not going to write an analysis of a book with which every one who reads this biography is sure to be acquainted; much less a criticism upon a work, which the great flood of public opinion has lifted up from the obscurity in which it first appeared, and laid high and safe on the everlasting hills of fame.

Before me lies a packet of extracts from newspapers and periodicals, which Mr. Brontë has sent me. It is touching to look them over, and see how there is hardly any notice, however short and clumsily-worded, in any obscure provincial paper, but what has been cut out and carefully ticketed with its date by the poor, bereaved father,---so proud when he first read them---so desolate now. For one and all are full of praise of this great, unknown genius, which suddenly appeared amongst us. Conjecture as to the authorship ran about like wild-fire. People in London, smooth and polished as the Athenians of old, and like them "spending their time in nothing else, but either to tell or to hear some new thing," were astonished and delighted to find that a fresh sensation, a new pleasure, was in reserve for them in the uprising of an author, capable of depicting with accurate and Titanic power the strong, self-reliant, racy, and individual characters which were not, after all, extinct species, but lingered still in existence in the North. They thought that there was some exaggeration mixed with the peculiar force of delineation. Those nearer to the spot, where the scene of the story was apparently laid, were sure, from the very truth and accuracy of the writing, that the writer was no Southeron; for though "dark, and cold, and rugged is the North," the old strength of the

Scandinavian races yet abides there, and glowed out in every character depicted in "Jane Eyre." Farther than this, curiosity, both honourable and dishonourable, was at fault.

When the second edition appeared, in the January of the following year, with the dedication to Mr. Thackeray, people looked at each other and wondered afresh. But Currer Bell knew no more of William Makepeace Thackeray as an individual man---of his life, age, fortunes, or circumstances---than she did of those of Mr. Michael Angelo Titmarsh. The one had placed his name as author upon the title-page of Vanity Fair, the other had not. She was thankful for the opportunity of expressing her high admiration of a writer, whom, as she says, she regarded "as the social regenerator of his day---as the very master of that working corps who would restore to rectitude the warped state of things. . . . His wit is bright, his humour attractive, but both bear the same relation to his serious genius, that the mere lambent sheet-lightning, playing under the edge of the summer cloud, does to the electric death-spark hid in its womb."

Anne Brontë had been more than usually delicate all the summer, and her sensitive spirit had been deeply affected by the great anxiety of her home. But now that "Jane Eyre" gave such indications of success, Charlotte began to plan schemes of future pleasure,---perhaps relaxation from care, would be the more correct expression,---for their darling younger sister, the "little one" of the household. But, although Anne was cheered for a time by Charlotte's success, the fact was, that neither her spirits nor her bodily strength were such as to incline her to much active exertion, and she led far too sedentary a life, continually stooping either over her book, or work, or at her desk. "It is with difficulty," writes her sister, "that we can prevail upon her to take a walk, or induce her to converse. I look forward to next summer with the confident intention that she shall, if possible, make at least a brief sojourn at the sea-side." In this same letter, is a sentence, telling how dearly home, even with its present terrible drawback, lay at the roots of her heart; but it is too much blended with reference to the affairs of others to bear quotation.

Any author of a successful novel is liable to an inroad of letters from unknown readers, containing commendation---sometimes of so fulsome and indiscriminating a character as to remind the recipient of Dr. Johnson's famous speech to one who offered presumptuous and injudicious praise---sometimes saying merely a few words, which have power to stir the heart "as with the sound of a trumpet," and in the high humility they excite, to call forth strong resolutions to make all future efforts worthy of such praise; and occasionally containing that true appreciation of both merits and demerits, together with the sources of each, which forms the very criticism and help for which an inexperienced writer thirsts. Of each of these kinds of communication Currer Bell received her full share; and her warm heart, and true sense and high standard of what she aimed at, affixed to each its true value. Among other letters of hers, some to Mr. G. H. Lewes have been kindly placed by him at my service; and as I know Miss Brontë highly prized his letters of encouragement and advice, I shall give extracts from her replies, as their dates occur, because they will indicate the kind of criticism she valued, and also because throughout, in anger, as in agreement and harmony, they show her character unblinded by any self-flattery, full of clear-sighted modesty as to what she really did well, and what she failed in, grateful for friendly interest, and only sore and irritable when the question of sex in authorship was, as she thought, roughly or unfairly treated. As to the rest, the letters speak for themselves, to those who know how to listen, far better than I can interpret their meaning into my poorer and weaker words. Mr. Lewes has politely sent me the following explanation of that letter of his, to which the succeeding one of Miss Brontë is a reply.

"When 'Jane Eyre' first appeared, the publishers courteously sent me a copy. The enthusiasm with which I read it, made me go down to Mr. Parker, and propose to write a review of it for Frazer's Magazine. He would not consent to an unknown novel---for the papers had not yet declared themselves---receiving such importance, but thought it might make one on 'Recent Novels: English and French'---which appeared in Frazer, December, 1847. Meanwhile I had written to Miss Brontë to tell her the delight with which her book filled me; and seem to have sermonised her, to judge from her reply."

To G. H. LEWES, ESQ.

"Nov. 6th, 1847.

"Dear Sir,---Your letter reached me yesterday; I beg to assure you, that I appreciate fully the intention with which it was written, and I thank you sincerely both for its cheering commendation and valuable advice.

"You warn me to beware of melodrama, and you exhort me to adhere to the real. When I first began to write, so impressed was I with the truth of the principles you advocate, that I determined to take Nature and Truth as my sole guides, and to follow in their very footprints; I restrained imagination, eschewed romance, repressed excitement; over-bright colouring, too, I avoided, and sought to produce something which should be soft, grave, and true.

"My work (a tale in one volume) being completed, I offered it to a publisher. He said it was original, faithful to nature, but he did not feel warranted in accepting it; such a work would not sell. I tried six publishers in succession; they all told me it was deficient in 'startling incident' and 'thrilling excitement,' that it would never suit the circulating libraries, and, as it was on those libraries the success of works of fiction mainly depended, they could not undertake to publish what would be overlooked there.

"'Jane Eyre' was rather objected to at first, on the same grounds, but finally found acceptance.

"I mention this to you, not with a view of pleading exemption from censure, but in order to direct your attention to the root of certain literary evils. If, in your forthcoming article in Frazer, you would bestow a few words of enlightenment on the public who support the circulating libraries, you might, with your powers, do some good.

"You advise me, too, not to stray far from the ground of experience, as I become weak when I enter the region of fiction; and you say, 'real experience is perennially interesting, and to all men.'

"I feel that this also is true; but, dear Sir, is not the real experience of each individual very limited? And, if a writer dwells upon that solely or principally, is he not in danger of repeating himself, and also of becoming an egotist? Then, too, imagination is a strong, restless faculty, which claims to be heard and exercised: are we to be quite deaf to her cry, and insensate to her struggles? When she shows us bright pictures, are we never to look at them, and try to reproduce them? And when she is eloquent, and speaks rapidly and urgently in our ear, are we not to write to her dictation?

"I shall anxiously search the next number of Fraser for your opinions on these points.--- Believe me, dear Sir, yours gratefully,

"C. BELL."

But while gratified by appreciation as an author, she was cautious as to the person from whom she received it; for much of the value of the praise depended on the sincerity and capability of the person rendering it. Accordingly, she applied to Mr. Williams (a gentleman connected with her publishers' firm) for information as to who and what Mr. Lewes was. Her reply, after she had learnt something of the character of her future critic, and while awaiting his criticism, must not be omitted. Besides the reference to him, it contains some amusing allusions to the perplexity which began to be excited respecting the "identity of the brothers Bell," and some notice of the conduct of another publisher towards her sister, which I refrain from characterising, because I understand that truth is considered a libel in speaking of such people. To W. S. WILLIAMS, ESQ.

"Nov. 10th, 1847.

"Dear Sir,---I have received the Britannia and the Sun, but not the Spectator which I rather regret, as censure, though not pleasant, is often wholesome.

"Thank you for your information regarding Mr. Lewes. I am glad to hear that he is a clever and sincere man: such being the case, I can await his critical sentence with fortitude; even if it goes against me, I shall not murmur; ability and honesty have a right to condemn, where they think condemnation is deserved. From what you say, however, I trust rather to obtain at least a modified approval.

"Your account of the various surmises respecting the identity of the brothers Bell, amused me much: were the enigma solved, it would probably be found not worth the trouble of solution; but I will let it alone; it suits ourselves to remain quiet, and certainly injures no one else.

"The reviewer who noticed the little book of poems, in the Dublin Magazine, conjectured that the soi-disant three personages were in reality but one, who, endowed with an unduly prominent organ of self-esteem, and consequently impressed with a somewhat weighty notion of his own merits, thought them too vast to be concentrated in a single individual, and accordingly divided himself into three, out of consideration, I suppose, for the nerves of the much-to-be-astounded public! This was an ingenious thought in the reviewer,---very original and striking, but not accurate. We are three.

"A prose work, by Ellis and Acton, will soon appear: it should have been out, indeed, long since; for the first proof-sheets were already in the press at the commencement of last August, before Currer Bell had placed the MS. of "Jane Eyre" in your hands. Mr.------, however, does not do business like Messrs. Smith and Elder; a different spirit seems to preside at ------ Street, to that which guides the helm at 65, Cornhill. . . . My relations have suffered from exhausting delay and procrastination, while I have to acknowledge the benefits of a management at once business-like and gentleman-like, energetic and considerate.

"I should like to know if Mr. ------ often acts as he has done to my relations, or whether this is an exceptional instance of his method. Do you know, and can you tell me anything about him? You must excuse me for going to the point at once, when I want to learn anything: if my questions are importunate, you are, of course, at liberty to decline answering them.---I am, yours respectfully,

C. BELL."

To G. H. LEWES, ESQ.
"Nov. 22nd, 1847.

"Dear Sir,---I have now read 'Ranthorpe.' I could not get it till a day or two ago; but I have got it and read it at last; and in reading 'Ranthorpe,' I have read a new book,---not a reprint---not a reflection of any other book, but a NEW BOOK.

"I did not know such books were written now. It is very different to any of the popular works of fiction: it fills the mind with fresh knowledge. Your experience and your convictions are made the reader's; and to an author, at least, they have a value and an interest quite unusual. I await your criticism on 'Jane Eyre' now with other sentiments than I entertained before the perusal of 'Ranthorpe.'

"You were a stranger to me. I did not particularly respect you. I did not feel that your praise or blame would have any special weight. I knew little of your right to condemn or approve. NOW I am informed on these points.

"You will be severe; your last letter taught me as much. Well! I shall try to extract good out of your severity: and besides, though I am now sure you are a just, discriminating man, yet, being mortal, you must be fallible; and if any part of your censure galls me too keenly to the quick---gives me deadly pain---I shall for the present disbelieve it, and put it quite aside, till such time as I feel able to receive it without torture.---I am, dear Sir, yours very respectfully,

C. BELL."

In December, 1847, "Wuthering Heights" and "Agnes Grey" appeared. The first-named of these stories has revolted many readers by the power with which wicked and exceptional characters are depicted. Others, again, have felt the attraction of remarkable genius, even when displayed on grim and terrible criminals. Miss Brontë herself says, with regard to this tale, "Where delineation of human character is concerned, the case is different. I am bound to avow that she had scarcely more practical knowledge of the peasantry amongst whom she lived, than a nun has of the country-people that pass her convent gates. My sister's disposition was not naturally gregarious: circumstances favoured and fostered her tendency to seclusion; except to go to church, or take a walk on the hills, she rarely crossed the threshold of home. Though the feeling for the people around her was benevolent, intercourse with them she never sought, nor, with very few exceptions, ever experienced and yet she knew them, knew their ways, their language, and their family histories; she could hear of them with interest, and talk of them with detail minute, graphic, and accurate; but WITH them she rarely exchanged a word. Hence it ensued, that what her mind has gathered of the real concerning them, was too exclusively confined to those tragic and terrible traits, of which, in listening to the secret annals of every rude vicinage, the memory is sometimes compelled to receive the impress. Her imagination, which was a spirit more sombre than sunny---more powerful than sportive--- found in such traits material whence it wrought creations like Heathcliff, like Earnshaw, like Catherine. Having formed these beings, she did not know what she had done. If the auditor of her work, when read in manuscript, shuddered under the grinding influence of natures so relentless and implacable---of spirits so lost and fallen; if it was complained that the mere hearing of certain vivid and fearful scenes banished sleep by night, and disturbed mental peace by day, Ellis Bell would wonder what was meant, and suspect the complainant of affectation. Had she but lived, her mind would of itself have grown like a strong tree---loftier, straighter, wider-spreading---and its matured fruits would have attained a mellower ripeness and sunnier bloom; but on that mind time and experience alone could work; to the influence of other intellects she was not amenable."

Whether justly or unjustly, the productions of the two younger Miss Brontës were not received with much favour at the time of their publication. "Critics failed to do them justice. The immature, but very real, powers revealed in 'Wuthering Heights,' were scarcely recognised; its import and nature were misunderstood; the identity of its author was misrepresented: it was said that this was an earlier and ruder attempt of the same pen which had produced 'Jane Eyre.'" . . . "Unjust and grievous error! We laughed at it at first, but I deeply lament it now."

Henceforward Charlotte Brontë's existence becomes divided into two parallel currents---her life as Currer Bell, the author; her life as Charlotte Brontë, the woman. There were separate duties belonging to each character---not opposing each other; not impossible, but difficult to be reconciled. When a man becomes an author, it is probably merely a change of employment to him. He takes a portion of that time which has hitherto been devoted to some other study or pursuit; he gives up something of the legal or medical profession, in which he has hitherto endeavoured to serve others, or relinquishes part of the trade or business by which he has been striving to gain a livelihood; and another merchant or lawyer, or doctor, steps into his vacant place, and probably does as well as he. But no other can take up the quiet, regular duties of the daughter, the wife, or the mother, as well as she whom God has appointed to fill that particular place: a woman's principal work in life is hardly left to her own choice; nor can she drop the domestic charges devolving on her as an individual, for the exercise of the most splendid talents that were ever bestowed. And yet she must not shrink from the extra responsibility implied by the very fact of her possessing such talents. She must not hide her gift in a napkin; it was meant for the use and service of others. In an humble and faithful spirit must she labour to do what is not impossible, or God would not have set her to do it.

I put into words what Charlotte Brontë put into actions.

The year 1848 opened with sad domestic distress. It is necessary, however painful, to remind the reader constantly of what was always present to the hearts of father and sisters at this time. It is well that the thoughtless critics, who spoke of the sad and gloomy views of life presented by the Brontës in their tales, should know how such words were wrung out of them by the living recollection of the long agony they suffered. It is well, too, that they who have objected to the representation of coarseness and shrank from it with repugnance, as if such conceptions arose out of the writers, should learn, that, not from the imagination---not from internal conception---but from the hard cruel facts, pressed down, by external life, upon their very senses, for long months and years together, did they write out what they saw, obeying the stern dictates of their consciences. They might be mistaken. They might err in writing at all, when their affections were so great that they could not write otherwise than they did of life. It is possible that it would have been better to have described only good and pleasant people, doing only good and pleasant things (in which case they could hardly have written at any time): all I say is, that never, I believe, did women, possessed of such wonderful gifts, exercise them with a fuller feeling of responsibility for their use. As to mistakes, stand now---as authors as well as women---before the judgment-seat of God.

"Jan. 11th, 1848.

"We have not been very comfortable here at home lately. Branwell has, by some means, contrived to get more money from the old quarter, and has led us a sad life. . . . Papa is harassed day and night; we have little peace, he is always sick; has two or three times fallen down in fits; what will be the ultimate end, God knows. But who is without their drawback, their scourge, their skeleton behind the curtain? It remains only to do one's best, and endure with patience what God sends."

I suppose that she had read Mr. Lewes' review on "Recent Novels," when it appeared in the December of the last year, but I find no allusion to it till she writes to him on January 12th, 1848.

"Dear Sir,---I thank you then sincerely for your generous review; and it is with the sense of double content I express my gratitude, because I am now sure the tribute is not superfluous or obtrusive. You were not severe on 'Jane Eyre;' you were very lenient. I am glad you told me my faults plainly in private, for in your public notice you touch on them so lightly, I should perhaps have passed them over thus indicated, with too little reflection.

"I mean to observe your warning about being careful how I undertake new works; my stock of materials is not abundant, but very slender; and, besides, neither my experience, my acquirements, nor my powers, are sufficiently varied to justify my ever becoming a frequent writer. I tell you this, because your article in Frazer left in me an uneasy impression that you were disposed to think better of the author of 'Jane Eyre' than that individual deserved; and I would rather you had a correct than a flattering opinion of me, even though I should never see you.

"If I ever DO write another book, I think I will have nothing of what you call 'melodrama;' I think so, but I am not sure. I THINK, too, I will endeavour to follow the counsel which shines out of Miss Austen's 'mild eyes,' 'to finish more and be more subdued;' but neither am I sure of that. When authors write best, or, at least, when they write most fluently, an influence seems to waken in them, which becomes their master---which will have its own way---putting out of view all behests but its own, dictating certain words, and insisting on their being used, whether vehement or measured in their nature; new-moulding characters, giving unthought of turns to incidents, rejecting carefully-elaborated old ideas, and suddenly creating and adopting new ones.

"Is it not so? And should we try to counteract this influence? Can we indeed counteract it?

"I am glad that another work of yours will soon appear; most curious shall I be to see whether you will write up to your own principles, and work out your own theories. You did not do it altogether in 'Ranthorpe'---at least not in the latter part; but the first portion was, I think, nearly without fault; then it had a pith, truth, significance in it, which gave the book sterling value; but to write so, one must have seen and known a great deal, and I have seen and known very little.

"Why do you like Miss Austen so very much? I am puzzled on that point. What induced you to say that you would have rather written "Pride and Prejudice,' or 'Tom Jones,' than any of the 'Waverley Novels'?

"I had not seen 'Pride and Prejudice' till I read that sentence of yours, and then I got the book. And what did I find? An accurate, daguerreotyped portrait of a commonplace face; a carefully-fenced, highly-cultivated garden, with neat borders and delicate flowers; but no glance of a bright, vivid physiognomy, no open country, no fresh air, no blue hill, no bonny beck. I should hardly like to live with her ladies and gentlemen, in their elegant but confined houses. These observations will probably irritate you, but I shall run the risk.

"Now I can understand admiration of George Sand; for though I never saw any of her works which I admired throughout (even 'Consuelo,' which is the best, or the best that I have read, appears to me to couple strange extravagance with wondrous excellence), yet she has a grasp of mind, which, if I cannot fully comprehend, I can very deeply respect; she is sagacious and profound;---Miss Austen is only shrewd and observant.

"Am I wrong---or, were you hasty in what you said? If you have time, I should be glad to hear further on this subject; if not, or if you think the questions frivolous, do not trouble yourself to reply.---I am, yours respectfully,

C. BELL."

To G. H. LEWES, ESQ.
"Jan. 18th, 1848.
"Dear Sir,---I must write one more note, though I had not intended to trouble you again so soon. I have to agree with you, and to differ from you.
"You correct my crude remarks on the subject of the 'influence'; well, I accept your definition of what the effects of that influence should be; I recognise the wisdom of your rules for its regulation. . . .
"What a strange lecture comes next in your letter! You say I must familiarise my mind with the fact, that 'Miss Austen is not a poetess, has no "sentiment" (you scornfully enclose the word in inverted commas), no eloquence, none of the ravishing enthusiasm of poetry,'---and then you add, I MUST 'learn to acknowledge her as ONE OF THE GREATEST ARTISTS, OF THE GREATEST PAINTERS OF HUMAN CHARACTER, and one of the writers with the nicest sense of means to an end that ever lived.'
"The last point only will I ever acknowledge.
"Can there be a great artist without poetry?
"What I call---what I will bend to, as a great artist then---cannot be destitute of the divine gift. But by POETRY, I am sure, you understand something different to what I do, as you do by 'sentiment.' It is POETRY, as I comprehend the word, which elevates that masculine George Sand, and makes out of something coarse, something Godlike. It is 'sentiment,' in my sense of the term---sentiment jealously hidden, but genuine, which extracts the venom from that formidable Thackeray, and converts what might be corrosive poison into purifying elixir.

"If Thackeray did not cherish in his large heart deep feeling for his kind, he would delight to exterminate; as it is, I believe, he wishes only to reform. Miss Austen being, as you say, without 'sentiment,' without Poetry, maybe IS sensible, real (more REAL than TRUE), but she cannot be great.

"I submit to your anger, which I have now excited (for have I not questioned the perfection of your darling?); the storm may pass over me. Nevertheless, I will, when I can (I do not know when that will be, as I have no access to a circulating library), diligently peruse all Miss Austen's works, as you recommend. . . . You must forgive me for not always being able to think as you do, and still believe me, yours gratefully,

C. BELL."

I have hesitated a little, before inserting the following extract from a letter to Mr. Williams, but it is strikingly characteristic; and the criticism contained in it is, from that circumstance, so interesting (whether we agree with it or not), that I have determined to do so, though I thereby displace the chronological order of the letters, in order to complete this portion of a correspondence which is very valuable, as showing the purely intellectual side of her character.

To W. S. WILLIAMS, BSQ.

"April 26th, 1848.

"My dear Sir,---I have now read 'Rose, Blanche, and Violet,' and I will tell you, as well as I can, what I think of it. Whether it is an improvement on 'Ranthorpe' I do not know, for I liked 'Ranthorpe' much; but, at any rate, it contains more of a good thing. I find in it the same power, but more fully developed.

"The author's character is seen in every page, which makes the book interesting---far more interesting than any story could do; but it is what the writer himself says that attracts far more than what he puts into the mouths of his characters. G. H. Lewes is, to my perception, decidedly the most original character in the book. . . . The didactic passages seem to me the best---far the best---in the work; very acute, very profound, are some of the views there given, and very clearly they are offered to the reader. He is a just thinker; he is a sagacious observer; there is wisdom in his theory, and, I doubt not, energy in his practice. But why, then, are you often provoked with him while you read? How does he manage, while teaching, to make his hearer feel as if his business was, not quietly to receive the doctrines propounded, but to combat them? You acknowledge that he offers you gems of pure truth; why do you keep perpetually scrutinising them for flaws?

"Mr. Lewes, I divine, with all his talents and honesty, must have some faults of manner; there must be a touch too much of dogmatism; a dash extra of confidence in him, sometimes. This you think while you are reading the book; but when you have closed it and laid it down, and sat a few minutes collecting your thoughts, and settling your impressions, you find the idea or feeling predominant in your mind to be pleasure at the fuller acquaintance you have made with a fine mind and a true heart, with high abilities and manly principles. I hope he will not be long ere he publishes another book. His emotional scenes are somewhat too uniformly vehement: would not a more subdued style of treatment often have produced a more masterly effect? Now and then Mr. Lewes takes a French pen into his hand, wherein he differs from Mr. Thackeray, who always uses an English quill. However, the French pen does not far mislead Mr. Lewes; he wields it with British muscles. All honour to him for the excellent general tendency of his book!

"He gives no charming picture of London literary society, and especially the female part of it; but all coteries, whether they be literary, scientific, political, or religious, must, it seems to me, have a tendency to change truth into affectation. When people belong to a clique, they must, I suppose, in some measure, write, talk, think, and live for that clique; a harassing and narrowing necessity. I trust, the press and the public show themselves disposed to give the book the reception it merits, and that is a very cordial one, far beyond anything due to a Bulwer or D'Israeli production."

Let us return from Currer Bell to Charlotte Brontë. The winter in Haworth had been a sickly season. Influenza had prevailed amongst the villagers, and where there was a real need for the presence of the clergyman's daughters, they were never found wanting, although they were shy of bestowing mere social visits on the parishioners. They had themselves suffered from the epidemic; Anne severely, as in her case it had been attended with cough and fever enough to make her elder sisters very anxious about her.

There is no doubt that the proximity of the crowded church-yard rendered the Parsonage unhealthy, and occasioned much illness to its inmates. Mr. Brontë represented the unsanitary state at Haworth pretty forcibly to the Board of Health; and, after the requisite visits from their officers, obtained a recommendation that all future interments in the churchyard should be forbidden, a new graveyard opened on the hill-side, and means set on foot for obtaining a water-supply to each house, instead of the weary, hard-worked housewives having to carry every bucketful, from a distance of several hundred yards, up a steep street. But he was baffled by the rate-payers; as, in many a similar instance, quantity carried it against quality, numbers against intelligence. And thus we find that illness often assumed a low typhoid form in Haworth, and fevers of various kinds visited the place with sad frequency.

In February, 1848, Louis Philippe was dethroned. The quick succession of events at that time called forth the following expression of Miss Brontë's thoughts on the subject, in a letter addressed to Miss Wooler, and dated March 31st.

"I remember well wishing my lot had been cast in the troubled times of the late war, and seeing in its exciting incidents a kind of stimulating charm, which it made my pulses beat fast to think of I remember even, I think; being a little impatient, that you would not fully sympathise with my feelings on those subjects; that you heard my aspirations and speculations very tranquilly, and by no means seemed to think the flaming swords could be any pleasant addition to Paradise. I have now out-lived youth; and, though I dare not say that I have outlived all its illusions---that the romance is quite gone from life---the veil fallen from truth, and that I see both in naked reality---yet, certainly, many things are not what they were ten years ago: and, amongst the rest, the pomp and circumstance of war have quite lost in my eyes their fictitious glitter. I have still no doubt that the shock of moral earthquakes wakens a vivid sense of life, both in nations and individuals; that the fear of dangers on a broad national scale, diverts men's minds momentarily from brooding over small private perils, and for the time gives them something like largeness of views; but, as little doubt have I, that convulsive revolutions put back the world in all that is good, check civilisation, bring the dregs of society to its surface; in short, it appears to me that insurrections and battles are the acute diseases of nations, and that their tendency is to exhaust, by their violence, the vital energies of the countries where they occur. That England may be spared the spasms, cramps, and frenzy-fits now contorting the Continent, and threatening Ireland, I earnestly pray. With the French and Irish I have no sympathy. With the Germans and Italians I think the case is different; as different as the love of freedom is from the lust for license."

Her birthday came round. She wrote to the friend whose birthday was within a week of hers; wrote the accustomed letter; but, reading it with our knowledge of what she had done, we perceive the difference between her thoughts and what they were a year or two ago, when she said "I have done nothing." There must have been a modest consciousness of having "done something" present in her mind, as she wrote this year:---

"I am now thirty-two. Youth is gone---gone,---and will never come back: can't help it. . . . It seems to me, that sorrow must come some time to everybody, and those who scarcely taste it in their youth, often have a more brimming and bitter cup to drain in after life; whereas, those who exhaust the dregs early, who drink the lees before the wine, may reasonably hope for more palatable draughts to succeed."

The authorship of "Jane Eyre" was as yet a close secret in the Brontë family; not even this friend, who was all but a sister knew more about it than the rest of the world. She might conjecture, it is true, both from her knowledge of previous habits, and from the suspicious fact of the proofs having been corrected at B------, that some literary project was afoot; but she knew nothing, and wisely said nothing, until she heard a report from others, that Charlotte Brontë was an author---had published a novel! Then she wrote to her; and received the two following letters; confirmatory enough, as it seems to me now, in their very vehemence and agitation of intended denial, of the truth of the report.

"April 28th, 1848.

"Write another letter, and explain that last note of yours distinctly. If your allusions are to myself, which I suppose they are, understand this,---I have given no one a right to gossip about me, and am not to be judged by frivolous conjectures, emanating from any quarter whatever. Let me know what you heard, and from whom you heard it."

"May 3rd, 1848.

"All I can say to you about a certain matter is this: the report---if report there be---and if the lady, who seems to have been rather mystified, had not dreamt what she fancied had been told to her---must have had its origin in some absurd misunderstanding. I have given NO ONE a right either to affirm, or to hint, in the most distant manner, that I was 'publishing'--- (humbug!) Whoever has said it---if any one has, which I doubt---is no friend of mine. Though twenty books were ascribed to me, I should own none. I scout the idea utterly. Whoever, after I have distinctly rejected the charge, urges it upon me, will do an unkind and an ill-bred thing. The most profound obscurity is infinitely preferable to vulgar notoriety; and that notoriety I neither seek nor will have. If then any B---an, or G---an, should presume to bore you on the subject,---to ask you what 'novel' Miss Brontë has been 'publishing,' you can just say, with the distinct firmness of which you are perfect mistress when you choose, that you are authorised by Miss Brontë to say, that she repels and disowns every accusation of the kind. You may add, if you please, that if any one has her confidence, you believe you have, and she has made no drivelling confessions to you on the subject. I am at a loss to conjecture from what source this rumour has come; and, I fear, it has far from a friendly origin. I am not certain, however, and I should be very glad if I could gain certainty. Should you hear anything more, please let me know. Your offer of 'Simeon's Life' is a very kind one, and I thank you for it. I dare say Papa would like to see the work very much, as he knew Mr. Simeon. Laugh or scold A------ out of the publishing notion; and believe me, through all chances and changes, whether calumniated or let alone,---Yours faithfully,

C. BRONTË."

The reason why Miss Brontë was so anxious to preserve her secret, was, I am told, that she had pledged her word to her sisters that it should not be revealed through her.

The dilemmas attendant on the publication of the sisters' novels, under assumed names, were increasing upon them. Many critics insisted on believing, that all the fictions published as by three Bells were the works of one author, but written at different periods of his development and maturity. No doubt, this suspicion affected the reception of the books. Ever since the completion of Anne Brontë's tale of "Agnes Grey", she had been labouring at a second, "The Tenant of Wildfell Hall." It is little known; the subject---the deterioration of a character, whose profligacy and ruin took their rise in habits of intemperance, so slight as to be only considered "good fellowship"---was painfully discordant to one who would fain have sheltered herself from all but peaceful and religious ideas. "She had" (says her sister of that gentle "little one"), "in the course of her life, been called on to contemplate near at hand, and for a long time, the terrible effects of talents misused and faculties abused; hers was naturally a sensitive, reserved, and dejected nature; what she saw sunk very deeply into her mind; it did her harm. She brooded over it till she believed it to be a duty to reproduce every detail (of course, with fictitious characters, incidents, and situations), as a warning to others. She hated her work, but would pursue it. When reasoned with on the subject, she regarded such reasonings as a temptation to self-indulgence. She must be honest; she must not varnish, soften, or conceal. This well-meant resolution brought on her misconstruction, and some abuse, which she bore, as it was her custom to bear whatever was unpleasant with mild steady patience. She was a very sincere and practical Christian, but the tinge of religious melancholy communicated a sad shade to her brief blameless life."

In the June of this year, 'The Tenant of Wildfell Hall' was sufficiently near its completion to be submitted to the person who had previously published for Ellis and Acton Bell.

In consequence of his mode of doing business, considerable annoyance was occasioned both to Miss Brontë and to them. The circumstances, as detailed in a letter of hers to a friend in New Zealand, were these:---One morning, at the beginning of July, a communication was received at the Parsonage from Messrs. Smith and Elder, which disturbed its quiet inmates not a little, as, though the matter brought under their notice was merely referred to as one which affected their literary reputation, they conceived it to have a bearing likewise upon their character. "Jane Eyre" had had a great run in America, and a publisher there had consequently bid high for early sheets of the next work by "Currer Bell." These Messrs. Smith and Elder had promised to let him have. He was therefore greatly astonished, and not well pleased, to learn that a similar agreement had been entered into with another American house, and that the new tale was very shortly to appear. It turned out, upon inquiry, that the mistake had originated in Acton and Ellis Bell's publisher having assured this American house that, to the best of his belief, "Jane Eyre", "Wuthering Heights", and "The Tenant of Wildfell Hall" (which he pronounced superior to either of the other two) were all written by the same author.

Though Messrs. Smith and Elder distinctly stated in their letter that they did not share in such "belief," the sisters were impatient till they had shown its utter groundlessness, and set themselves perfectly straight. With rapid decision, they resolved that Charlotte and Anne should start, for London, that very day, in order to prove their separate identity to Messrs. Smith and Elder, and demand from the credulous publisher his reasons for a "belief" so directly at variance with an assurance which had several times been given to him. Having arrived at this determination, they made their preparations with resolute promptness. There were many household duties to be performed that day; but they were all got through. The two sisters each packed up a change of dress in a small box, which they sent down to Keighley by an opportune cart; and after early tea they set off to walk thither---no doubt in some excitement; for, independently of the cause of their going to London, it was Anne's first visit there. A great thunderstorm overtook them on their way that summer evening to the station; but they had no time to seek shelter. They only just caught the train at Keighley, arrived at Leeds, and were whirled up by the night train to London.

About eight o'clock on the Saturday morning, they arrived at the Chapter Coffee-house, Paternoster Row---a strange place, but they did not well know where else to go. They refreshed themselves by washing, and had some breakfast. Then they sat still for a few minutes, to consider what next should be done.

When they had been discussing their project in the quiet of Haworth Parsonage the day before, and planning the mode of setting about the business on which they were going to London, they had resolved to take a cab, if they should find it desirable, from their inn to Cornhill; but that, amidst the bustle and "queer state of inward excitement" in which they found themselves, as they sat and considered their position on the Saturday morning, they quite forgot even the possibility of hiring a conveyance; and when they set forth, they became so dismayed by the crowded streets, and the impeded crossings, that they stood still repeatedly, in complete despair of making progress, and were nearly an hour in walking the half-mile they had to go. Neither Mr. Smith nor Mr. Williams knew that they were coming; they were entirely unknown to the publishers of "Jane Eyre", who were not, in fact, aware whether the "Bells" were men or women, but had always written to them as to men.

On reaching Mr. Smith's, Charlotte put his own letter into his hands; the same letter which had excited so much disturbance at Haworth Parsonage only twenty-four hours before. "Where did you get this?" said he,---as if he could not believe that the two young ladies dressed in black, of slight figures and diminutive stature, looking pleased yet agitated, could be the embodied Currer and Acton Bell, for whom curiosity had been hunting so eagerly in vain. An explanation ensued, and Mr. Smith at once began to form plans for their amusement and pleasure during their stay in London. He urged them to meet a few literary friends at his house; and this was a strong temptation to Charlotte, as amongst them were one or two of the writers whom she particularly wished to see; but her resolution to remain unknown induced her firmly to put it aside.

The sisters were equally persevering in declining Mr. Smith's invitations to stay at his house. They refused to leave their quarters, saying they were not prepared for a long stay.

When they returned back to their inn, poor Charlotte paid for the excitement of the interview, which had wound up the agitation and hurry of the last twenty-four hours, by a racking headache and harassing sickness. Towards evening, as she rather expected some of the ladies of Mr. Smith's family to call, she prepared herself for the chance, by taking a strong dose of sal-volatile, which roused her a little, but still, as she says, she was "in grievous bodily case," when their visitors were announced, in full evening costume. The sisters had not understood that it had been settled that they were to go to the Opera, and therefore were not ready. Moreover, they had no fine elegant dresses either with them, or in the world. But Miss Brontë resolved to raise no objections in the acceptance of kindness. So, in spite of headache and weariness, they made haste to dress themselves in their plain high-made country garments.

Charlotte says, in an account which she gives to her friend of this visit to London, describing the entrance of her party into the Opera-house:---

"Fine ladies and gentlemen glanced at us, as we stood by the box-door, which was not yet opened, with a slight, graceful superciliousness, quite warranted by the circumstances. Still I felt pleasurably excited in spite of headache, sickness, and conscious clownishness; and I saw Anne was calm and gentle, which she always is. The performance was Rossini's 'Barber of Seville,'---very brilliant, though I fancy there are things I should like better. We got home after one o'clock. We had never been in bed the night before; had been in constant excitement for twenty-four hours; you may imagine we were tired. The next day, Sunday, Mr. Williams came early to take us to church; and in the afternoon Mr. Smith and his mother fetched us in a carriage, and took us to his house to dine.

"On Monday we went to the Exhibition of the Royal Academy, the National Gallery, dined again at Mr. Smith's, and then went home to tea with Mr. Williams at his house.

"On Tuesday morning, we left London, laden with books Mr. Smith had given us, and got safely home. A more jaded wretch than I looked, it would be difficult to conceive. I was thin when I went, but I was meagre indeed when I returned, my face looking grey and very old, with strange deep lines ploughed in it---my eyes stared unnaturally. I was weak and yet restless. In a while, however, these bad effects of excitement went off, and I regained my normal condition."

The impression Miss Brontë made upon those with whom she first became acquainted during this visit to London, was of a person with clear judgment and fine sense; and though reserved, possessing unconsciously the power of drawing out others in conversation. She never expressed an opinion without assigning a reason for it; she never put a question without a definite purpose; and yet people felt at their ease in talking with her. All conversation with her was genuine and stimulating; and when she launched forth in praise or reprobation of books, or deeds, or works of art, her eloquence was indeed burning. She was thorough in all that she said or did; yet so open and fair in dealing with a subject, or contending with an opponent, that instead of rousing resentment, she merely convinced her hearers of her earnest zeal for the truth and right.

Not the least singular part of their proceedings was the place at which the sisters had chosen to stay.

Paternoster Row was for many years sacred to publishers. It is a narrow flagged street, lying under the shadow of St. Paul's; at each end there are posts placed, so as to prevent the passage of carriages, and thus preserve a solemn silence for the deliberations of the "Fathers of the Row." The dull warehouses on each side are mostly occupied at present by wholesale stationers; if they be publishers' shops, they show no attractive front to the dark and narrow street. Half-way up, on the left-hand side, is the Chapter Coffee-house. I visited it last June. It was then unoccupied. It had the appearance of a dwelling-house, two hundred years old or so, such as one sometimes sees in ancient country towns; the ceilings of the small rooms were low, and had heavy beams running across them; the walls were wainscotted breast high; the staircase was shallow, broad, and dark, taking up much space in the centre of the house. This then was the Chapter Coffee-house, which, a century ago, was the resort of all the booksellers and publishers; and where the literary hacks, the critics, and even the wits, used to go in search of ideas or employment. This was the place about which Chatterton wrote, in those delusive letters he sent to his mother at Bristol, while he was starving in London. "I am quite familiar at the Chapter Coffee-house, and know all the geniuses there." Here he heard of chances of employment; here his letters were to be left.

Years later, it became the tavern frequented by university men and country clergymen, who were up in London for a few days, and, having no private friends or access into society, were glad to learn what was going on in the world of letters, from the conversation which they were sure to hear in the Coffee-room. In Mr. Brontë's few and brief visits to town, during his residence at Cambridge, and the period of his curacy in Essex, he had stayed at this house; hither he had brought his daughters, when he was convoying them to Brussels; and here they came now, from very ignorance where else to go. It was a place solely frequented by men; I believe there was but one female servant in the house. Few people slept there; some of the stated meetings of the Trade were held in it, as they had been for more than a century; and, occasionally country booksellers, with now and then a clergyman, resorted to it; but it was a strange desolate place for the Miss Brontës to have gone to, from its purely business and masculine aspect. The old "grey-haired elderly man," who officiated as waiter seems to have been touched from the very first with the quiet simplicity of the two ladies, and he tried to make them feel comfortable and at home in the long, low, dingy room up-stairs, where the meetings of the Trade were held. The high narrow windows looked into the gloomy Row; the sisters, clinging together on the most remote window-seat, (as Mr. Smith tells me he found them, when he came, that Saturday evening, to take them to the Opera,) could see nothing of motion, or of change, in the grim, dark houses opposite, so near and close, although the whole breadth of the Row was between. The mighty roar of London was round them, like the sound of an unseen ocean, yet every footfall on the pavement below might be heard distinctly, in that unfrequented street. Such as it was, they preferred remaining at the Chapter Coffee-house, to accepting the invitation which Mr. Smith and his mother urged upon them, and, in after years, Charlotte says:---

"Since those days, I have seen the West End, the parks, the fine squares; but I love the City far better. The City seems so much more in earnest; its business, its rush, its roar, are such serious things, sights, sounds. The City is getting its living---the West End but enjoying its pleasure. At the West End you may be amused; but in the City you are deeply excited." (Villette, vol. i. p. 89.)

Their wish had been to hear Dr. Croly on the Sunday morning, and Mr. Williams escorted them to St. Stephen's, Walbrook; but they were disappointed, as Dr. Croly did not preach. Mr. Williams also took them (as Miss Brontë has mentioned) to drink tea at his house. On the way thither, they had to pass through Kensington Gardens, and Miss Brontë was much "struck with the beauty of the scene, the fresh verdure of the turf, and the soft rich masses of foliage." From remarks on the different character of the landscape in the South to what it was in the North, she was led to speak of the softness and varied intonation of the voices of those with whom she conversed in London, which seem to have made a strong impression on both sisters. All this time those who came in contact with the "Miss Browns" (another pseudonym, also beginning with B), seem only to have regarded them as shy and reserved little country-women, with not much to say. Mr. Williams tells me that on the night when he accompanied the party to the Opera, as Charlotte ascended the flight of stairs leading from the grand entrance up to the lobby of the first tier of boxes, she was so much struck with the architectural effect of the splendid decorations of that vestibule and saloon, that involuntarily she slightly pressed his arm, and whispered, "You know I am not accustomed to this sort of thing." Indeed, it must have formed a vivid contrast to what they were doing and seeing an hour or two earlier the night before, when they were trudging along, with beating hearts and high-strung courage, on the road between Haworth and Keighley, hardly thinking of the thunder-storm that beat about their heads, for the thoughts which filled them of how they would go straight away to London, and prove that they were really two people, and not one imposter. It was no wonder that they returned to Haworth utterly fagged and worn out, after the fatigue and excitement of this visit.

The next notice I find of Charlotte's life at this time is of a different character to anything telling of enjoyment.

"July 28th.

"Branwell is the same in conduct as ever. His constitution seems much shattered. Papa, and sometimes all of us, have sad nights with him. He sleeps most of the day, and consequently will lie awake at night. But has not every house its trial?"

While her most intimate friends were yet in ignorance of the fact of her authorship of "Jane Eyre," she received a letter from one of them, making inquiries about Casterton School. It is but right to give her answer, written on August 28th, 1848.

"Since you wish to hear from me while you are from home, I will write without further delay. It often happens that when we linger at first in answering a friend's letter, obstacles occur to retard us to an inexcusably late period. In my last, I forgot to answer a question which you asked me, and was sorry afterwards for the omission. I will begin, therefore, by replying to it, though I fear what information I can give will come a little late. You said Mrs. ------ had some thoughts of sending ------ to school, and wished to know whether the Clergy Daughters' School at Casterton was an eligible place. My personal knowledge of that institution is very much out of date, being derived from the experience of twenty years ago. The establishment was at that time in its infancy, and a sad rickety infancy it was. Typhus fever decimated the school periodically; and consumption and scrofula, in every variety of form bad air and water, bad and insufficient diet can generate, preyed on the ill-fated pupils. It would not THEN have been a fit place for any of Mrs. ------'s children; but I understand it is very much altered for the better since those days. The school is removed from Cowan Bridge (a situation as unhealthy as it was picturesque---low, damp, beautiful with wood and water) to Casterton. The accommodations, the diet, the discipline, the system of tuition---all are, I believe, entirely altered and greatly improved. I was told that such pupils as behaved well, and remained at the school till their education was finished, were provided with situations as governesses, if they wished to adopt the vocation and much care was exercised in the selection, it was added, that they were also furnished with an excellent wardrobe on leaving Casterton. . . . The oldest family in Haworth failed lately, and have quitted the neighbourhood where their fathers resided before them for, it is said, thirteen generations. . . . Papa, I am most thankful to say, continues in very good health, considering his age; his sight, too, rather, I think, improves than deteriorates. My sisters likewise are pretty well."

But the dark cloud was hanging over that doomed household, and gathering blackness every hour.

On October the 9th, she thus writes:---

"The past three weeks have been a dark interval in our humble home. Branwell's constitution had been failing fast all the summer; but still, neither the doctors nor himself thought him so near his end as he was. He was entirely confined to his bed but for one single day, and was in the village two days before his death. He died, after twenty minutes' struggle, on Sunday morning, September 24th. He was perfectly conscious till the last agony came on. His mind had undergone the peculiar change which frequently precedes death, two days previously; the calm of better feelings filled it; a return of natural affection marked his last moments. He is in God's hands now; and the All-Powerful is likewise the All-Merciful. A deep conviction that he rests at last---rests well, after his brief, erring, suffering, feverish life---fills and quiets my mind now. The final separation, the spectacle of his pale corpse, gave me more acute bitter pain than I could have imagined. Till the last hour comes, we never how know much we can forgive, pity, regret a near relative. All his vices were and are nothing now. We remember only his woes. Papa was acutely distressed at first, but, on the whole, has borne the event well. Emily and Anne are pretty well, though Anne is always delicate, and Emily has a cold and cough at present. It was my fate to sink at the crisis, when I should have collected my strength. Headache and sickness came on first on the Sunday; I could not regain my appetite. Then internal pain attacked me. I became at once much reduced. It was impossible to touch a morsel. At last, bilious fever declared itself. I was confined to bed a week,---a dreary week. But, thank God! health seems now returning. I can sit up all day, and take moderate nourishment. The doctor said at first, I should be very slow in recovering, but I seem to get on faster than he anticipated. I am truly MUCH BETTER."

I have heard, from one who attended Branwell in his last illness, that he resolved on standing up to die. He had repeatedly said, that as long as there was life there was strength of will to do what it chose; and when the last agony came on, he insisted on assuming the position just mentioned. I have previously stated, that when his fatal attack came on, his pockets were found filled with old letters from the woman to whom he was attached. He died! she lives still,---in May Fair. The Eumenides, I suppose, went out of existence at the time when the wail was heard, "Great Pan is dead." I think we could better have spared him than those awful Sisters who sting dead conscience into life.

I turn from her for ever. Let us look once more into the Parsonage at Haworth.

"Oct. 29th, 1848.

"I think I have now nearly got over the effects of my late illness, and am almost restored to my normal condition of health. I sometimes wish that it was a little higher, but we ought to be content with such blessings as we have, and not pine after those that are out of our reach. I feel much more uneasy about my sister than myself just now. Emily's cold and cough are very obstinate. I fear she has pain in her chest, and I sometimes catch a shortness in her breathing, when she has moved at all quickly. She looks very thin and pale. Her reserved nature occasions me great uneasiness of mind. It is useless to question her; you get no answers. It is still more useless to recommend remedies; they are never adopted. Nor can I shut my eyes to Anne's great delicacy of constitution. The late sad event has, I feel, made me more apprehensive than common. I cannot help feeling much depressed sometimes. I try to leave all in God's hands; to trust in His goodness; but faith and resignation are difficult to practise under some circumstances. The weather has been most unfavourable for invalids of late; sudden changes of temperature, and cold penetrating winds have been frequent here. Should the atmosphere become more settled, perhaps a favourable effect might be produced on the general health, and these harassing colds and coughs be removed. Papa has not quite escaped, but he has so far stood it better than any of us. You must not mention my going to ------ this winter. I could not, and would not, leave home on any account. Miss ------ has been for some years out of health now. These things make one FEEL, as well as KNOW, that this world is not our abiding-place. We should not knit human ties too close, or clasp human affections too fondly. They must leave us, or we must leave them, one day. God restore health and strength to all who need it!"

I go on now with her own affecting words in the biographical notice of her sisters.

"But a great change approached. Affliction came in that shape which to anticipate is dread; to look back on grief. In the very heat and burden of the day, the labourers failed over their work. My sister Emily first declined. . . . Never in all her life had she lingered over any task that lay before her, and she did not linger now. She sank rapidly. She made haste to leave us. . . . Day by day, when I, saw with what a front she met suffering, I looked on her with an anguish of wonder and love: I have seen nothing like it; but, indeed, I have never seen her parallel in anything. Stronger than a man, simpler than a child, her nature stood alone. The awful point was that, while full of ruth for others, on herself she had no pity; the spirit was inexorable to the flesh; from the trembling hands, the unnerved limbs, the fading eyes, the same service was exacted as they had rendered in health. To stand by and witness this, and not dare to remonstrate, was a pain no words can render."

In fact, Emily never went out of doors after the Sunday succeeding Branwell's death. She made no complaint; she would not endure questioning; she rejected sympathy and help. Many a time did Charlotte and Anne drop their sewing, or cease from their writing, to listen with wrung hearts to the failing step, the laboured breathing, the frequent pauses, with which their sister climbed the short staircase; yet they dared not notice what they observed, with pangs of suffering even deeper than hers. They dared not notice it in words, far less by the caressing assistance of a helping arm or hand. They sat, still and silent.

"Nov. 23rd, 1848.

"I told you Emily was ill, in my last letter. She has not rallied yet. She is VERY ill. I believe, if you were to see her, your impression would be that there is no hope. A more hollow, wasted, pallid aspect I have not beheld. The deep tight cough continues; the breathing after the least exertion is a rapid pant; and these symptoms are accompanied by pains in the chest and side. Her pulse, the only time she allowed it be to felt, was found to beat 115 per minute. In this state she resolutely refuses to see a doctor; she will give no explanation of her feelings, she will scarcely allow her feelings to be alluded to. Our position is, and has been for some weeks, exquisitely painful. God only knows how all this is to terminate. More than once, I have been forced boldly to regard the terrible event of her loss as possible, and even probable. But nature shrinks from such thoughts. I think Emily seems the nearest thing to my heart in the world."

When a doctor had been sent for, and was in the very house, Emily refused to see him. Her sisters could only describe to him what symptoms they had observed; and the medicines which he sent she would not take, denying that she was ill.

"Dec. 10th, 1848.

"I hardly know what to say to you about the subject which now interests me the most keenly of anything in this world, for, in truth, I hardly know what to think myself. Hope and fear fluctuate daily. The pain in her side and chest is better; the cough, the shortness of breath, the extreme emaciation continue. I have endured, however, such tortures of uncertainty on this subject that, at length, I could endure it no longer; and as her repugnance to seeing a medical man continues immutable,---as she declares 'no poisoning doctor' shall come near her,---I have written unknown to her, to an eminent physician in London, giving as minute a statement of her case and symptoms as I could draw up, and requesting an opinion. I expect an answer in a day or two. I am thankful to say, that my own health at present is very tolerable. It is well such is the case; for Anne, with the best will in the world to be useful, is really too delicate to do or bear much. She, too, at present, has frequent pains in the side. Papa is also pretty well, though Emily's state renders him very anxious.

"The ------s (Anne Brontë's former pupils) were here about a week ago. They are attractive and stylish-looking girls. They seemed overjoyed to see Anne: when I went into the room, they were clinging round her like two children---she, meantime, looking perfectly quiet and passive. . . . I. and H. took it into their heads to come here. I think it probable offence was taken on that occasion,---from what cause, I know not; and as, if such be the case, the grudge must rest upon purely imaginary grounds,---and since, besides, I have other things to think about, my mind rarely dwells upon the subject. If Emily were but well, I feel as if I should not care who neglected, misunderstood, or abused me. I would rather you were not of the number either. The crab-cheese arrived safely. Emily has just reminded me to thank you for it: it looks very nice. I wish she were well enough to eat it."

But Emily was growing rapidly worse. I remember Miss Brontë's shiver at recalling the pang she felt when, after having searched in the little hollows and sheltered crevices of the moors for a lingering spray of heather---just one spray, however withered---to take in to Emily, she saw that the flower was not recognised by the dim and indifferent eyes. Yet, to the last, Emily adhered tenaciously to her habits of independence. She would suffer no one to assist her. Any effort to do so roused the old stern spirit. One Tuesday morning, in December, she arose and dressed herself as usual, making many a pause, but doing everything for herself, and even endeavouring to take up her employment of sewing: the servants looked on, and knew what the catching, rattling breath, and the glazing of the eye too surely foretold; but she kept at her work; and Charlotte and Anne, though full of unspeakable dread, had still the faintest spark of hope. On that morning Charlotte wrote thus---probably in the very presence of her dying sister:---

"Tuesday.

"I should have written to you before, if I had had one word of hope to say; but I have not. She grows daily weaker. The physician's opinion was expressed too obscurely to be of use. He sent some medicine, which she would not take. Moments so dark as these I have never known. I pray for God's support to us all. Hitherto He has granted it."

The morning drew on to noon. Emily was worse: she could only whisper in gasps. Now, when it was too late, she said to Charlotte, "If you will send for a doctor, I will see him now." About two o'clock she died.

"Dec. 21st, 1848.

"Emily suffers no more from pain or weakness now. She never will suffer more in this world. She is gone, after a hard short conflict. She died on TUESDAY, the very day I wrote to you. I thought it very possible she might be with us still for weeks; and a few hours afterwards, she was in eternity. Yes; there is no Emily in time or on earth now. Yesterday we put her poor, wasted, mortal frame quietly under the church pavement. We are very calm at present. Why should we be otherwise? The anguish of seeing her suffer is over; the spectacle of the pains of death is gone by; the funeral day is past. We feel she is at peace. No need now to tremble for the hard frost and the keen wind. Emily does not feel them. She died in a time of promise. We saw her taken from life in its prime. But it is God's will, and the place where she is gone is better than that she has left.

"God has sustained me, in a way that I marvel at, through such agony as I had not conceived. I now look at Anne, and wish she were well and strong; but she is neither; nor is papa. Could you now come to us for a few days? I would not ask you to stay long. Write and tell me if you could come next week, and by what train. I would try to send a gig for you to Keighley. You will, I trust, find us tranquil. Try to come. I never so much needed the consolation of a friend's presence. Pleasure, of course, there would be none for you in the visit, except what your kind heart would teach you to find in doing good to others."

As the old, bereaved father and his two surviving children followed the coffin to the grave, they were joined by Keeper, Emily's fierce, faithful bull-dog. He walked alongside of the mourners, and into the church, and stayed quietly there all the time that the burial service was being read. When he came home, he lay down at Emily's chamber door, and howled pitifully for many days. Anne Brontë drooped and sickened more rapidly from that time; and so ended the year 1848.

CHAPTER III.

An article on "Vanity Fair" and "Jane Eyre" had appeared in the Quarterly Review of December, 1848. Some weeks after, Miss Brontë wrote to her publishers, asking why it had not been sent to her; and conjecturing that it was unfavourable, she repeated her previous request, that whatever was done with the laudatory, all critiques adverse to the novel might be forwarded to her without fail. The Quarterly Review was accordingly sent. I am not aware that Miss Brontë took any greater notice of the article than to place a few sentences out of it in the mouth of a hard and vulgar woman in "Shirley," where they are so much in character, that few have recognised them as a quotation. The time when the article was read was good for Miss Brontë; she was numbed to all petty annoyances by the grand severity of Death. Otherwise she might have felt more keenly than they deserved the criticisms which, while striving to be severe, failed in logic, owing to the misuse of prepositions; and have smarted under conjectures as to the authorship of "Jane Eyre," which, intended to be acute, were merely flippant. But flippancy takes a graver name when directed against an author by an anonymous writer. We call it then cowardly insolence.

Every one has a right to form his own conclusion respecting the merits and demerits of a book. I complain not of the judgment which the reviewer passes on "Jane Eyre." Opinions as to its tendency varied then, as they do now. While I write, I receive a letter from a clergyman in America in which he says: "We have in our sacred of sacreds a special shelf, highly adorned, as a place we delight to honour, of novels which we recognise as having had a good influence on character OUR character. Foremost is 'Jane Eyre.'"

Nor do I deny the existence of a diametrically opposite judgment. And so (as I trouble not myself about the reviewer's style of composition) I leave his criticisms regarding the merits of the work on one side. But when---forgetting the chivalrous spirit of the good and noble Southey, who said: "In reviewing anonymous works myself, when I have known the authors I have never mentioned them, taking it for granted they had sufficient reasons for avoiding the publicity"---the Quarterly reviewer goes on into gossiping conjectures as to who Currer Bell really is, and pretends to decide on what the writer may be from the book, I protest with my whole soul against such want of Christian charity. Not even the desire to write a "smart article," which shall be talked about in London, when the faint mask of the anonymous can be dropped at pleasure if the cleverness of the review be admired---not even this temptation can excuse the stabbing cruelty of the judgment. Who is he that should say of an unknown woman: "She must be one who for some sufficient reason has long forfeited the society of her sex"? Is he one who has led a wild and struggling and isolated life,---seeing few but plain and outspoken Northerns, unskilled in the euphuisms which assist the polite world to skim over the mention of vice? Has he striven through long weeping years to find excuses for the lapse of an only brother; and through daily contact with a poor lost profligate, been compelled into a certain familiarity with the vices that his soul abhors? Has he, through trials, close following in dread march through his household, sweeping the hearthstone bare of life and love, still striven hard for strength to say, "It is the Lord! let Him do what seemeth to Him good"---and sometimes striven in vain, until the kindly Light returned? If through all these dark waters the scornful reviewer have passed clear, refined, free from stain,---with a soul that has never in all its agonies cried "lama sabachthani,"---still, even then let him pray with the Publican rather than judge with the Pharisee.

"Jan. 10th, 1849.

"Anne had a very tolerable day yesterday, and a pretty quiet night last night, though she did not sleep much. Mr. Wheelhouse ordered the blister to be put on again. She bore it without sickness. I have just dressed it, and she is risen and come down-stairs. She looks somewhat pale and sickly. She has had one dose of the cod-liver oil; it smells and tastes like train oil. I am trying to hope, but the day is windy, cloudy, and stormy. My spirits fall at intervals very low; then I look where you counsel me to look, beyond earthly tempests and sorrows. I seem to get strength, if not consolation. It will not do to anticipate. I feel that hourly. In the night, I awake and long for morning; then my heart is wrung. Papa continues much the same; he was very faint when he came down to breakfast. . . . Dear E------, your friendship is some comfort to me. I am thankful for it. I see few lights through the darkness of the present time, but amongst them the constancy of a kind heart attached to me is one of the most cheering and serene."

"Jan. 15th, 1849.

"I can scarcely say that Anne is worse, nor can I say she is better. She varies often in the course of a day, yet each day is passed pretty much the same. The morning is usually the best time; the afternoon and the evening the most feverish. Her cough is the most troublesome at night, but it is rarely violent. The pain in her arm still disturbs her. She takes the cod-liver oil and carbonate of iron regularly; she finds them both nauseous, but especially the oil. Her appetite is small indeed. Do not fear that I shall relax in my care of her. She is too precious not to be cherished with all the fostering strength I have. Papa, I am thankful to say, has been a good deal better this last day or two.

"As to your queries about myself, I can only say, that if I continue as I am I shall do very well. I have not yet got rid of the pains in my chest and back. They oddly return with every change of weather; and are still sometimes accompanied with a little soreness and hoarseness, but I combat them steadily with pitch plasters and bran tea. I should think it silly and wrong indeed not to be regardful of my own health at present; it would not do to be ill NOW.

"I avoid looking forward or backward, and try to keep looking upward. This is not the time to regret, dread, or weep. What I have and ought to do is very distinctly laid out for me; what I want, and pray for, is strength to perform it. The days pass in a slow, dark march; the nights are the test; the sudden wakings from restless sleep, the revived knowledge that one lies in her grave, and another not at my side, but in a separate and sick bed. However, God is over all."

"Jan. 22nd, 1849.

"Anne really did seem to be a little better during some mild days last week, but to-day she looks very pale and languid again. She perseveres with the cod-liver oil, but still finds it very nauseous.

"She is truly obliged to you for the soles for her shoes, and finds them extremely comfortable. I am to commission you to get her just such a respirator as Mrs. ------ had. She would not object to give a higher price, if you thought it better. If it is not too much trouble, you may likewise get me a pair of soles; you can send them and the respirator when you send the box. You must put down the price of all, and we will pay you in a Post Office order. "Wuthering Heights" was given to you. I have sent ------ neither letter nor parcel. I had nothing but dreary news to write, so preferred that others should tell her. I have not written to ------ either. I cannot write, except when I am quite obliged."

"Feb. 11th, 1849.

"We received the box and its contents quite safely to-day. The penwipers are very pretty, and we are very much obliged to you for them. I hope the respirator will be useful to Anne, in case she should ever be well enough to go out again. She continues very much in the same state---I trust not greatly worse, though she is becoming very thin. I fear it would be only self-delusion to fancy her better. What effect the advancing season may have on her, I know not; perhaps the return of really warm weather may give nature a happy stimulus. I tremble at the thought of any change to cold wind or frost. Would that March were well over! Her mind seems generally serene, and her sufferings hitherto are nothing like Emily's. The thought of what may be to come grows more familiar to my mind; but it is a sad, dreary guest."

"March 16th, 1849.

"We have found the past week a somewhat trying one; it has not been cold, but still there have been changes of temperature whose effect Anne has felt unfavourably. She is not, I trust, seriously worse, but her cough is at times very hard and painful, and her strength rather diminished than improved. I wish the month of March was well over. You are right in conjecturing that I am somewhat depressed; at times I certainly am. It was almost easier to bear up when the trial was at its crisis than now. The feeling of Emily's loss does not diminish as time wears on; it often makes itself most acutely recognised. It brings too an inexpressible sorrow with it; and then the future is dark. Yet I am well aware, it will not do either to complain, or sink, and I strive to do neither. Strength, I hope and trust, will yet be given in proportion to the burden; but the pain of my position is not one likely to lessen with habit. Its solitude and isolation are oppressive circumstances, yet I do not wish for any friends to stay with me; I could not do with any one---not even you---to share the sadness of the house; it would rack me intolerably. Meantime, judgment is still blent with mercy. Anne's sufferings still continue mild. It is my nature, when left alone, to struggle on with a certain perseverance, and I believe God will help me."

Anne had been delicate all her life; a fact which perhaps made them less aware than they would otherwise have been of the true nature of those fatal first symptoms. Yet they seem to have lost but little time before they sent for the first advice that could be procured. She was examined with the stethoscope, and the dreadful fact was announced that her lungs were affected, and that tubercular consumption had already made considerable progress. A system of treatment was prescribed, which was afterwards ratified by the opinion of Dr. Forbes.

For a short time they hoped that the disease was arrested. Charlotte---herself ill with a complaint that severely tried her spirits---was the ever-watchful nurse of this youngest, last sister. One comfort was that Anne was the patientest, gentlest invalid that could be. Still, there were hours, days, weeks of inexpressible anguish to be borne; under the pressure of which Charlotte could only pray and pray she did, right earnestly. Thus she writes on March 24th;---

"Anne's decline is gradual and fluctuating; but its nature is not doubtful. . . . In spirit she is resigned: at heart she is, I believe, a true Christian. . . . May God support her and all of us through the trial of lingering sickness, and aid her in the last hour when the struggle which separates soul from body must be gone through! We saw Emily torn from the midst of us when our hearts clung to her with intense attachment. . . She was scarce buried when Anne's health failed. . . . These things would be too much, if reason, unsupported by religion, were condemned to bear them alone. I have cause to be most thankful for the strength that has hitherto been vouchsafed both to my father and to myself. God, I think, is especially merciful to old age; and for my own part, trials, which in perspective would have seemed to me quite intolerable, when they actually came I endured without prostration. Yet I must confess that, in the time which has elapsed since Emily's death, there have been moments of solitary, deep, inert affliction, far harder to bear than those which immediately followed our loss. The crisis of bereavement has an acute pang which goads to exertion; the desolate after-feeling sometimes paralyses. I have learnt that we are not to find solace in our own strength; we must seek it in God's omnipotence. Fortitude is good; but fortitude itself must be shaken under us to teach us how weak we are!"

All through this illness of Anne's, Charlotte had the comfort of being able to talk to her about her state; a comfort rendered inexpressibly great by the contrast which it presented to the recollection of Emily's rejection of all sympathy. If a proposal for Anne's benefit was made, Charlotte could speak to her about it, and the nursing and dying sister could consult with each other as to its desirability. I have seen but one of Anne's letters; it is the only time we seem to be brought into direct personal contact with this gentle, patient girl. In order to give the requisite preliminary explanation, I must state that the family of friends, to which E------ belonged, proposed that Anne should come to them; in order to try what change of air and diet, and the company of kindly people could do towards restoring her to health. In answer to this proposal, Charlotte writes:---

"March 24th.

"I read your kind note to Anne, and she wishes me to thank you sincerely for your friendly proposal. She feels, of course, that it would not do to take advantage of it, by quartering an invalid upon the inhabitants of ------; but she intimates there is another way in which you might serve her, perhaps with some benefit to yourself as well as to her. Should it, a month or two hence, be deemed advisable that she should go either to the sea-side, or to some inland watering-place---and should papa be disinclined to move, and I consequently obliged to remain at home---she asks, could you be her companion? Of course I need not add that in the event of such an arrangement being made, you would be put to no expense. This, dear E., is Anne's proposal; I make it to comply with her wish; but for my own part, I must add that I see serious objections to your accepting it---objections I cannot name to her. She continues to vary; is sometimes worse, and sometimes better, as the weather changes; but, on the whole, I fear she loses strength. Papa says her state is most precarious; she may be spared for some time, or a sudden alteration might remove her before we are aware. Were such an alteration to take place while she was far from home, and alone with you, it would be terrible. The idea of it distresses me inexpressibly, and I tremble whenever she alludes to the project of a journey. In short, I wish we could gain time, and see how she gets on. If she leaves home it certainly should not be in the capricious month of May, which is proverbially trying to the weak. June would be a safer month. If we could reach June, I should have good hopes of her getting through the summer. Write such an answer to this note as I can show Anne. You can write any additional remarks to me on a separate piece of paper. Do not consider yourself as confined to discussing only our sad affairs. I am interested in all that interests you."

FROM ANNE BRONTË

"April 5th, 1849.

"My dear Miss ------,---I thank you greatly for your kind letter, and your ready compliance with my proposal, as far as the WILL can go at least. I see, however, that your friends are unwilling that you should undertake the responsibility of accompanying me under present circumstances. But I do not think there would be any great responsibility in the matter. I know, and everybody knows, that you would be as kind and helpful as any one could possibly be, and I hope I should not be very troublesome. It would be as a companion, not as a nurse, that I should wish for your company; otherwise I should not venture to ask it. As for your kind and often-repeated invitation to ------, pray give my sincere thanks to your mother and sisters, but tell them I could not think of inflicting my presence upon them as I now am. It is very kind of them to make so light of the trouble, but still there must be more or less, and certainly no pleasure, from the society of a silent invalid stranger. I hope, however, that Charlotte will by some means make it possible to accompany me after all. She is certainly very delicate, and greatly needs a change of air and scene to renovate her constitution. And then your going with me before the end of May, is apparently out of the question, unless you are disappointed in your visitors; but I should be reluctant to wait till then, if the weather would at all permit an earlier departure. You say May is a trying month, and so say others. The earlier part is often cold enough, I acknowledge, but, according to my experience, we are almost certain of some fine warm days in the latter half, when the laburnums and lilacs are in bloom; whereas June is often cold, and July generally wet. But I have a more serious reason than this for my impatience of delay. The doctors say that change of air or removal to a better climate would hardly ever fail of success in consumptive cases, if the remedy were taken IN TIME; but the reason why there are so many disappointments is, that it is generally deferred till it is too late. Now I would not commit this error; and, to say the truth, though I suffer much less from pain and fever than I did when you were with us, I am decidedly weaker, and very much thinner. My cough still troubles me a good deal, especially in the night, and, what seems worse than all, I am subject to great shortness of breath on going up-stairs or any slight exertion. Under these circumstances, I think there is no time to be lost. I have no horror of death: if I thought it inevitable, I think I could quietly resign myself to the prospect, in the hope that you, dear Miss ------, would give as much of your company as you possibly could to Charlotte, and be a sister to her in my stead. But I wish it would please God to spare me, not only for papa's and Charlotte's sakes, but because I long to do some good in the world before I leave it. I have many schemes in my head for future practice---humble and limited indeed---but still I should not like them all to come to nothing, and myself to have lived to so little purpose. But God's will be done. Remember me respectfully to your mother and sisters, and believe me, dear Miss ------, yours most affectionately,

"ANNE BRONTË."

It must have been about this time that Anne composed her last verses, before "the desk was closed, and the pen laid aside for ever."

I.

"I hoped that with the brave and strong
My portioned task might lie;
To toil amid the busy throng,
With purpose pure and high.

II.

"But God has fixed another part,
And He has fixed it well:
I said so with my bleeding heart,
When first the anguish fell.

III.

"Thou God, hast taken our delight,
Our treasured hope, away;
Thou bid'st us now weep through the night
And sorrow through the day.

IV.

"These weary hours will not be lost,
These days of misery,---
These nights of darkness, anguish-tost,---
Can I but turn to Thee.

IV.

"With secret labour to sustain
In humble patience every blow;
To gather fortitude from pain,

And hope and holiness from woe.

VI.

"Thus let me serve Thee from my heart,
Whate'er may be my written fate;
Whether thus early to depart,
Or yet a while to wait.

VII.

"If Thou should'st bring me back to life,
More humbled I should be;
More wise---more strengthened for the strife,
More apt to lean on Thee.

VIII.

"Should death be standing at the gate,
Thus should I keep my vow;
But, Lord, whatever be my fate,
Oh let me serve Thee now!"

I take Charlotte's own words as the best record of her thoughts and feelings during all this terrible time.

"April 12th.

"I read Anne's letter to you; it was touching enough, as you say. If there were no hope beyond this world,---no eternity, no life to come,---Emily's fate, and that which threatens Anne, would be heart-breaking. I cannot forget Emily's death-day; it becomes a more fixed, a darker, a more frequently recurring idea in my mind than ever. It was very terrible. She was torn, conscious, panting, reluctant, though resolute, out of a happy life. But it WILL NOT do to dwell on these things.

"I am glad your friends object to your going with Anne: it would never do. To speak truth, even if your mother and sisters had consented, I never could. It is not that there is any laborious attention to pay her; she requires, and will accept, but little nursing; but there would be hazard, and anxiety of mind, beyond what you ought to be subject to. If, a month or six weeks hence, she continues to wish for a change as much as she does now, I shall (D. V.) go with her myself. It will certainly be my paramount duty; other cares must be made subservient to that. I have consulted Mr. T------: he does not object, and recommends Scarborough, which was Anne's own choice. I trust affairs may be so ordered, that you may be able to be with us at least part of the time. . . . Whether in lodgings or not, I should wish to be boarded. Providing oneself is, I think, an insupportable nuisance. I don't like keeping provisions in a cupboard, locking up, being pillaged, and all that. It is a petty, wearing annoyance."

The progress of Anne's illness was slower than that of Emily's had been; and she was too unselfish to refuse trying means, from which, if she herself had little hope of benefit, her friends might hereafter derive a mournful satisfaction.

"I began to flatter myself she was getting strength. But the change to frost has told upon her; she suffers more of late. Still her illness has none of the fearful rapid symptoms which appalled in Emily's case. Could she only get over the spring, I hope summer may do much for her, and then early removal to a warmer locality for the winter might, at least, prolong her life. Could we only reckon upon another year, I should be thankful; but can we do this for the healthy? A few days ago I wrote to have Dr. Forbes' opinion. . . . He warned us against entertaining sanguine hopes of recovery. The cod-liver oil he considers a peculiarly efficacious medicine. He, too, disapproved of change of residence for the present. There is some feeble consolation in thinking we are doing the very best that can be done. The agony of forced, total neglect, is not now felt, as during Emily's illness. Never may we be doomed to feel such agony again. It was terrible. I have felt much less of the disagreeable pains in my chest lately, and much less also of the soreness and hoarseness. I tried an application of hot vinegar, which seemed to do good."

"May 1st.

"I was glad to hear that when we go to Scarborough, you will be at liberty to go with us, but the journey and its consequences still continue a source of great anxiety to me, I must try to put it off two or three weeks longer if I can; perhaps by that time the milder season may have given Anne more strength,perhaps it will be otherwise; I cannot tell. The change to fine weather has not proved beneficial to her so far. She has sometimes been so weak, and suffered so much from pain in the side, during the last few days, that I have not known what to think. . . . She may rally again, and be much better, but there must be SOME improvement before I can feel justified in taking her away from home. Yet to delay is painful; for, as is ALWAYS the case, I believe, under her circumstances, she seems herself not half conscious of the necessity for such delay. She wonders, I believe, why I don't talk more about the journey: it grieves me to think she may even be hurt by my seeming tardiness. She is very much emaciated,---far more than when you were with us; her arms are no thicker than a little child's. The least exertion brings a shortness of breath. She goes out a little every day, but we creep rather than walk. . . . Papa continues pretty well;---I hope I shall be enabled to bear up. So far, I have reason for thankfulness to God."

May had come, and brought the milder weather longed for; but Anne was worse for the very change. A little later on it became colder, and she rallied, and poor Charlotte began to hope that, if May were once over, she might last for a long time. Miss Brontë wrote to engage the lodgings at Scarborough,---a place which Anne had formerly visited with the family to whom she was governess. They took a good-sized sitting-room, and an airy double-bedded room (both commanding a sea-view), in one of the best situations of the town. Money was as nothing in comparison with life; besides, Anne had a small legacy left to her by her godmother, and they felt that she could not better employ this than in obtaining what might prolong life, if not restore health. On May 16th, Charlotte writes:

"It is with a heavy heart I prepare; and earnestly do I wish the fatigue of the journey were well over. It may be borne better than I expect; for temporary stimulus often does much; but when I see the daily increasing weakness, I know not what to think. I fear you will be shocked when you see Anne; but be on your guard, dear E------, not to express your feelings; indeed, I can trust both your self-possession and your kindness. I wish my judgment sanctioned the step of going to Scarborough, more fully than it does. You ask how I have arranged about leaving Papa. I could make no special arrangement. He wishes me to go with Anne, and would not hear of Mr. N------'s coming, or anything of that kind; so I do what I believe is for the best, and leave the result to Providence."

They planned to rest and spend a night at York; and, at Anne's desire, arranged to make some purchases there. Charlotte ends the letter to her friend, in which she tells her all this, with---

"May 23rd.

"I wish it seemed less like a dreary mockery in us to talk of buying bonnets, etc. Anne was very ill yesterday. She had difficulty of breathing all day, even when sitting perfectly still. To-day she seems better again. I long for the moment to come when the experiment of the sea-air will be tried. Will it do her good? I cannot tell; I can only wish. Oh! if it would please God to strengthen and revive Anne, how happy we might be together: His will, however, be done!"

The two sisters left Haworth on Thursday, May 24th. They were to have done so the day before, and had made an appointment with their friend to meet them at the Leeds Station, in order that they might all proceed together. But on Wednesday morning Anne was so ill, that it was impossible for the sisters to set out; yet they had no means of letting their friend know of this, and she consequently arrived at Leeds station at the time specified. There she sate waiting for several hours. It struck her as strange at the time---and it almost seems ominous to her fancy now---that twice over, from two separate arrivals on the line by which she was expecting her friends, coffins were carried forth, and placed in hearses which were in waiting for their dead, as she was waiting for one in four days to become so.

The next day she could bear suspense no longer, and set out for Haworth, reaching there just in time to carry the feeble, fainting invalid into the chaise which stood at the gate to take them down to Keighley. The servant who stood at the Parsonage gates, saw Death written on her face, and spoke of it. Charlotte saw it and did not speak of it,---it would have been giving the dread too distinct a form; and if this last darling yearned for the change to Scarborough, go she should, however Charlotte's heart might be wrung by impending fear. The lady who accompanied them, Charlotte's beloved friend of more than twenty years, has kindly written out for me the following account of the journey---and of the end.

"She left her home May 24th, 1849---died May 28th. Her life was calm, quiet, spiritual: SUCH was her end. Through the trials and fatigues of the journey, she evinced the pious courage and fortitude of a martyr. Dependence and helplessness were ever with her a far sorer trial than hard, racking pain.

"The first stage of our journey was to York; and here the dear invalid was so revived, so cheerful, and so happy, we drew consolation, and trusted that at least temporary improvement was to be derived from the change which SHE had so longed for, and her friends had so dreaded for her.

"By her request we went to the Minster, and to her it was an overpowering pleasure; not for its own imposing and impressive grandeur only, but because it brought to her susceptible nature a vital and overwhelming sense of omnipotence. She said, while gazing at the structure, 'If finite power can do this, what is the . . . ?' and here emotion stayed her speech, and she was hastened to a less exciting scene.

"Her weakness of body was great, but her gratitude for every mercy was greater. After such an exertion as walking to her bed-room, she would clasp her hands and raise her eyes in silent thanks, and she did this not to the exclusion of wonted prayer, for that too was performed on bended knee, ere she accepted the rest of her couch.

"On the 25th we arrived at Scarborough; our dear invalid having, during the journey, directed our attention to every prospect worthy of notice.

"On the 26th she drove on the sands for an hour; and lest the poor donkey should be urged by its driver to a greater speed than her tender heart thought right, she took the reins, and drove herself. When joined by her friend, she was charging the boy-master of the donkey to treat the poor animal well. She was ever fond of dumb things, and would give up her own comfort for them.

"On Sunday, the 27th, she wished to go to church, and her eye brightened with the thought of once more worshipping her God amongst her fellow-creatures. We thought it prudent to dissuade her from the attempt, though it was evident her heart was longing to join in the public act of devotion and praise.

"She walked a little in the afternoon, and meeting with a sheltered and comfortable seat near the beach, she begged we would leave her, and enjoy the various scenes near at hand, which were new to us but familiar to her. She loved the place, and wished us to share her preference.

"The evening closed in with the most glorious sunset ever witnessed. The castle on the cliff stood in proud glory gilded by the rays of the declining sun. The distant ships glittered like burnished gold; the little boats near the beach heaved on the ebbing tide, inviting occupants. The view was grand beyond description. Anne was drawn in her easy chair to the window, to enjoy the scene with us. Her face became illumined almost as much as the glorious scene she gazed upon. Little was said, for it was plain that her thoughts were driven by the imposing view before her to penetrate forwards to the regions of unfading glory. She again thought of public worship, and wished us to leave her, and join those who were assembled at the House of God. We declined, gently urging the duty and pleasure of staying with her, who was now so dear and so feeble. On returning to her place near the fire, she conversed with her sister upon the propriety of returning to their home. She did not wish it for her own sake, she said she was fearing others might suffer more if her decease occurred where she was. She probably thought the task of accompanying her lifeless remains on a long journey was more than her sister could bear---more than the bereaved father could bear, were she borne home another, and a third tenant of the family-vault in the short space of nine months.

"The night was passed without any apparent accession of illness. She rose at seven o'clock, and performed most of her toilet herself, by her expressed wish. Her sister always yielded such points, believing it was the truest kindness not to press inability when it was not acknowledged. Nothing occurred to excite alarm till about 11 A. M. She then spoke of feeling a change. She believed she had not long to live. Could she reach home alive, if we prepared immediately for departure? A physician was sent for. Her address to him was made with perfect composure. She begged him to say how long he thought she might live;---not to fear speaking the truth, for she was not afraid to die. The doctor reluctantly admitted that the angel of death was already arrived, and that life was ebbing fast. She thanked him for his truthfulness, and he departed to come again very soon. She still occupied her easy chair, looking so serene, so reliant there was no opening for grief as yet, though all knew the separation was at hand. She clasped her hands, and reverently invoked a blessing from on high; first upon her sister, then upon her friend, to whom she said, 'Be a sister in my stead. Give Charlotte as much of your company as you can.' She then thanked each for her kindness and attention.

"Ere long the restlessness of approaching death appeared, and she was borne to the sofa; on being asked if she were easier, she looked gratefully at her questioner, and said, 'It is not YOU who can give me ease, but soon all will be well, through the merits of our Redeemer.' Shortly after this, seeing that her sister could hardly restrain her grief, she said, 'Take courage, Charlotte; take courage.' Her faith never failed, and her eye never dimmed till about two o'clock, when she calmly and without a sigh passed from the temporal to the eternal. So still, and so hallowed were her last hours and moments. There was no thought of assistance or of dread. The doctor came and went two or three times. The hostess knew that death was near, yet so little was the house disturbed by the presence of the dying, and the sorrow of those so nearly bereaved, that dinner was announced as ready, through the half-opened door, as the living sister was closing the eyes of the dead one. She could now no more stay the welled-up grief of her sister with her emphatic and dying 'Take courage,' and it burst forth in brief but agonising strength. Charlotte's affection, however, had another channel, and there it turned in thought, in care, and in tenderness. There was bereavement, but there was not solitude;--- sympathy was at hand, and it was accepted. With calmness, came the consideration of the removal of the dear remains to their home resting-place. This melancholy task, however, was never performed; for the afflicted sister decided to lay the flower in the place where it had fallen. She believed that to do so would accord with the wishes of the departed. She had no preference for place. She thought not of the grave, for that is but the body's goal, but of all that is beyond it.

"Her remains rest,

'Where the south sun warms the now dear sod, Where the ocean billows lave and strike the steep and turf-covered rock.'"

Anne died on the Monday. On the Tuesday Charlotte wrote to her father; but, knowing that his presence was required for some annual Church solemnity at Haworth, she informed him that she had made all necessary arrangements for the interment and that the funeral would take place so soon, that he could hardly arrive in time for it. The surgeon who had visited Anne on the day of her death, offered his attendance, but it was respectfully declined.

Mr. Brontë wrote to urge Charlotte's longer stay at the seaside. Her health and spirits were sorely shaken; and much as he naturally longed to see his only remaining child, he felt it right to persuade her to take, with her friend, a few more weeks' change of scene,---though even that could not bring change of thought. Late in June the friends returned homewards,---parting rather suddenly (it would seem) from each other, when their paths diverged.

"July, 1849.

"I intended to have written a line to you to-day, if I had not received yours. We did indeed part suddenly; it made my heart ache that we were severed without the time to exchange a word;

and yet perhaps it was better. I got here a little before eight o'clock. All was clean and bright waiting for me. Papa and the servants were well; and all received me with an affection which should have consoled. The dogs seemed in strange ecstasy. I am certain they regarded me as the harbinger of others. The dumb creatures thought that as I was returned, those who had been so long absent were not far behind.

"I left Papa soon, and went into the dining-room: I shut the door---I tried to be glad that I was come home. I have always been glad before---except once---even then I was cheered. But this time joy was not to be the sensation. I felt that the house was all silent---the rooms were all empty. I remembered where the three were laid---in what narrow dark dwellings---never more to reappear on earth. So the sense of desolation and bitterness took possession of me. The agony that WAS to be undergone, and WAS NOT to be avoided, came on. I underwent it, and passed a dreary evening and night, and a mournful morrow; to-day I am better.

"I do not know how life will pass, but I certainly do feel confidence in Him who has upheld me hitherto. Solitude may be cheered, and made endurable beyond what I can believe. The great trial is when evening closes and night approaches. At that hour, we used to assemble in the dining-room---we used to talk. Now I sit by myself---necessarily I am silent. I cannot help thinking of their last days, remembering their sufferings, and what they said and did, and how they looked in mortal affliction. Perhaps all this will become less poignant in time.

"Let me thank you once more, dear E------, for your kindness to me, which I do not mean to forget. How did you think all looking at your home? Papa thought me a little stronger; he said my eyes were not so sunken."

"July 14th, 1849.

"I do not much like giving an account of myself. I like better to go out of myself, and talk of something more cheerful. My cold, wherever I got it, whether at Easton or elsewhere, is not vanished yet. It began in my head, then I had a sore throat, and then a sore chest, with a cough, but only a trifling cough, which I still have at times. The pain between my shoulders likewise amazed me much. Say nothing about it, for I confess I am too much disposed to be nervous. This nervousness is a horrid phantom. I dare communicate no ailment to Papa; his anxiety harasses me inexpressibly.

"My life is what I expected it to be. Sometimes when I wake in the morning, and know that Solitude, Remembrance, and Longing are to be almost my sole companions all day through--- that at night I shall go to bed with them, that they will long keep me sleepless---that next morning I shall wake to them again,---sometimes, Nell, I have a heavy heart of it. But crushed I am not, yet; nor robbed of elasticity, nor of hope, nor quite of endeavour. I have some strength to fight the battle of life. I am aware, and can acknowledge, I have many comforts, many mercies. Still I can GET ON. But I do hope and pray, that never may you, or any one I love, be placed as I am. To sit in a lonely room---the clock ticking loud through a still house--- and have open before the mind's eye the record of the last year, with its shocks, sufferings, losses---is a trial.

"I write to you freely, because I believe you will hear me with moderation---that you will not take alarm or think me in any way worse off than I am."

CHAPTER IV.

The tale of "Shirley" had been begun soon after the publication of "Jane Eyre." If the reader will refer to the account I have given of Miss Brontë's schooldays at Roe Head, he will there see how every place surrounding that house was connected with the Luddite riots, and will learn how stories and anecdotes of that time were rife among the inhabitants of the neighbouring villages; how Miss Wooler herself, and the elder relations of most of her schoolfellows, must have known the actors in those grim disturbances. What Charlotte had heard there as a girl came up in her mind when, as a woman, she sought a subject for her next work; and she sent to Leeds for a file of the Mercuries of 1812, '13, and '14; in order to understand the spirit of those eventful times. She was anxious to write of things she had known and seen; and among the number was the West Yorkshire character, for which any tale laid among the Luddites would afford full scope. In "Shirley" she took the idea of most of her characters from life, although the incidents and situations were, of course, fictitious. She thought that if these last were purely imaginary, she might draw from the real without detection, but in this she was mistaken; her studies were too closely accurate. This occasionally led her into difficulties. People recognised themselves, or were recognised by others, in her graphic descriptions of their personal appearance, and modes of action and turns of thought; though they were placed in new positions, and figured away in scenes far different to those in which their actual life had been passed. Miss Brontë was struck by the force or peculiarity of the character of some one whom she knew; she studied it, and analysed it with subtle power; and having traced it to its germ, she took that germ as the nucleus of an imaginary character, and worked outwards;---thus reversing the process of analysation, and unconsciously reproducing the same external development. The "three curates" were real living men, haunting Haworth and the neighbouring district; and so obtuse in perception that, after the first burst of anger at having their ways and habits chronicled was over, they rather enjoyed the joke of calling each other by the names she had given them. "Mrs. Pryor" was well known to many who loved the original dearly. The whole family of the Yorkes were, I have been assured, almost daguerreotypes. Indeed Miss Brontë told me that, before publication, she had sent those parts of the novel in which these remarkable persons are introduced, to one of the sons; and his reply, after reading it, was simply that "she had not drawn them strong enough." From those many-sided sons, I suspect, she drew all that there was of truth in the characters of the heroes in her first two works. They, indeed, were almost the only young men she knew intimately, besides her brother. There was much friendship, and still more confidence between the Brontë family and them,---although their intercourse was often broken and irregular. There was never any warmer feeling on either side.

The character of Shirley herself, is Charlotte's representation of Emily. I mention this, because all that I, a stranger, have been able to learn about her has not tended to give either me, or my readers, a pleasant impression of her. But we must remember how little we are acquainted with her, compared to that sister, who, out of her more intimate knowledge, says that she "was genuinely good, and truly great," and who tried to depict her character in Shirley Keeldar, as what Emily Brontë would have been, had she been placed in health and prosperity.

Miss Brontë took extreme pains with "Shirley." She felt that the fame she had acquired imposed upon her a double responsibility. She tried to make her novel like a piece of actual life,---feeling sure that, if she but represented the product of personal experience and observation truly, good would come out of it in the long run. She carefully studied the different reviews and criticisms that had appeared on "Jane Eyre," in hopes of extracting precepts and advice from which to profit.

Down into the very midst of her writing came the bolts of death. She had nearly finished the second volume of her tale when Branwell died,---after him Emily,---after her Anne;---the pen, laid down when there were three sisters living and loving, was taken up when one alone remained. Well might she call the first chapter that she wrote after this, "The Valley of the Shadow of Death."

I knew in part what the unknown author of "Shirley" must have suffered, when I read those pathetic words which occur at the end of this and the beginning of the succeeding chapter:---

"Till break of day, she wrestled with God in earnest prayer.

"Not always do those who dare such divine conflict prevail. Night after night the sweat of agony may burst dark on the forehead; the supplicant may cry for mercy with that soundless voice the soul utters when its appeal is to the Invisible. 'Spare my beloved,' it may implore. 'Heal my life's life. Rend not from me what long affection entwines with my whole nature. God of Heaven---bend---hear---be clement!' And after this cry and strife, the sun may rise and see him worsted. That opening morn, which used to salute him with the whispers of zephyrs, the carol of skylarks, may breathe, as its first accents, from the dear lips which colour and heat have quitted,---'Oh! I have had a suffering night. This morning I am worse. I have tried to rise. I cannot. Dreams I am unused to have troubled me.'

"Then the watcher approaches the patient's pillow, and sees a new and strange moulding of the familiar features, feels at once that the insufferable moment draws nigh, knows that it is God's will his idol should be broken, and bends his head, and subdues his soul to the sentence he cannot avert, and scarce can bear. . . .

"No piteous, unconscious moaning sound---which so wastes our strength that, even if we have sworn to be firm, a rush of unconquerable tears sweeps away the oath---preceded her waking. No space of deaf apathy followed. The first words spoken were not those of one becoming estranged from this world, and already permitted to stray at times into realms foreign to the living."

She went on with her work steadily. But it was dreary to write without any one to listen to the progress of her tale,---to find fault or to sympathise,---while pacing the length of the parlour in the evenings, as in the days that were no more. Three sisters had done this,---then two, the other sister dropping off from the walk,---and now one was left desolate, to listen for echoing steps that never came,---and to hear the wind sobbing at the windows, with an almost articulate sound.

But she wrote on, struggling against her own feelings of illness; "continually recurring feelings of slight cold; slight soreness in the throat and chest, of which, do what I will," she writes, "I cannot get rid."

In August there arose a new cause for anxiety, happily but temporary.

"Aug. 23rd, 1849.

"Papa has not been well at all lately. He has had another attack of bronchitis. I felt very uneasy about him for some days---more wretched indeed than I care to tell you. After what has happened, one trembles at any appearance of sickness; and when anything ails Papa, I feel too keenly that he is the LAST---the only near and dear relative I have in the world. Yesterday and to-day he has seemed much better, for which I am truly thankful. . . .

"From what you say of Mr. ------, I think I should like him very much. ------ wants shaking to be put out about his appearance. What does it matter whether her husband dines in a dress-coat, or a market-coat, provided there be worth, and honesty, and a clean shirt underneath?"

"Sept. 10th, 1849.

"My piece of work is at last finished, and despatched to its destination. You must now tell me when there is a chance of your being able to come here. I fear it will now be difficult to arrange, as it is so near the marriage-day. Note well, it would spoil all my pleasure, if you put yourself or any one else to inconvenience to come to Haworth. But when it is CONVENIENT, I shall be truly glad to see you. . . . Papa, I am thankful to say, is better, though not strong. He is often troubled with a sensation of nausea. My cold is very much less troublesome, I am sometimes quite free from it. A few days since, I had a severe bilious attack, the consequence of sitting too closely to my writing; but it is gone now. It is the first from which I have suffered since my return from the sea-side. I had them every month before."

"Sept. 13th, 1849.

"If duty and the well-being of others require that you should stay at home, I cannot permit myself to complain, still, I am very, VERY sorry that circumstances will not permit us to meet just now. I would without hesitation come to ------, if Papa were stronger; but uncertain as are both his health and spirits, I could not possibly prevail on myself to leave him now. Let us hope that when we do see each other our meeting will be all the more pleasurable for being delayed. Dear E------, you certainly have a heavy burden laid on your shoulders, but such burdens, if well borne, benefit the character; only we must take the GREATEST, CLOSEST, MOST WATCHFUL care not to grow proud of our strength, in case we should be enabled to bear up under the trial. That pride, indeed, would be sign of radical weakness. The strength, if strength we have, is certainly never in our own selves; it is given us."

To W. S. WILLIAMS, ESQ.

"Sept. 21st, 1849.

"My dear Sir,---I am obliged to you for preserving my secret, being at least as anxious as ever (MORE anxious I cannot well be) to keep quiet. You asked me in one of your letters lately, whether I thought I should escape identification in Yorkshire. I am so little known, that I think I shall. Besides, the book is far less founded on the Real, than perhaps appears. It would be difficult to explain to you how little actual experience I have had of life, how few persons I have known, and how very few have known me.

"As an instance how the characters have been managed, take that of Mr. Helstone. If this character had an original, it was in the person of a clergyman who died some years since at the advanced age of eighty. I never saw him except once---at the consecration of a church---when I was a child of ten years old. I was then struck with his appearance, and stern, martial air. At a subsequent period, I heard him talked about in the neighbourhood where he had resided: some mention him with enthusiasm---others with detestation. I listened to various anecdotes, balanced evidence against evidence, and drew an inference. The original of Mr. Hall I have seen; he knows me slightly; but he would as soon think I had closely observed him or taken him for a character---he would as soon, indeed, suspect me of writing a hook---a novel---as he would his dog, Prince. Margaret Hall called "Jane Eyre" a 'wicked book,' on the authority of the Quarterly; an expression which, coming from her, I will here confess, struck somewhat deep. It opened my eyes to the harm the Quarterly had done. Margaret would not have called it 'wicked,' if she had not been told so.

"No matter,---whether known or unknown---misjudged, or the contrary,---I am resolved not to write otherwise. I shall bend as my powers tend. The two human beings who understood me, and whom I understood, are gone: I have some that love me yet, and whom I love, without expecting, or having a right to expect, that they shall perfectly understand me. I am satisfied; but I must have my own way in the matter of writing. The loss of what we possess nearest and dearest to us in this world, produces an effect upon the character we search out what we have yet left that can support, and, when found, we cling to it with a hold of new-strung tenacity. The faculty of imagination lifted me when I was sinking, three months ago; its active exercise has kept my head above water since; its results cheer me now, for I feel they have enabled me to give pleasure to others. I am thankful to God, who gave me the faculty; and it is for me a part of my religion to defend this gift, and to profit by its possession.---Yours sincerely,

"**CHARLOTTE BRONTË.**"

At the time when this letter was written, both Tabby and the young servant whom they had to assist her were ill in bed; and, with the exception of occasional aid, Miss Brontë had all the household work to perform, as well as to nurse the two invalids.

The serious illness of the younger servant was at its height, when a cry from Tabby called Miss Brontë into the kitchen, and she found the poor old woman of eighty laid on the floor, with her head under the kitchen-grate; she had fallen from her chair in attempting to rise. When I saw her, two years later, she described to me the tender care which Charlotte had taken of her at this time; and wound up her account of "how her own mother could not have had more thought for her nor Miss Brontë had," by saying, "Eh! she's a good one---she IS!"

But there was one day when the strung nerves gave way---when, as she says, "I fairly broke down for ten minutes; sat and cried like a fool. Tabby could neither stand nor walk. Papa had just been declaring that Martha was in imminent danger. I was myself depressed with headache and sickness. That day I hardly knew what to do, or where to turn. Thank God! Martha is now convalescent: Tabby, I trust, will be better soon. Papa is pretty well. I have the satisfaction of knowing that my publishers are delighted with what I sent them. This supports me. But life is a battle. May we all be enabled to fight it well!"

The kind friend, to whom she thus wrote, saw how the poor over-taxed system needed bracing, and accordingly sent her a shower-bath---a thing for which she had long been wishing. The receipt of it was acknowledged as follows:---

"Sept. 28th, 1849. ". . . Martha is now almost well, and Tabby much better. A huge monster-package, from 'Nelson, Leeds,' came yesterday. You want chastising roundly and soundly. Such are the thanks you get for all your trouble. . . . Whenever you come to Haworth, you shall certainly have a thorough drenching in your own shower-bath. I have not yet unpacked the wretch.---"Yours, as you deserve,

C. B."

There was misfortune of another kind impending over her. There were some railway shares, which, so early as 1846, she had told Miss Wooler she wished to sell, but had kept because she could not persuade her sisters to look upon the affair as she did, and so preferred running the risk of loss, to hurting Emily's feelings by acting in opposition to her opinion. The depreciation of these same shares was now verifying Charlotte's soundness of judgment. They were in the York and North-Midland Company, which was one of Mr. Hudson's pet lines, and had the full benefit of his peculiar system of management. She applied to her friend and publisher, Mr. Smith, for information on the subject; and the following letter is in answer to his reply:---

"Oct. 4th, 1849.

"My dear Sir,---I must not THANK you for, but acknowledge the receipt of your letter. The business is certainly very bad; worse than I thought, and much worse than my father has any idea of. In fact, the little railway property I possessed, according to original prices, formed already a small competency for me, with my views and habits. Now, scarcely any portion of it can, with security, be calculated upon. I must open this view of the case to my father by degrees; and, meanwhile, wait patiently till I see how affairs are likely to turn. . . . However the matter may terminate, I ought perhaps to be rather thankful than dissatisfied. When I look at my own case, and compare it with that of thousands besides, I scarcely see room for a murmur. Many, very many, are by the late strange railway system deprived almost of their daily bread. Such then as have only lost provision laid up for the future, should take care how they complain. The thought that 'Shirley' has given pleasure at Cornhill, yields me much quiet comfort. No doubt, however, you are, as I am, prepared for critical severity; but I have good hopes that the vessel is sufficiently sound of construction to weather a gale or two, and to make a prosperous voyage for you in the end."

Towards the close of October in this year, she went to pay a visit to her friend; but her enjoyment in the holiday, which she had so long promised herself when her work was completed, was deadened by a continual feeling of ill-health; either the change of air or the foggy weather produced constant irritation at the chest. Moreover, she was anxious about the impression which her second work would produce on the public mind. For obvious reasons an author is more susceptible to opinions pronounced on the book which follows a great success, than he has ever been before. Whatever be the value of fame, he has it in his possession, and is not willing to have it dimmed or lost.

"Shirley" was published on October 26th.

When it came out, but before reading it, Mr. Lewes wrote to tell her of his intention of reviewing it in the Edinburgh. Her correspondence with him had ceased for some time: much had occurred since.

To G. H. LEWES, ESQ.

"Nov. 1st, 1849.

"My dear Sir,---It is about a year and a half since you wrote to me; but it seems a longer period, because since then it has been my lot to pass some black milestones in the journey of life. Since then there have been intervals when I have ceased to care about literature and critics and fame; when I have lost sight of whatever was prominent in my thoughts at the first publication of 'Jane Eyre;' but now I want these things to come back vividly, if possible: consequently, it was a pleasure to receive your note. I wish you did not think me a woman. I wish all reviewers believed 'Currer Bell' to be a man; they would be more just to him. You will, I know, keep measuring me by some standard of what you deem becoming to my sex; where I am not what you consider graceful, you will condemn me. All mouths will be open against that first chapter; and that first chapter is true as the Bible, nor is it exceptionable. Come what will, I cannot, when I write, think always of myself and of what is elegant and charming in femininity; it is not on those terms, or with such ideas, I ever took pen in hand: and if it is only on such terms my writing will be tolerated, I shall pass away from the public and trouble it no more. Out of obscurity I came, to obscurity I can easily return. Standing afar off, I now watch to see what will become of 'Shirley.' My expectations are very low, and my anticipations somewhat sad and bitter; still, I earnestly conjure you to say honestly what you think; flattery would be worse than vain; there is no consolation in flattery. As for condemnation I cannot, on reflection, see why I should much fear it; there is no one but myself to suffer therefrom, and both happiness and suffering in this life soon pass away. Wishing you all success in your Scottish expedition,---I am, dear Sir, yours sincerely,

C. BELL."

Miss Brontë, as we have seen, had been as anxious as ever to preserve her incognito in "Shirley." She even fancied that there were fewer traces of a female pen in it than in "Jane Eyre"; and thus, when the earliest reviews were published, and asserted that the mysterious writer must be a woman, she was much disappointed. She especially disliked the lowering of the standard by which to judge a work of fiction, if it proceeded from a feminine pen; and praise mingled with pseudo-gallant allusions to her sex, mortified her far more than actual blame.

But the secret, so jealously preserved, was oozing out at last. The publication of "Shirley" seemed to fix the conviction that the writer was an inhabitant of the district where the story was laid. And a clever Haworth man, who had somewhat risen in the world, and gone to settle in Liverpool, read the novel, and was struck with some of the names of places mentioned, and knew the dialect in which parts of it were written. He became convinced that it was the production of some one in Haworth. But he could not imagine who in that village could have written such a work except Miss Brontë. Proud of his conjecture, he divulged the suspicion (which was almost certainty) in the columns of a Liverpool paper; thus the heart of the mystery came slowly creeping out; and a visit to London, which Miss Brontë paid towards the end of the year 1849, made it distinctly known. She had been all along on most happy terms with her publishers; and their kindness had beguiled some of those weary, solitary hours which had so often occurred of late, by sending for her perusal boxes of books more suited to her tastes than any she could procure from the circulating library at Keighley. She often writes such sentences as the following, in her letters to Cornhill:---

"I was indeed very much interested in the books you sent 'Eckermann's Conversations with Goethe,' 'Guesses as Truth,' 'Friends in Council,' and the little work on English social life, pleased me particularly, and the last not least. We sometimes take a partiality to books as to characters, not on account of any brilliant intellect or striking peculiarity they boast, but for the sake of something good, delicate, and genuine. I thought that small book the production of a lady, and an amiable, sensible woman, and I liked it. You must not think of selecting any more works for me yet; my stock is still far from exhausted.

"I accept your offer respecting the 'Athenaeum;' it is a paper I should like much to see, providing that you can send it without trouble. It shall be punctually returned."

In a letter to her friend she complains of the feelings of illness from which she was seldom or never free.

"Nov. 16th, 1849.

You are not to suppose any of the characters in 'Shirley' intended as literal portraits. It would not suit the rules of art, nor of my own feelings; to write in that style. We only suffer reality to SUGGEST, never to DICTATE. The heroines are abstractions and the heroes also. Qualities I have seen, loved, and admired, are here and there put in as decorative gems, to be preserved in that sitting. Since you say you could recognise the originals of all except the heroines, pray whom did you suppose the two Moores to represent? I send you a couple of reviews; the one is in the Examiner, written by Albany Fonblanque, who is called the most brilliant political writer of the day, a man whose dictum is much thought of in London. The other, in the Standard of Freedom, is written by William Howitt, a Quaker! . . . I should be pretty well, if it were not for headaches and indigestion. My chest has been better lately."

In consequence of this long-protracted state of languor, headache, and sickness, to which the slightest exposure to cold added sensations of hoarseness and soreness at the chest, she determined to take the evil in time, as much for her father's sake as for her own, and to go up to London and consult some physician there. It was not her first intention to visit anywhere; but the friendly urgency of her publishers prevailed, and it was decided that she was to become the guest of Mr. Smith. Before she went, she wrote two characteristic letters about "Shirley," from which I shall take a few extracts.

"'Shirley' makes her way. The reviews shower in fast. . . . The best critique which has yet appeared is in the Revue des deux Mondes, a sort of European Cosmopolitan periodical, whose head-quarters are at Paris. Comparatively few reviewers, even in their praise, evince a just comprehension of the author's meaning. Eugene Forcarde, the reviewer in question, follows Currer Bell through every winding, discerns every point, discriminates every shade, proves himself master of the subject, and lord of the aim. With that man I would shake hands, if I saw him. I would say, 'You know me, Monsieur; I shall deem it an honour to know you.' I could not say so much of the mass of the London critics. Perhaps I could not say so much to five hundred men and women in all the millions of Great Britain. That matters little. My own conscience I satisfy first; and having done that, if I further content and delight a Forsarde, a Fonblanque, and a Thackeray, my ambition has had its ration, it is fed; it lies down for the present satisfied; my faculties have wrought a day's task, and earned a day's wages. I am no teacher; to look on me in that light is to mistake me. To teach is not my vocation. What I AM, it is useless to say. Those whom it concerns feel and find it out. To all others I wish only to be an obscure, steady-going, private character. To you, dear E ------, I wish to be a sincere friend. Give me your faithful regard; I willingly dispense with admiration."

"Nov. 26th.

"It is like you to pronounce the reviews not good enough, and belongs to that part of your character which will not permit you to bestow unqualified approbation on any dress, decoration, etc., belonging to you. Know that the reviews are superb; and were I dissatisfied with them, I should be a conceited ape. Nothing higher is ever said, FROM PERFECTLY DISINTERESTED MOTIVES, of any living authors. If all be well, I go to London this week; Wednesday, I think. The dress-maker has done my small matters pretty well, but I wish you could have looked them over, and given a dictum. I insisted on the dresses being made quite plainly."

At the end of November she went up to the "big Babylon," and was immediately plunged into what appeared to her a whirl; for changes, and scenes, and stimulus which would have been a trifle to others, were much to her. As was always the case with strangers, she was a little afraid at first of the family into which she was now received, fancying that the ladies looked on her with a mixture of respect and alarm; but in a few days, if this state of feeling ever existed, her simple, shy, quiet manners, her dainty personal and household ways, had quite done away with it, and she says that she thinks they begin to like her, and that she likes them much, for "kindness is a potent heart-winner." She had stipulated that she should not be expected to see many people. The recluse life she had led, was the cause of a nervous shrinking from meeting any fresh face, which lasted all her life long. Still, she longed to have an idea of the personal appearance and manners of some of those whose writings or letters had interested her. Mr. Thackeray was accordingly invited to meet her, but it so happened that she had been out for the greater part of the morning, and, in consequence, missed the luncheon hour at her friend's house. This brought on a severe and depressing headache in one accustomed to the early, regular hours of a Yorkshire Parsonage; besides, the excitement of meeting, hearing, and sitting next a man to whom she looked up with such admiration as she did to the author of "Vanity Fair," was of itself overpowering to her frail nerves. She writes about this dinner as follows:---

"Dec. 10th, 1849.

"As to being happy, I am under scenes and circumstances of excitement; but I suffer acute pain sometimes,---mental pain, I mean. At the moment Mr. Thackeray presented himself, I was thoroughly faint from inanition, having eaten nothing since a very slight breakfast, and it was then seven o'clock in the evening. Excitement and exhaustion made savage work of me that evening. What he thought of me I cannot tell."

She told me how difficult she found it, this first time of meeting Mr. Thackeray, to decide whether he was speaking in jest or in earnest, and that she had (she believed) completely misunderstood an inquiry of his, made on the gentlemen's coming into the drawing-room. He asked her "if she had perceived the secret of their cigars;" to which she replied literally, discovering in a minute afterwards, by the smile on several faces, that he was alluding to a passage in "Jane Eyre". Her hosts took pleasure in showing her the sights of London. On one of the days which had been set apart for some of these pleasant excursions, a severe review of "Shirley" was published in the Times. She had heard that her book would be noticed by it, and guessed that there was some particular reason for the care with which her hosts mislaid it on that particular morning. She told them that she was aware why she might not see the paper. Mrs. Smith at once admitted that her conjecture was right, and said that they had wished her to go to the day's engagement before reading it. But she quietly persisted in her request to be allowed to have the paper. Mrs. Smith took her work, and tried not to observe the countenance, which the other tried to hide between the large sheets; but she could not help becoming aware of tears stealing down the face and dropping on the lap. The first remark Miss Brontë made was to express her fear lest so severe a notice should check the sale of the book, and injuriously affect her publishers. Wounded as she was, her first thought was for others. Later on (I think that very afternoon) Mr. Thackeray called; she suspected (she said) that he came to see how she bore the attack on "Shirley;" but she had recovered her composure, and conversed very quietly with him: he only learnt from the answer to his direct inquiry that she had read the Times' article. She acquiesced in the recognition of herself as the authoress of "Jane Eyre," because she perceived that there were some advantages to be derived from dropping her pseudonym. One result was an acquaintance with Miss Martineau. She had sent her the novel just published, with a curious note, in which Currer Bell offered a copy of "Shirley" to Miss Martineau, as an acknowledgment of the gratification he had received from her works. From "Deerbrook" he had derived a new and keen pleasure, and experienced a genuine benefit. In HIS mind "Deerbrook," etc.

Miss Martineau, in acknowledging this note and the copy of "Shirley," dated her letter from a friend's house in the neighbourhood of Mr. Smith's residence; and when, a week or two afterwards, Miss Brontë found how near she was to her correspondent, she wrote, in the name of Currer Bell, to propose a visit to her. Six o'clock, on a certain Sunday afternoon (Dec. 10th), was the time appointed. Miss Martineau's friends had invited the unknown Currer Bell to their early tea; they were ignorant whether the name was that of a man or a woman; and had had various conjectures as to sex, age, and appearance. Miss Martineau had, indeed, expressed her private opinion pretty distinctly by beginning her reply, to the professedly masculine note referred to above, with "Dear Madam;" but she had addressed it to "Currer Bell, Esq." At every ring the eyes of the party turned towards the door. Some stranger (a gentleman, I think) came in; for an instant they fancied he was Currer Bell, and indeed an Esq.; he stayed some time---went away. Another ring; "Miss Brontë was announced; and in came a young-looking lady, almost child-like in stature, in a deep mourning dress, neat as a Quaker's, with her beautiful hair smooth and brown, her fine eyes blazing with meaning and her sensible face indicating a habit of self-control." She came,---hesitated one moment at finding four or five people assembled,---then went straight to Miss Martineau with intuitive recognition, and, with the free-masonry of good feeling and gentle breeding, she soon became as one of the family seated round the tea-table; and, before she left, she told them, in a simple, touching manner, of her sorrow and isolation, and a foundation was laid for her intimacy with Miss Martineau.

After some discussion on the subject, and a stipulation that she should not be specially introduced to any one, some gentlemen were invited by Mr. Smith to meet her at dinner the evening before she left town. Her natural place would have been at the bottom of the table by her host; and the places of those who were to be her neighbours were arranged accordingly; but, on entering the dining-room, she quickly passed up so as to sit next to the lady of the house, anxious to shelter herself near some one of her own sex. This slight action arose out of the same womanly seeking after protection on every occasion, when there was no moral duty involved in asserting her independence, that made her about this time write as follows: "Mrs. ------ watches me very narrowly when surrounded by strangers. She never takes her eye from me. I like the surveillance; it seems to keep guard over me."

Respecting this particular dinner-party she thus wrote to the Brussels schoolfellow of former days, whose friendship had been renewed during her present visit to London:---

"The evening after I left you passed better than I expected. Thanks to my substantial lunch and cheering cup of coffee, I was able to wait the eight o'clock dinner with complete resignation, and to endure its length quite courageously, nor was I too much exhausted to converse; and of this I was glad, for otherwise I know my kind host and hostess would have been much disappointed. There were only seven gentlemen at dinner besides Mr. Smith, but of these five were critics---men more dreaded in the world of letters than you can conceive. I did not know how much their presence and conversation had excited me till they were gone, and the reaction commenced. When I had retired for the night, I wished to sleep---the effort to do so was vain. I could not close my eyes. Night passed; morning came, and I rose without having known a moment's slumber. So utterly worn out was I when I got to Derby, that I was again obliged to stay there all night."

"Dec. 17th.

"Here I am at Haworth once more. I feel as if I had come out of an exciting whirl. Not that the hurry and stimulus would have seemed much to one accustomed to society and change, but to me they were very marked. My strength and spirits too often proved quite insufficient to the demand on their exertions. I used to bear up as long as I possibly could, for, when I flagged, I could see Mr. Smith became disturbed; he always thought that something had been said or done to annoy me---which never once happened, for I met with perfect good breeding even from antagonists---men who had done their best or worst to write me down. I explained to him over and over again, that my occasional silence was only failure of the power to talk, never of the will. . . .

"Thackeray is a Titan of mind. His presence and powers impress one deeply in an intellectual sense; I do not see him or know him as a man. All the others are subordinate. I have esteem for some, and, I trust, courtesy for all. I do not, of course, know what they thought of me, but I believe most of them expected me to come out in a more marked, eccentric, striking light. I believe they desired more to admire and more to blame. I felt sufficiently at my ease with all but Thackeray; with him I was fearfully stupid."

She returned to her quiet home, and her noiseless daily duties. Her father had quite enough of the spirit of hero-worship in him to make him take a vivid pleasure in the accounts of what she had heard and whom she had seen. It was on the occasion of one of her visits to London that he had desired her to obtain a sight of Prince Albert's armoury, if possible. I am not aware whether she managed to do this; but she went to one or two of the great national armouries in order that she might describe the stern steel harness and glittering swords to her father, whose imagination was forcibly struck by the idea of such things; and often afterwards, when his spirits flagged and the languor of old age for a time got the better of his indomitable nature, she would again strike on the measure wild, and speak about the armies of strange weapons she had seen in London, till he resumed his interest in the old subject, and was his own keen, warlike, intelligent self again.

CHAPTER V.

Her life at Haworth was so unvaried that the postman's call was the event of her day. Yet she dreaded the great temptation of centring all her thoughts upon this one time, and losing her interest in the smaller hopes and employments of the remaining hours. Thus she conscientiously denied herself the pleasure of writing letters too frequently, because the answers (when she received them) took the flavour out of the rest of her life; or the disappointment, when the replies did not arrive, lessened her energy for her home duties.

The winter of this year in the north was hard and cold; it affected Miss Brontë's health less than usual, however, probably because the change and the medical advice she had taken in London had done her good; probably, also, because her friend had come to pay her a visit, and enforced that attention to bodily symptoms which Miss Brontë was too apt to neglect, from a fear of becoming nervous herself about her own state and thus infecting her father. But she could scarcely help feeling much depressed in spirits as the anniversary of her sister Emily's death came round; all the recollections connected with it were painful, yet there were no outward events to call off her attention, and prevent them from pressing hard upon her. At this time, as at many others, I find her alluding in her letters to the solace which she found in the books sent her from Cornhill.

"What, I sometimes ask, could I do without them? I have recourse to them as to friends; they shorten and cheer many an hour that would be too long and too desolate otherwise; even when my tired sight will not permit me to continue reading, it is pleasant to see them on the shelf, or on the table. I am still very rich, for my stock is far from exhausted. Some other friends have sent me books lately. The perusal of Harriet Martineau's 'Eastern Life' has afforded me great pleasure; and I have found a deep and interesting subject of study in Newman's work on the Soul. Have you read this work? It is daring,---it may be mistaken,---but it is pure and elevated. Froude's 'Nemesis of Faith' I did not like; I thought it morbid; yet in its pages, too, are found sprinklings of truth."

By this time, "Airedale, Wharfedale, Calderdale, and Ribblesdale" all knew the place of residence of Currer Bell. She compared herself to the ostrich hiding its head in the sand; and says that she still buries hers in the heath of Haworth moors; but "the concealment is but self-delusion." Indeed it was. Far and wide in the West Riding had spread the intelligence that Currer Bell was no other than a daughter of the venerable clergyman of Haworth; the village itself caught up the excitement.

"Mr. ------, having finished 'Jane Eyre,' is now crying out for the 'other book;' he is to have it next week. . . . Mr. R ------ has finished 'Shirley;' he is delighted with it. John ------'s wife seriously thought him gone wrong in the head, as she heard him giving vent to roars of laughter as he sat alone, clapping and stamping on the floor. He would read all the scenes about the curates aloud to papa." . . . "Martha came in yesterday, puffing and blowing, and much excited. 'I've heard sich news!' she began. 'What about?' 'Please, ma'am, you've been and written two books---the grandest books that ever was seen. My father has heard it at Halifax, and Mr. G------ T------ and Mr. G------ and Mr. M------ at Bradford; and they are going to have a meeting at the Mechanics' Institute, and to settle about ordering them.' 'Hold your tongue, Martha, and be off.' I fell into a cold sweat. "Jane Eyre" will be read by J------ B------, by Mrs. T-----, and B------. Heaven help, keep, and deliver me!" . . . "The Haworth people have been making great fools of themselves about Shirley; they have taken it in an enthusiastic light. When they got the volumes at the Mechanics' Institute, all the members wanted them. They cast lots for the whole three, and whoever got a volume was only allowed to keep it two days, and was to be fined a shilling per diem for longer detention. It would be mere nonsense and vanity to tell you what they say."

The tone of these extracts is thoroughly consonant with the spirit of Yorkshire and Lancashire people, who try as long as they can to conceal their emotions of pleasure under a bantering exterior, almost as if making fun of themselves. Miss Brontë was extremely touched in the secret places of her warm heart by the way in which those who had known her from her childhood were proud and glad of her success. All round about the news had spread; strangers came "from beyond Burnley" to see her, as she went quietly and unconsciously into church and the sexton "gained many a half-crown" for pointing her out.

But there were drawbacks to this hearty and kindly appreciation which was so much more valuable than fame. The January number of the Edinburgh Review had contained the article on Shirley, of which her correspondent, Mr. Lewes, was the writer. I have said that Miss Brontë was especially anxious to be criticised as a writer, without relation to her sex as a woman. Whether right or wrong, her feeling was strong on this point. Now in this review of Shirley, the heading of the first two pages ran thus: "Mental Equality of the Sexes?" "Female Literature," and through the whole article the fact of the author's sex is never forgotten.

A few days after the review appeared, Mr. Lewes received the following note,---rather in the style of Anne Countess of Pembroke, Dorset, and Montgomery.

To G. H. LEWES, ESQ.

"I can be on my guard against my enemies, but God deliver me from my friends!

CURRER BELL."

In some explanatory notes on her letters to him, with which Mr. Lewes has favoured me, he says:---

"Seeing that she was unreasonable because angry, I wrote to remonstrate with her on quarrelling with the severity or frankness of a review, which certainly was dictated by real admiration and real friendship; even under its objections the friend's voice could be heard."

The following letter is her reply:---

To G. H. LEWES, ESQ.

"Jan. 19th, 1850.

"My dear Sir,---I will tell you why I was so hurt by that review in the Edinburgh; not because its criticism was keen or its blame sometimes severe; not because its praise was stinted (for, indeed, I think you give me quite as much praise as I deserve), but because after I had said earnestly that I wished critics would judge me as an AUTHOR, not as a woman, you so roughly---I even thought so cruelly---handled the question of sex. I dare say you meant no harm, and perhaps you will not now be able to understand why I was so grieved at what you will probably deem such a trifle; but grieved I was, and indignant too.

"There was a passage or two which you did quite wrong to write.

"However, I will not bear malice against you for it; I know what your nature is: it is not a bad or unkind one, though you would often jar terribly on some feelings with whose recoil and quiver you could not possibly sympathise. I imagine you are both enthusiastic and implacable, as you are at once sagacious and careless; you know much and discover much, but you are in such a hurry to tell it all you never give yourself time to think how your reckless eloquence may affect others; and, what is more, if you knew how it did affect them, you would not much care.

"However, I shake hands with you: you have excellent points; you can be generous. I still feel angry, and think I do well to be angry; but it is the anger one experiences for rough play rather than for foul play.---I am yours, with a certain respect, and more chagrin,

CURRER BELL."

As Mr. Lewes says, "the tone of this letter is cavalier." But I thank him for having allowed me to publish what is so characteristic of one phase of Miss Brontë's mind. Her health, too, was suffering at this time. "I don't know what heaviness of spirit has beset me of late" (she writes, in pathetic words, wrung out of the sadness of her heart), "made my faculties dull, made rest weariness, and occupation burdensome. Now and then, the silence of the house, the solitude of the room, has pressed on me with a weight I found it difficult to bear, and recollection has not failed to be as alert, poignant, obtrusive, as other feelings were languid. I attribute this state of things partly to the weather. Quicksilver invariably falls low in storms and high winds, and I have ere this been warned of approaching disturbance in the atmosphere by a sense of bodily weakness, and deep, heavy mental sadness, such as some would call PRESENTIMENT,---presentiment indeed it is, but not at all super-natural. . . . I cannot help feeling something of the excitement of expectation till the post hour comes, and when, day after day, it brings nothing, I get low. This is a stupid, disgraceful, unmeaning state of things. I feel bitterly vexed at my own dependence and folly; but it is so bad for the mind to be quite alone, and to have none with whom to talk over little crosses and disappointments, and to laugh them away. If I could write, I dare say I should be better, but I cannot write a line. However (by God's help), I will contend against this folly.

"I had rather a foolish letter the other day from ------. Some things in it nettled me, especially an unnecessarily earnest assurance that, in spite of all I had done in the writing line, I still retained a place in her esteem. My answer took strong and high ground at once. I said I had been troubled by no doubts on the subject; that I neither did her nor myself the injustice to suppose there was anything in what I had written to incur the just forfeiture of esteem. . . .

"A few days since, a little incident happened which curiously touched me. Papa put into my hands a little packet of letters and papers,---telling me that they were mamma's, and that I might read them. I did read them, in a frame of mind I cannot describe. The papers were yellow with time, all having been written before I was born it was strange now to peruse, for the first time, the records of a mind whence my own sprang; and most strange, and at once sad

68

and sweet, to find that mind of a truly fine, pure, and elevated order. They were written to papa before they were married. There is a rectitude, a refinement a constancy, a modesty, a sense, a gentleness about them indescribable. I wished that she had lived, and that I had known her. . . . All through this month of February, I have had a crushing time of it. I could not escape from or rise above certain most mournful recollections,---the last days, the sufferings, the remembered words---most sorrowful to me, of those who, Faith assures me, are now happy. At evening and bed-time, such thoughts would haunt me, bringing a weary heartache."

The reader may remember the strange prophetic vision, which dictated a few words, written on the occasion of the death of a pupil of hers in January, 1840:

"Wherever I seek for her now in this world, she cannot be found; no more than a flower or a leaf which withered twenty years ago. A bereavement of this kind gives one a glimpse of the feeling those must have, who have seen all drop round them---friend after friend, and are left to end their pilgrimage alone."

Even in persons of naturally robust health, and with no

"Ricordarsi di tempo felice Nella miseria---"

to wear, with slow dropping but perpetual pain, upon their spirits, the nerves and appetite will give way in solitude. How much more must it have been so with Miss Brontë, delicate and frail in constitution, tried by much anxiety and sorrow in early life, and now left to face her life alone. Owing to Mr. Brontë's great age, and long-formed habits of solitary occupation when in the house, his daughter was left to herself for the greater part of the day. Ever since his serious attacks of illness, he had dined alone; a portion of her dinner, regulated by strict attention to the diet most suitable for him, being taken into his room by herself. After dinner she read to him for an hour or so, as his sight was too weak to allow of his reading long to himself. He was out of doors among his parishioners for a good part of each day; often for a longer time than his strength would permit. Yet he always liked to go alone, and consequently her affectionate care could be no check upon the length of his walks to the more distant hamlets which were in his cure. He would come back occasionally utterly fatigued; and be obliged to go to bed, questioning himself sadly as to where all his former strength of body had gone to. His strength of will was the same as ever. That which he resolved to do he did, at whatever cost of weariness; but his daughter was all the more anxious from seeing him so regardless of himself and his health. The hours of retiring for the night had always been early in the Parsonage; now family prayers were at eight o'clock; directly after which Mr. Brontë and old Tabby went to bed, and Martha was not long in following. But Charlotte could not have slept if she had gone,---could not have rested on her desolate couch. She stopped up,---it was very tempting,---late and later, striving to beguile the lonely night with some employment, till her weak eyes failed to read or to sew, and could only weep in solitude over the dead that were not. No one on earth can even imagine what those hours were to her. All the grim superstitions of the North had been implanted in her during her childhood by the servants, who believed in them. They recurred to her now,---with no shrinking from the spirits of the Dead, but with such an intense longing once more to stand face to face with the souls of her sisters, as no one but she could have felt. It seemed as if the very strength of her yearning should have compelled them to appear. On windy nights, cries, and sobs, and wailings seemed to go round the house, as of the dearly-beloved striving to force their way to her. Some one conversing with her once objected, in my presence, to that part of "Jane Eyre" in which she hears Rochester's voice crying out to her in a great crisis of her life, he being many, many miles distant at the time. I do not know what incident was in Miss Brontë's recollection when she replied, in a low voice, drawing in her breath, "But it is a true thing; it really happened."

The reader, who has even faintly pictured to himself her life at this time,---the solitary days,---the waking, watching nights,---may imagine to what a sensitive pitch her nerves were strung, and how such a state was sure to affect her health.

It was no bad thing for her that about this time various people began to go over to Haworth, curious to see the scenery described in "Shirley," if a sympathy with the writer, of a more generous kind than to be called mere curiosity, did not make them wish to know whether they could not in some way serve or cheer one who had suffered so deeply.

Among this number were Sir James and Lady Kay Shuttleworth. Their house lies over the crest of the moors which rise above Haworth, at about a dozen miles' distance as the crow flies, though much further by the road. But, according to the acceptation of the word in that uninhabited district, they were neighbours, if they so willed it. Accordingly, Sir James and his wife drove over one morning, at the beginning of March, to call upon Miss Brontë and her father. Before taking leave, they pressed her to visit them at Gawthorpe Hall, their residence on the borders of East Lancashire. After some hesitation, and at the urgency of her father, who was extremely anxious to procure for her any change of scene and society that was offered, she consented to go. On the whole, she enjoyed her visit very much, in spite of her shyness, and the difficulty she always experienced in meeting the advances of those strangers whose kindness she did not feel herself in a position to repay.

She took great pleasure in the "quiet drives to old ruins and old halls, situated among older hills and woods; the dialogues by the old fireside in the antique oak-panneled drawing-room, while they suited him, did not too much oppress and exhaust me. The house, too, is much to my taste; near three centuries old, grey, stately, and picturesque. On the whole, now that the visit is over, I do not regret having paid it. The worst of it is, that there is now some menace hanging over my head of an invitation to go to them in London during the season. This, which would be a great enjoyment to some people, is a perfect terror to me. I should highly prize the advantages to be gained in an extended range of observation; but I tremble at the thought of the price I must necessarily pay in mental distress and physical wear and tear."

On the same day on which she wrote the above, she sent the following letter to Mr. Smith.
"March 16th, 1850.

"I return Mr. H------'s note, after reading it carefully. I tried very hard to understand all he says about art; but, to speak truth, my efforts were crowned with incomplete success. There is a certain jargon in use amongst critics on this point through which it is physically and morally impossible to me to see daylight. One thing however, I see plainly enough, and that is, Mr. Currer Bell needs improvement, and ought to strive after it; and this (D. V.) he honestly intends to do---taking his time, however, and following as his guides Nature and Truth. If these lead to what the critics call art, it is all very well; but if not, that grand desideratum has no chance of being run after or caught. The puzzle is, that while the people of the South object to my delineation of Northern life and manners, the people of Yorkshire and Lancashire approve. They say it is precisely the contrast of rough nature with highly artificial cultivation which forms one of their main characteristics. Such, or something very similar, has been the observation made to me lately, whilst I have been from home, by members of some of the ancient East Lancashire families, whose mansions lie on the hilly border-land between the two counties. The question arises, whether do the London critics, or the old Northern squires, understand the matter best?

"Any promise you require respecting the books shall be willingly given, provided only I am allowed the Jesuit's principle of a mental reservation, giving licence to forget and promise whenever oblivion shall appear expedient. The last two or three numbers of Pendennis will not, I dare say, be generally thought sufficiently exciting, yet I like them. Though the story lingers, (for me) the interest does not flag. Here and there we feel that the pen has been guided by a tired hand, that the mind of the writer has been somewhat chafed and depressed by his recent illness, or by some other cause; but Thackeray still proves himself greater when he is weary than other writers are when they are fresh. The public, of course, will have no compassion for his fatigue, and make no allowance for the ebb of inspiration; but some true-hearted readers here and there, while grieving that such a man should be obliged to write when he is not in the mood, will wonder that, under such circumstances, he should write so well. The parcel of books will come, I doubt not, at such time as it shall suit the good pleasure of the railway officials to send it on,---or rather to yield it up to the repeated and humble solicitations of Haworth carriers;---till when I wait in all reasonable patience and resignation, looking with docility to that model of active self-helpfulness Punch friendly offers the 'Women of England,' in his 'Unprotected Female.'"

The books lent her by her publishers were, as I have before said, a great solace and pleasure to her. There was much interest in opening the Cornhill parcel. But there was pain too; for, as she untied the cords, and took out the volumes one by one, she could scarcely fail to be reminded of those who once, on similar occasions, looked on so eagerly. "I miss familiar voices, commenting mirthfully and pleasantly; the room seems very still---very empty; but yet there is consolation in remembering that Papa will take pleasure in some of the books. Happiness quite unshared can scarcely be called happiness; it has no taste." She goes on to make remarks upon the kind of books sent.

"I wonder how you can choose so well; on no account would I forestall the choice. I am sure any selection I might make for myself would be less satisfactory than the selection others so kindly and judiciously make for me; besides, if I knew all that was coming, it would be comparatively flat. I would much rather not know.

"Amongst the especially welcome works are 'Southey's Life', the 'Women of France,' Hazlitt's 'Essays,' Emerson's 'Representative Men;' but it seems invidious to particularise when all are good. . . . I took up a second small book, Scott's 'Suggestions on Female Education;' that, too, I read, and with unalloyed pleasure. It is very good; justly thought, and clearly and felicitously expressed. The girls of this generation have great advantages; it seems to me that they receive much encouragement in the acquisition of knowledge, and the cultivation of their minds; in these days, women may be thoughtful and well read, without being universally stigmatised as 'Blues' and 'Pedants.' Men begin to approve and aid, instead of ridiculing or checking them in their efforts to be wise. I must say that, for my own part, whenever I have been so happy as to share the conversation of a really intellectual man, my feeling has been, not that the little I knew was accounted a superfluity and impertinence, but that I did not know enough to satisfy just expectation. I have always to explain, 'In me you must not look for great attainments: what seems to you the result of reading and study is chiefly spontaneous and intuitive.' . . . Against the teaching of some (even clever) men, one instinctively revolts. They may possess attainments, they may boast varied knowledge of life and of the world; but if of the finer perceptions, of the more delicate phases of feeling, they be destitute and incapable, of what avail is the rest? Believe me, while hints well worth consideration may come from unpretending sources, from minds not highly cultured, but naturally fine and delicate, from hearts kindly, feeling, and unenvious, learned dictums delivered with pomp and sound may be perfectly empty, stupid, and contemptible. No man ever yet 'by aid of Greek climbed Parnassus,' or taught others to climb it. . . . I enclose for your perusal a scrap of paper which came into my hands without the knowledge of the writer. He is a poor working man of this village---a thoughtful, reading, feeling being, whose mind is too keen for his frame, and wears it out. I have not spoken to him above thrice in my life, for he is a Dissenter, and has rarely come in my way. The document is a sort of record of his feelings, after the perusal of "Jane Eyre;" it is artless and earnest; genuine and generous. You must return it to me, for I value it more than testimonies from higher sources. He said, 'Miss Brontë, if she knew he had written it, would scorn him;' but, indeed, Miss Brontë does not scorn him; she only grieves that a mind of which this is the emanation, should be kept crushed by the leaden hand of poverty---by the trials of uncertain health, and the claims of a large family.

'As to the Times, as you say, the acrimony of its critique has proved, in some measure, its own antidote; to have been more effective, it should have been juster. I think it has had little weight up here in the North it may be that annoying remarks, if made, are not suffered to reach my ear; but certainly, while I have heard little condemnatory of Shirley, more than once have I been deeply moved by manifestations of even enthusiastic approbation. I deem it unwise to dwell much on these matters; but for once I must permit myself to remark, that the generous pride many of the Yorkshire people have taken in the matter, has been such as to awake and claim my gratitude---especially since it has afforded a source of reviving pleasure to my father in his old age. The very curates, poor fellows! show no resentment each characteristically finds solace for his own wounds in crowing over his brethren. Mr. Donne was at first a little disturbed; for a week or two he was in disquietude, but he is now soothed down; only yesterday I had the pleasure of making him a comfortable cup of tea, and seeing him sip it with revived complacency. It is a curious fact that, since he read 'Shirley,' he has come to the house oftener than ever, and been remarkably meek and assiduous to please. Some people's natures are veritable enigmas I quite expected to have had one good scene at least with him; but as yet nothing of the sort has occurred."

CHAPTER VI.

During the earlier months of this spring, Haworth was extremely unhealthy. The weather was damp, low fever was prevalent, and the household at the Parsonage suffered along with its neighbours. Charlotte says, "I have felt it (the fever) in frequent thirst and infrequent appetite; Papa too, and even Martha, have complained." This depression of health produced depression of spirits, and she grew more and more to dread the proposed journey to London with Sir James and Lady Kay Shuttleworth. "I know what the effect and what the pain will be, how wretched I shall often feel, and how thin and haggard I shall get; but he who shuns suffering will never win victory. If I mean to improve, I must strive and endure. . . . Sir James has been a physician, and looks at me with a physician's eye: he saw at once that I could not stand much fatigue, nor bear the presence of many strangers. I believe he would partly understand how soon my stock of animal spirits was brought to a low ebb; but none---not the most skilful physician---can get at more than the outside of these things: the heart knows its own bitterness, and the frame its own poverty, and the mind its own struggles. Papa is eager and restless for me to go; the idea of a refusal quite hurts him."

But the sensations of illness in the family increased; the symptoms were probably aggravated, if not caused, by the immediate vicinity of the church-yard, "paved with rain-blackened tomb-stones." On April 29th she writes:---

"We have had but a poor week of it at Haworth. Papa continues far from well; he is often very sickly in the morning, a symptom which I have remarked before in his aggravated attacks of bronchitis; unless he should get much better, I shall never think of leaving him to go to London. Martha has suffered from tic-douloureux, with sickness and fever, just like you. I have a bad cold, and a stubborn sore throat; in short, everybody but old Tabby is out of sorts. When ------ was here, he complained of a sudden headache, and the night after he was gone I had something similar, very bad, lasting about three hours."

A fortnight later she writes:---

"I did not think Papa well enough to be left, and accordingly begged Sir James and Lady Kay Shuttleworth to return to London without me. It was arranged that we were to stay at several of their friends' and relatives' houses on the way; a week or more would have been taken up on the journey. I cannot say that I regret having missed this ordeal; I would as lief have walked among red-hot plough-shares; but I do regret one great treat, which I shall now miss. Next Wednesday is the anniversary dinner of the Royal Literary Fund Society, held in Freemasons' Hall. Octavian Blewitt, the secretary, offered me a ticket for the ladies' gallery. I should have seen all the great literati and artists gathered in the hall below, and heard them speak; Thackeray and Dickens are always present among the rest. This cannot now be. I don't think all London can afford another sight to me so interesting."

It became requisite, however, before long, that she should go to London on business; and as Sir James Kay Shuttleworth was detained in the country by indisposition, she accepted Mrs. Smith's invitation to stay quietly at her house, while she transacted her affairs.

In the interval between the relinquishment of the first plan and the adoption of the second, she wrote the following letter to one who was much valued among her literary friends:---

"May 22nd.

"I had thought to bring the Leader and the Athenaeum myself this time, and not to have to send them by post, but it turns out otherwise; my journey to London is again postponed, and this time indefinitely. Sir James Kay Shuttleworth's state of health is the cause---a cause, I fear, not likely to be soon removed. . . . Once more, then, I settle myself down in the quietude of Haworth Parsonage, with books for my household companions, and an occasional letter for a visitor; a mute society, but neither quarrelsome, nor vulgarising, nor unimproving.

"One of the pleasures I had promised myself consisted in asking you several questions about the Leader, which is really, in its way, an interesting paper. I wanted, amongst other things, to ask you the real names of some of the contributors, and also what Lewes writes besides his Apprenticeship of Life. I always think the article headed 'Literature' is his. Some of the communications in the 'Open Council' department are odd productions; but it seems to me very fair and right to admit them. Is not the system of the paper altogether a novel one? I do not remember seeing anything precisely like it before.

"I have just received yours of this morning; thank you for the enclosed note. The longings for liberty and leisure which May sunshine wakens in you, stir my sympathy. I am afraid Cornhill is little better than a prison for its inmates on warm spring or summer days. It is a pity to think of you all toiling at your desks in such genial weather as this. For my part, I am free to walk on the moors; but when I go out there alone, everything reminds me of the times when others were with me, and then the moors seem a wilderness, featureless, solitary, saddening. My sister Emily had a particular love for them, and there is not a knoll of heather, not a branch of fern, not a young bilberry leaf, not a fluttering lark or linnet, but reminds me of her. The distant prospects were Anne's delight, and when I look round, she is in the blue tints, the pale mists, the waves and shadows of the horizon. In the hill-country silence, their poetry comes by lines and stanzas into my mind: once I loved it; now I dare not read it, and am driven often to wish I could taste one draught of oblivion, and forget much that, while mind remains, I never shall forget. Many people seem to recall their departed relatives with a sort of melancholy complacency, but I think these have not watched them through lingering sickness, nor witnessed their last moments: it is these reminiscences that stand by your bedside at night, and rise at your pillow in the morning. At the end of all, however, exists the Great Hope. Eternal Life is theirs now."

She had to write many letters, about this time, to authors who sent her their books, and strangers who expressed their admiration of her own. The following was in reply to one of the latter class, and was addressed to a young man at Cambridge:---

"May 23rd, 1850.

"Apologies are indeed unnecessary for a 'reality of feeling, for a genuine unaffected impulse of the spirit,' such as prompted you to write the letter which I now briefly acknowledge.

"Certainly it is 'something to me' that what I write should be acceptable to the feeling heart and refined intellect; undoubtedly it is much to me that my creations (such as they are) should find harbourage, appreciation, indulgence, at any friendly hand, or from any generous mind. You are very welcome to take Jane, Caroline, and Shirley for your sisters, and I trust they will often speak to their adopted brother when he is solitary, and soothe him when he is sad. If they cannot make themselves at home in a thoughtful, sympathetic mind, and diffuse through its twilight a cheering, domestic glow, it is their fault; they are not, in that case, so amiable, so benignant, not so real as they ought to be. If they CAN, and can find household altars in human hearts, they will fulfil the best design of their creation, in therein maintaining a genial flame, which shall warm but not scorch, light but not dazzle.

"What does it matter that part of your pleasure in such beings has its source in the poetry of your own youth rather than in any magic of theirs? What, that perhaps, ten years hence, you may smile to remember your present recollections, and view under another light both 'Currer Bell' and his writings? To me this consideration does not detract from the value of what you now feel. Youth has its romance, and maturity its wisdom, as morning and spring have their freshness, noon and summer their power, night and winter their repose. Each attribute is good in its own season. Your letter gave me pleasure, and I thank you for it.

"CURRER BELL."

Miss Brontë went up to town at the beginning of June, and much enjoyed her stay there; seeing very few persons, according to the agreement she made before she went; and limiting her visit to a fortnight, dreading the feverishness and exhaustion which were the inevitable consequences of the slightest excitement upon her susceptible frame.

"June 12th.

"Since I wrote to you last, I have not had many moments to myself, except such as it was absolutely necessary to give to rest. On the whole, however, I have thus far got on very well, suffering much less from exhaustion than I did last time.

"Of course I cannot give you in a letter a regular chronicle of how my time has been spent. I can only---just notify. what I deem three of its chief incidents: a sight of the Duke of Wellington at the Chapel Royal (he is a real grand old man), a visit to the House of Commons (which I hope to describe to you some day when I see you), and last, not least, an interview with Mr. Thackeray. He made a morning call, and sat above two hours. Mr. Smith only was in the room the whole time. He described it afterwards as a 'queer scene,' and---I suppose it was. The giant sate before me; I was moved to speak to him of some of his short-comings (literary of course); one by one the faults came into my head, and one by one I brought them out, and sought some explanation or defence. He did defend himself, like a great Turk and heathen; that is to say, the excuses were often worse than the crime itself. The matter ended in decent amity; if all be well, I am to dine at his house this evening.

"I have seen Lewes too. . . . I could not feel otherwise to him than half-sadly, half-tenderly,---a queer word that last, but I use it because the aspect of Lewes's face almost moves me to tears; it is so wonderfully like Emily,---her eyes, her features, the very nose, the somewhat prominent mouth, the forehead, even, at moments, the expression: whatever Lewes says, I believe I cannot hate him. Another likeness I have seen, too, that touched me sorrowfully. You remember my speaking of a Miss K., a young authoress, who supported her mother by writing? Hearing that she had a longing to see me, I called on her yesterday. . . . She met me half-frankly, half-tremblingly; we sate down together, and when I had talked with her five minutes, her face was no longer strange, but mournfully familiar;---it was Martha in every lineament. I shall try to find a moment to see her again. . . . I do not intend to stay here, at the furthest, more than a week longer; but at the end of that time I cannot go home, for the house at Haworth is just now unroofed; repairs were become necessary."

She soon followed her letter to the friend to whom it was written; but her visit was a very short one, for, in accordance with a plan made before leaving London, she went on to Edinburgh to join the friends with whom she had been staying in town. She remained only a few days in Scotland, and those were principally spent in Edinburgh, with which she was delighted, calling London a "dreary place" in comparison.

"My stay in Scotland" (she wrote some weeks later) "was short, and what I saw was chiefly comprised in Edinburgh and the neighbourhood, in Abbotsford and in Melrose, for I was obliged to relinquish my first intention of going from Glasgow to Oban, and thence through a portion of the Highlands; but though the time was brief, and the view of objects limited, I found such a charm of situation, association, and circumstance, that I think the enjoyment experienced in that little space equalled in degree, and excelled in kind, all which London yielded during a month's sojourn. Edinburgh, compared to London, is like a vivid page of history compared to a large dull treatise on political economy; and as to Melrose and Abbotsford, the very names possess music and magic."

And again, in a letter to a different correspondent, she says:---

"I would not write to you immediately on my arrival at home, because each return to this old house brings with it a phase of feeling which it is better to pass through quietly before beginning to indite letters. The six weeks of change and enjoyment are past, but they are not lost; memory took a sketch of each as it went by, and, especially, a distinct daguerreotype of the two days I spent in Scotland. Those were two very pleasant days. I always liked Scotland as an idea, but now, as a reality, I like it far better; it furnished me with some hours as happy almost as any I ever spent. Do not fear, however, that I am going to bore you with description; you will, before now, have received a pithy and pleasant report of all things, to which any addition of mine would be superfluous. My present endeavours are directed towards recalling my thoughts, cropping their wings, drilling them into correct discipline, and forcing them to settle to some useful work: they are idle, and keep taking the train down to London, or making a foray over the Border---especially are they prone to perpetrate that last excursion; and who, indeed, that has once seen Edinburgh, with its couchant crag-lion, but must see it again in dreams, waking or sleeping? My dear sir, I do not think I blaspheme, when I tell you that your great London, as compared to Dun-Edin, 'mine own romantic town,' is as prose compared to poetry, or as a great rumbling, rambling, heavy epic compared to a lyric, brief, bright, clear and vital as a flash of lightning. You have nothing like Scott's monument, or, if you had that, and all the glories of architecture assembled together, you have nothing like Arthur's Seat, and, above all, you have not the Scotch national character; and it is that grand character after all which gives the land its true charm, its true greatness.

On her return from Scotland, she again spent a few days with her friends, and then made her way to Haworth.

"July 15th.

I got home very well, and full glad was I that no insuperable obstacle had deferred my return one single day longer. Just at the foot of Bridgehouse hill, I met John, staff in hand; he fortunately saw me in the cab, stopped, and informed me he was setting off to B------, by Mr.

Brontë's orders, to see how I was, for that he had been quite miserable ever since he got Miss ------'s letter. I found, on my arrival, that Papa had worked himself up to a sad pitch of nervous excitement and alarm, in which Martha and Tabby were but too obviously joining him. . . . The house looks very clean, and, I think, is not damp; there is, however, still a great deal to do in the way of settling and arranging,---enough to keep me disagreeably busy for some time to come. I was truly thankful to find Papa pretty well, but I fear he is just beginning to show symptoms of a cold: my cold continues better. . . . An article in a newspaper I found awaiting me on my arrival, amused me; it was a paper published while I was in London. I enclose it to give you a laugh; it professes to be written by an Author jealous of Authoresses. I do not know who he is, but he must be one of those I met. . . . The 'ugly men,' giving themselves 'Rochester airs,' is no bad hit; some of those alluded to will not like it."

While Miss Brontë was staying in London, she was induced to sit for her portrait to Richmond. It is a crayon drawing; in my judgment an admirable likeness, though of course there is some difference of opinion on the subject; and, as usual, those best acquainted with the original were least satisfied with the resemblance. Mr. Brontë thought that it looked older than Charlotte did, and that her features had not been flattered; but he acknowledged that the expression was wonderfully good and life-like. She sent the following amusing account of the arrival of the portrait to the donor:---

"Aug. 1st.

"The little box for me came at the same time as the large one for Papa. When you first told me that you had had the Duke's picture framed, and had given it to me, I felt half provoked with you for performing such a work of supererogation, but now, when I see it again, I cannot but acknowledge that, in so doing, you were felicitously inspired. It is his very image, and, as Papa said when he saw it, scarcely in the least like the ordinary portraits; not only the expression, but even the form of the head is different, and of a far nobler character. I esteem it a treasure. The lady who left the parcel for me was, it seems, Mrs. Gore. The parcel contained one of her works, 'The Hamiltons,' and a very civil and friendly note, in which I find myself addressed as 'Dear Jane.' Papa seems much pleased with the portrait, as do the few other persons who have seen it, with one notable exception; viz., our old servant, who tenaciously maintains that it is not like---that it is too old-looking; but as she, with equal tenacity, asserts that the Duke of Wellington's picture is a portrait of 'the Master' (meaning Papa), I am afraid not much weight is to be ascribed to her opinion: doubtless she confuses her recollections of me as I was in childhood with present impressions. Requesting always to be very kindly remembered to your mother and sisters, I am, yours very thanklessly (according to desire),

"C. BRONTË."

It may easily be conceived that two people living together as Mr. Brontë and his daughter did, almost entirely dependent on each other for society, and loving each other deeply (although not demonstratively)---that these two last members of a family would have their moments of keen anxiety respecting each other's health. There is not one letter of hers which I have read, that does not contain some mention of her father's state in this respect. Either she thanks God with simple earnestness that he is well, or some infirmities of age beset him, and she mentions the fact, and then winces away from it, as from a sore that will not bear to be touched. He, in his turn, noted every indisposition of his one remaining child's, exaggerated its nature, and sometimes worked himself up into a miserable state of anxiety, as in the case she refers to, when, her friend having named in a letter to him that his daughter was suffering from a bad cold, he could not rest till he despatched a messenger, to go, "staff in hand" a distance of fourteen miles, and see with his own eyes what was her real state, and return and report.

She evidently felt that this natural anxiety on the part of her father and friend increased the nervous depression of her own spirits, whenever she was ill; and in the following letter she expresses her strong wish that the subject of her health should be as little alluded to as possible.

"Aug. 7th.

"I am truly sorry that I allowed the words to which you refer to escape my lips, since their effect on you has been unpleasant; but try to chase every shadow of anxiety from your mind, and, unless the restraint be very disagreeable to you, permit me to add an earnest request that you will broach the subject to me no more. It is the undisguised and most harassing anxiety of others that has fixed in my mind thoughts and expectations which must canker wherever they take root; against which every effort of religion or philosophy must at times totally fail; and subjugation to which is a cruel terrible fate---the fate, indeed, of him whose life was passed under a sword suspended by a horse-hair. I have had to entreat Papa's consideration on this point. My nervous system is soon wrought on. I should wish to keep it in rational strength and coolness; but to do so I must determinedly resist the kindly-meant, but too irksome expression of an apprehension, for the realisation or defeat of which I have no possible power to be responsible. At present, I am pretty well. Thank God! Papa, I trust, is no worse, but he complains of weakness."

CHAPTER VII.

Her father was always anxious to procure every change that was possible for her, seeing, as he did, the benefit which she derived from it, however reluctant she might have been to leave her home and him beforehand. This August she was invited to go for a week to the neighbourhood of Bowness, where Sir James Kay Shuttleworth had taken a house; but she says, "I consented to go, with reluctance, chiefly to please Papa, whom a refusal on my part would much have annoyed; but I dislike to leave him. I trust he is not worse, but his complaint is still weakness. It is not right to anticipate evil, and to be always looking forward with an apprehensive spirit; but I think grief is a two-edged sword, it cuts both ways; the memory of one loss is the anticipation of another."

It was during this visit at the Briery---Lady Kay Shuttleworth having kindly invited me to meet her there---that I first made acquaintance with Miss Brontë. If I copy out part of a letter, which I wrote soon after this to a friend, who was deeply interested in her writings, I shall probably convey my first impressions more truly and freshly than by amplifying what I then said into a longer description.

"Dark when I got to Windermere station; a drive along the level road to Low-wood; then a stoppage at a pretty house, and then a pretty drawing-room, in which were Sir James and Lady Kay Shuttleworth, and a little lady in a black-silk gown, whom I could not see at first for the dazzle in the room; she came up and shook hands with me at once. I went up to unbonnet, etc.; came down to tea; the little lady worked away and hardly spoke but I had time for a good look at her. She is (as she calls herself) UNDEVELOPED, thin, and more than half a head shorter than I am; soft brown hair, not very dark; eyes (very good and expressive, looking straight and open at you) of the same colour as her hair; a large mouth; the forehead square, broad and rather over-hanging. She has a very sweet voice; rather hesitates in choosing her expressions, but when chosen they seem without an effort admirable, and just befitting the occasion; there is nothing overstrained, but perfectly simple. . . . After breakfast, we four went out on the lake, and Miss Brontë agreed with me in liking Mr. Newman's Soul, and in liking Modern Painters, and the idea of the Seven Lamps; and she told me about Father Newman's lectures at the Oratory in a very quiet, concise, graphic way. . . . She is more like Miss ------ than any one in her ways---if you can fancy Miss ------ to have gone through suffering enough to have taken out every spark of merriment, and to be shy and silent from the habit of extreme, intense solitude. Such a life as Miss Brontë's I never heard of before. ------ described her home to me as in a village of grey stone houses, perched up on the north side of a bleak moor, looking over sweeps of bleak moors, etc., etc.

"We were only three days together; the greater part of which was spent in driving about, in order to show Miss Brontë the Westmoreland scenery, as she had never been there before. We were both included in an invitation to drink tea quietly at Fox How; and I then saw how severely her nerves were taxed by the effort of going amongst strangers. We knew beforehand that the number of the party would not exceed twelve; but she suffered the whole day from an acute headache brought on by apprehension of the evening.

"Brierly Close was situated high above Low-wood, and of course commanded an extensive view and wide horizon. I was struck by Miss Brontë's careful examination of the shape of the clouds and the signs of the heavens, in which she read, as from a book, what the coming weather would be. I told her that I saw she must have a view equal in extent at her own home. She said that I was right, but that the character of the prospect from Haworth was very different; that I had no idea what a companion the sky became to any one living in solitude,---more than any inanimate object on earth,---more than the moors themselves."

The following extracts convey some of her own impressions and feelings respecting this visit:---

"You said I should stay longer than a week in Westmoreland; you ought by this time to know me better. Is it my habit to keep dawdling at a place long after the time I first fixed on for departing? I have got home, and I am thankful to say Papa seems,---to say the least,---no worse than when I left him, yet I wish he were stronger. My visit passed off very well; I am glad I went. The scenery is, of course, grand; could I have wandered about amongst those hills ALONE, I could have drank in all their beauty; even in a carriage with company, it was very well. Sir James was all the while as kind and friendly as he could be: he is in much better health. . . . Miss Martineau was from home; she always leaves her house at Ambleside during the Lake season, to avoid the influx of visitors to which she would otherwise be subject.

"If I could only have dropped unseen out of the carriage, and gone away by myself in amongst those grand hills and sweet dales, I should have drank in the full power of this glorious scenery. In company this can hardly be. Sometimes, while ------ was warning me against the faults of the artist-class, all the while vagrant artist instincts were busy in the mind of his listener.

"I forget to tell you that, about a week before I went to Westmoreland, there came an invitation to Harden Grange; which, of course, I declined. Two or three days after, a large party made their appearance here, consisting of Mrs. F------ and sundry other ladies and two gentlemen; one tall and stately, black haired and whiskered, who turned out to be Lord John Manners,---the other not so distinguished-looking, shy, and a little queer, who was Mr. Smythe, the son of Lord Strangford. I found Mrs. F. a true lady in manners and appearance, very gentle and unassuming. Lord John Manners brought in his hand a brace of grouse for Papa, which was a well-timed present: a day or two before Papa had been wishing for some."

To these extracts I must add one other from a letter referring to this time. It is addressed to Miss Wooler, the kind friend of both her girlhood and womanhood, who had invited her to spend a fortnight with her at her cottage lodgings.

"Haworth, Sept. 27th, 1850.

"When I tell you that I have already been to the Lakes this season, and that it is scarcely more than a month since I returned, you will understand that it is no longer within my option to accept your kind invitation. I wish I could have gone to you. I have already had my excursion, and there is an end of it. Sir James Kay Shuttleworth is residing near Windermere, at a house called the 'Briery,' and it was there I was staying for a little time this August. He very kindly showed me the neighbourhood, as it can be seen from a carriage, and I discerned that the Lake country is a glorious region, of which I had only seen the similitude in dreams, waking or sleeping. Decidedly I find it does not agree with me to prosecute the search of the picturesque in a carriage. A waggon, a spring-cart, even a post-chaise might do; but the carriage upsets everything. I longed to slip out unseen, and to run away by myself in amongst the hills and dales. Erratic and vagrant instincts tormented me, and these I was obliged to control or rather suppress for fear of growing in any degree enthusiastic, and thus drawing attention to the 'lioness'---the authoress.

"You say that you suspect I have formed a large circle of acquaintance by this time. No: I cannot say that I have. I doubt whether I possess either the wish or the power to do so. A few friends I should like to have, and these few I should like to know well; If such knowledge brought proportionate regard, I could not help concentrating my feelings; dissipation, I think, appears synonymous with dilution. However, I have, as yet, scarcely been tried. During the month I spent in London in the spring, I kept very quiet, having the fear of lionising before my eyes. I only went out once to dinner; and once was present at an evening party; and the only visits I have paid have been to Sir James Kay Shuttleworth's and my publisher's. From this system I should not like to depart; as far as I can see, Indiscriminate visiting tends only to a waste of time and a vulgarising of character. Besides, it would be wrong to leave Papa often; he is now in his seventy-fifth year, the infirmities of age begin to creep upon him; during the summer he has been much harassed by chronic bronchitis, but I am thankful to say that he is now somewhat better. I think my own health has derived benefit from change and exercise.

"Somebody in D------ professes to have authority for saying, that 'when Miss Brontë was in London she neglected to attend Divine service on the Sabbath, and in the week spent her time in going about to balls, theatres, and operas.' On the other hand, the London quidnuncs make my seclusion a matter of wonder, and devise twenty romantic fictions to account for it. Formerly I used to listen to report with interest, and a certain credulity; but I am now grown deaf and sceptical: experience has taught me how absolutely devoid of foundation her stories may be."

I must now quote from the first letter I had the privilege of receiving from Miss Brontë. It is dated August the 27th.

"Papa and I have just had tea; he is sitting quietly in his room, and I in mine; 'storms of rain' are sweeping over the garden and churchyard: as to the moors, they are hidden in thick fog. Though alone, I am not unhappy; I have a thousand things to be thankful for, and, amongst the rest, that this morning I received a letter from you, and that this evening I have the privilege of answering it.

"I do not know the 'Life of Sydney Taylor;' whenever I have the opportunity I will get it. The little French book you mention shall also take its place on the list of books to be procured as soon as possible. It treats a subject interesting to all women---perhaps, more especially to single women; though, indeed, mothers, like you, study it for the sake of their daughters. The Westminster Review is not a periodical I see regularly, but some time since I got hold of a number---for last January, I think---in which there was an article entitled 'Woman's Mission' (the phrase is hackneyed), containing a great deal that seemed to me just and sensible. Men begin to regard the position of woman in another light than they used to do; and a few men, whose sympathies are fine and whose sense of justice is strong, think and speak of it with a candour that commands my admiration. They say, however---and, to an extent, truly---that the amelioration of our condition depends on ourselves. Certainly there are evils which our own efforts will best reach; but as certainly there are other evils---deep-rooted in the foundation of the social system---which no efforts of ours can touch: of which we cannot complain; of which it is advisable not too often to think.

"I have read Tennyson's 'In Memoriam,' or rather part of it; I closed the book when I had got about half way. It is beautiful; it is mournful; it is monotonous. Many of the feelings expressed bear, in their utterance, the stamp of truth; yet, if Arthur Hallam had been somewhat nearer Alfred Tennyson, his brother instead of his friend,---I should have distrusted this rhymed, and measured, and printed monument of grief. What change the lapse of years may work I do not know; but it seems to me that bitter sorrow, while recent, does not flow out in verse.

"I promised to send you Wordsworth's 'Prelude,' and, accordingly, despatch it by this post; the other little volume shall follow in a day or two. I shall be glad to hear from you whenever you have time to write to me, but you are never, on any account, to do this except when inclination prompts and leisure permits. I should never thank you for a letter which you had felt it a task to write."

A short time after we had met at the Briery, she sent me the volume of Currer, Ellis, and Acton Bell's poems; and thus alludes to them in the note that accompanied the parcel:---

"The little book of rhymes was sent by way of fulfilling a rashly-made promise; and the promise was made to prevent you from throwing away four shillings in an injudicious purchase. I do not like my own share of the work, nor care that it should be read: Ellis Bell's I think good and vigorous, and Acton's have the merit of truth and simplicity. Mine are chiefly juvenile productions; the restless effervescence of a mind that would not be still. In those days, the sea too often 'wrought and was tempestuous,' and weed, sand, shingle---all turned up in the tumult. This image is much too magniloquent for the subject, but you will pardon it."

Another letter of some interest was addressed, about this time, to a literary friend, on Sept. 5th:---

"The reappearance of the Athenaeum is very acceptable, not merely for its own sake,---though I esteem the opportunity of its perusal a privilege,---but because, as a weekly token of the remembrance of friends, it cheers and gives pleasure. I only fear that its regular transmission may become a task to you; in this case, discontinue it at once.

"I did indeed enjoy my trip to Scotland, and yet I saw little of the face of the country; nothing of its grandeur or finer scenic features; but Edinburgh, Melrose, Abbotsford---these three in themselves sufficed to stir feelings of such deep interest and admiration, that neither at the time did I regret, nor have I since regretted, the want of wider space over which to diffuse the sense of enjoyment. There was room and variety enough to be very happy, and 'enough,' the proverb says, 'is as good as a feast.' The queen, indeed, was right to climb Arthur's Seat with her husband and children. I shall not soon forget how I felt when, having reached its summit, we all sat down and looked over the city---towards the sea and Leith, and the Pentland Hills. No doubt you are proud of being a native of Scotland,---proud of your country, her capital, her children, and her literature. You cannot be blamed.

"The article in the Palladium is one of those notices over which an author rejoices trembling. He rejoices to find his work finely, fully, fervently appreciated, and trembles under the responsibility such appreciation seems to devolve upon him. I am counselled to wait and watch---D. V. I will do so; yet it is harder to wait with the hands bound, and the observant and reflective faculties at their silent and unseen work, than to labour mechanically.

"I need not say how I felt the remarks on 'Wuthering Heights;' they woke the saddest yet most grateful feelings; they are true, they are discriminating, they are full of late justice, but it is very late---alas! in one sense, TOO late. Of this, however, and of the pang of regret for a light prematurely extinguished, it is not wise to speak much. Whoever the author of this article may be, I remain his debtor.

"Yet, you see, even here, Shirley is disparaged in comparison with "Jane Eyre"; and yet I took great pains with Shirley. I did not hurry; I tried to do my best, and my own impression was that it was not inferior to the former work; indeed, I had bestowed on it more time, thought, and anxiety: but great part of it was written under the shadow of impending calamity; and the last volume, I cannot deny, was composed in the eager, restless endeavour to combat mental sufferings that were scarcely tolerable.

"You sent the tragedy of 'Galileo Galilei,' by Samuel Brown, in one of the Cornhill parcels; it contained, I remember, passages of very great beauty. Whenever you send any more books (but that must not be till I return what I now have) I should be glad if you would include amongst them the 'Life of Dr. Arnold.' Do you know also the 'Life of Sydney Taylor?' I am not familiar even with the name, but it has been recommended to me as a work meriting perusal. Of course, when I name any book, it is always understood that it should be quite convenient to send it."

CHAPTER VIII.

It was thought desirable about this time, to republish "Wuthering Heights" and "Agnes Grey", the works of the two sisters, and Charlotte undertook the task of editing them.

She wrote to Mr. Williams, September 29th, 1850, "It is my intention to write a few lines of remark on 'Wuthering Heights,' which, however, I propose to place apart as a brief preface before the tale. I am likewise compelling myself to read it over, for the first time of opening the book since my sister's death. Its power fills me with renewed admiration; but yet I am oppressed: the reader is scarcely ever permitted a taste of unalloyed pleasure; every beam of sunshine is poured down through black bars of threatening cloud; every page is surcharged with a sort of moral electricity; and the writer was unconscious of all this---nothing could make her conscious of it.

"And this makes me reflect,---perhaps I am too incapable of perceiving the faults and peculiarities of my own style.

"I should wish to revise the proofs, if it be not too great an inconvenience to send them. It seems to me advisable to modify the orthography of the old servant Joseph's speeches; for though, as it stands, it exactly renders the Yorkshire dialect to a Yorkshire ear, yet, I am sure Southerns must find it unintelligible; and thus one of the most graphic characters in the book is lost on them.

"I grieve to say that I possess no portrait of either of my sisters."

To her own dear friend, as to one who had known and loved her sisters, she writes still more fully respecting the painfulness of her task.

"There is nothing wrong, and I am writing you a line as you desire, merely to say that I AM busy just now. Mr. Smith wishes to reprint some of Emily's and Annie's works, with a few little additions from the papers they have left; and I have been closely engaged in revising, transcribing, preparing a preface, notice, etc. As the time for doing this is limited, I am obliged to be industrious. I found the task at first exquisitely painful and depressing; but regarding it in the light of a SACRED DUTY, I went on, and now can bear it better. It is work, however, that I cannot do in the evening, for if I did, I should have no sleep at night. Papa, I am thankful to say, is in improved health, and so, I think, am I; I trust you are the same.

"I have just received a kind letter from Miss Martineau. She has got back to Ambleside, and had heard of my visit to the Lakes. She expressed her regret, etc., at not being at home.

"I am both angry and surprised at myself for not being in better spirits; for not growing accustomed, or at least resigned, to the solitude and isolation of my lot. But my late occupation left a result for some days, and indeed still, very painful. The reading over of papers, the renewal of remembrances brought back the pang of bereavement, and occasioned a depression of spirits well nigh intolerable. For one or two nights, I scarcely knew how to get on till morning; and when morning came, I was still haunted with a sense of sickening distress. I tell you these things, because it is absolutely necessary to me to have some relief. You will forgive me, and not trouble yourself, or imagine that I am one whit worse than I say.

It is quite a mental ailment, and I believe and hope is better now. I think so, because I can speak about it, which I never can when grief is at its worst.

"I thought to find occupation and interest in writing, when alone at home, but hitherto my efforts have been vain; the deficiency of every stimulus is so complete. You will recommend me, I dare say, to go from home; but that does no good, even could I again leave Papa with an easy mind (thank God! he is better). I cannot describe what a time of it I had after my return from London, Scotland, etc. There was a reaction that sunk me to the earth; the deadly silence, solitude, desolation, were awful; the craving for companionship, the hopelessness of relief, were what I should dread to feel again.

"Dear ------, when I think of you, it is with a compassion and tenderness that scarcely cheer me. Mentally, I fear, you also are too lonely and too little occupied. It seems our doom, for the present at least. May God in His mercy help us to bear it!"

During her last visit to London, as mentioned in one of her letters, she had made the acquaintance of her correspondent, Mr. Lewes. That gentleman says:---

"Some months after" (the appearance of the review of "Shirley" in the Edinburgh), "Currer Bell came to London, and I was invited to meet her at your house. You may remember, she asked you not to point me out to her, but allow her to discover me if she could. She DID recognise me almost as soon as I came into the room. You tried me in the same way; I was less sagacious. However, I sat by her side a great part of the evening and was greatly interested by her conversation. On parting we shook hands, and she said, 'We are friends now, are we not?' 'Were we not always, then?' I asked. 'No! not always,' she said, significantly; and that was the only allusion she made to the offending article. I lent her some of Balzac's and George Sand's novels to take with her into the country; and the following letter was written when they were returned:"---

"I am sure you will have thought me very dilatory in returning the books you so kindly lent me. The fact is, having some other books to send, I retained yours to enclose them in the same parcel.

"Accept my thanks for some hours of pleasant reading. Balzac was for me quite a new author; and in making big acquaintance, through the medium of 'Modeste Mignon,' and 'Illusions perdues,' you cannot doubt I have felt some interest. At first, I thought he was going to be painfully minute, and fearfully tedious; one grew impatient of his long parade of detail, his slow revelation of unimportant circumstances, as he assembled his personages on the stage; but by and bye I seemed to enter into the mystery of his craft, and to discover, with delight, where his force lay: is it not in the analysis of motive; and in a subtle perception of the most obscure and secret workings of the mind? Still, admire Balzac as we may, I think we do not like him; we rather feel towards him as towards an ungenial acquaintance who is for ever holding up in strong light our defects, and who rarely draws forth our better qualities.

"Truly, I like George Sand better.

"Fantastic, fanatical, unpractical enthusiast as she often is---far from truthful as are many of her views of life---misled, as she is apt to be, by her feelings---George Sand has a better nature than M. de Balzac; her brain is larger, her heart warmer than his. The 'Lettres d'un Voyageur' are full of the writer's self; and I never felt so strongly, as in the perusal of this work, that most of her very faults spring from the excess of her good qualities: it is this excess which has often hurried her into difficulty, which has prepared for her enduring regret.

"But I believe her mind is of that order which disastrous experience teaches, without weakening or too much disheartening; and, in that case, the longer she lives the better she will grow. A hopeful point in all her writings is the scarcity of false French sentiment; I wish I could say its absence; but the weed flourishes here and there, even in the 'Lettres.'"

I remember the good expression of disgust which Miss Brontë made use of in speaking to me of some of Balzac's novels: "They leave such a bad taste in my mouth."

The reader will notice that most of the letters from which I now quote are devoted to critical and literary subjects. These were, indeed, her principal interests at this time; the revision of her sister's works, and writing a short memoir of them, was the painful employment of every day during the dreary autumn of 1850. Wearied out by the vividness of her sorrowful recollections, she sought relief in long walks on the moors. A friend of hers, who wrote to me on the appearance of the eloquent article in the Daily News upon the "Death of Currer Bell," gives an anecdote which may well come in here.

"They are mistaken in saying she was too weak to roam the hills for the benefit of the air. I do not think any one, certainly not any woman, in this locality, went so much on the moors as she did, when the weather permitted. Indeed, she was so much in the habit of doing so, that people, who live quite away on the edge of the common, knew her perfectly well. I remember on one occasion an old woman saw her at a little distance, and she called out, 'How! Miss Brontë! Hey yah (have you) seen ought o' my cofe (calf)?' Miss Brontë told her she could not say, for she did not know it. 'Well!' she said, 'Yah know, it's getting up like nah (now), between a cah (cow) and a cofe---what we call a stirk, yah know, Miss Brontë; will yah turn it this way if yah happen to see't, as yah're going back, Miss Brontë; nah DO, Miss Brontë.'"

It must have been about this time that a visit was paid to her by some neighbours, who were introduced to her by a mutual friend. This visit has been described in a letter from which I am permitted to give extracts, which will show the impression made upon strangers by the character of the country round her home, and other circumstances. "Though the weather was drizzly, we resolved to make our long-planned excursion to Haworth; so we packed ourselves into the buffalo-skin, and that into the gig, and set off about eleven. The rain ceased, and the day was just suited to the scenery,---wild and chill,---with great masses of cloud glooming over the moors, and here and there a ray of sunshine covertly stealing through, and resting with a dim magical light upon some high bleak village; or darting down into some deep glen, lighting up the tall chimney, or glistening on the windows and wet roof of the mill which lies couching in the bottom. The country got wilder and wilder as we approached Haworth; for the last four miles we were ascending a huge moor, at the very top of which lies the dreary black-looking village of Haworth. The village-street itself is one of the steepest hills I have ever seen, and the stones are so horribly jolting that I should have got out and walked with W------, if possible, but, having once begun the ascent, to stop was out of the question. At the top was the inn where we put up, close by the church; and the clergyman's house, we were told, was at the top of the churchyard. So through that we went,---a dreary, dreary place, literally PAVED with rain-blackened tombstones, and all on the slope, for at Haworth there is on the highest height a higher still, and Mr. Brontë's house stands considerably above the church. There was the house before us, a small oblong stone house, with not a tree to screen it from the cutting wind; but how were we to get at it from the churchyard we could not see! There was an old man in the churchyard, brooding like a Ghoul over the graves, with a sort of grim hilarity on his face. I thought he looked hardly human; however, he was human enough to tell us the way; and presently we found ourselves in the little bare parlour. Presently the door opened, and in came a superannuated mastiff, followed by an old gentleman very like Miss Brontë, who shook hands with us, and then went to call his daughter. A long interval, during which we coaxed the old dog, and looked at a picture of Miss Brontë, by Richmond, the solitary ornament of the room, looking strangely out of place on the bare walls, and at the books on the little shelves, most of them evidently the gift of the authors since Miss Brontë's celebrity. Presently she came in, and welcomed us very kindly, and took me upstairs to take off my bonnet, and herself brought me water and towels. The uncarpeted stone stairs and floors, the old drawers propped on wood, were all scrupulously clean and neat. When we went into the parlour again, we began talking very comfortably, when the door opened and Mr. Brontë looked in; seeing his daughter there, I suppose he thought it was all right, and he retreated to his study on the opposite side of the passage; presently emerging again to bring W------ a country newspaper. This was his last appearance till we went. Miss Brontë spoke with the greatest warmth of Miss Martineau, and of the good she had gained from her. Well! we talked about various things; the character of the people,---about her solitude, etc., till she left the room to help about dinner, I suppose, for she did not return for an age. The old dog had vanished; a fat curly-haired dog honoured us with his company for some time, but finally manifested a wish to get out, so we were left alone. At last she returned, followed by the maid and dinner, which made us all more comfortable; and we had some very pleasant conversation, in the midst of which time passed quicker than we supposed, for at last W------ found that it was half-past three, and we had fourteen or fifteen miles before us. So we hurried off, having obtained from her a promise to pay us a visit in the spring; and the old gentleman having issued once more from his study to say good-bye, we returned to the inn, and made the best of our way homewards.

"Miss Brontë put me so in mind of her own 'Jane Eyre.' She looked smaller than ever, and moved about so quietly, and noiselessly, just like a little bird, as Rochester called her, barring that all birds are joyous, and that joy can never have entered that house since it was first built; and yet, perhaps, when that old man married, and took home his bride, and children's voices and feet were heard about the house, even that desolate crowded grave-yard and biting blast could not quench cheerfulness and hope. Now there is something touching in the sight of that little creature entombed in such a place, and moving about herself like a spirit, especially when you think that the slight still frame encloses a force of strong fiery life, which nothing has been able to freeze or extinguish."

In one of the preceding letters, Miss Brontë referred to am article in the Palladium, which had rendered what she considered the due meed of merit to "Wuthering Heights", her sister Emily's tale. Her own works were praised, and praised with discrimination, and she was grateful for this. But her warm heart was filled to the brim with kindly feelings towards him who had done justice to the dead. She anxiously sought out the name of the writer; and having discovered that it was Mr. Sydney Dobell he immediately became one of her

"Peculiar people whom Death had made dear."

She looked with interest upon everything he wrote; and before long we shall find that they corresponded.

To W. S. WILLIAMS, ESQ.

"Oct. 25th.

"The box of books came last night, and, as usual, I have only gratefully to admire the selection made: 'Jeffrey's Essays,' 'Dr. Arnold's Life,' 'The Roman,' 'Alton Loche,' these were all wished for and welcome.

"You say I keep no books; pardon me---I am ashamed of my own rapaciousness I have kept 'Macaulay's History,' and Wordsworth's 'Prelude', and Taylor's 'Philip Van Artevelde.' I soothe my conscience by saying that the two last,---being poetry---do not count. This is a convenient doctrine for me I meditate acting upon it with reference to the Roman, so I trust nobody in Cornhill will dispute its validity or affirm that 'poetry' has a value, except for trunk-makers.

"I have already had 'Macaulay's Essays,' 'Sidney Smith's Lectures on Moral Philosophy,' and 'Knox on Race.' Pickering's work on the same subject I have not seen; nor all the volumes of Leigh Hunt's Autobiography. However, I am now abundantly supplied for a long time to come. I liked Hazlitt's Essays much.

"The autumn, as you say, has been very fine. I and solitude and memory have often profited by its sunshine on the moors.

"I had felt some disappointment at the non-arrival of the proof-sheets of 'Wuthering Heights;' a feverish impatience to complete the revision is apt to beset me. The work of looking over papers, etc., could not be gone through with impunity, and with unaltered spirits; associations too tender, regrets too bitter, sprang out of it. Meantime, the Cornhill books now, as heretofore, are my best medicine,---affording a solace which could not be yielded by the very same books procured from a common library.

"Already I have read the greatest part of the 'Roman;' passages in it possess a kindling virtue such as true poetry alone can boast; there are images of genuine grandeur; there are lines that at once stamp themselves on the memory. Can it be true that a new planet has risen on the heaven, whence all stars seemed fast fading? I believe it is; for this Sydney or Dobell speaks with a voice of his own, unborrowed, unmimicked. You hear Tennyson, indeed, sometimes, and Byron sometimes, in some passages of the Roman; but then again you have a new note,--- nowhere clearer than in a certain brief lyric, sang in a meeting of minstrels, a sort of dirge over a dead brother;---THAT not only charmed the ear and brain, it soothed the heart."

The following extract will be read with interest as conveying her thoughts after the perusal of Dr. Arnold's Life:---

"Nov. 6th.

"I have just finished reading the 'Life of Dr. Arnold;' but now when I wish, according to your request, to express what I think of it, I do not find the task very easy; proper terms seem wanting. This is not a character to be dismissed with a few laudatory words; it is not a one-sided character; pure panegyric would be inappropriate. Dr. Arnold (it seems to me) was not quite saintly; his greatness was cast in a mortal mould; he was a little severe, almost a little hard; he was vehement and somewhat oppugnant. Himself the most indefatigable of workers, I know not whether he could have understood, or made allowance for, a temperament that required more rest; yet not to one man in twenty thousand is given his giant faculty of labour; by virtue of it he seems to me the greatest of working men. Exacting he might have been, then, on this point; and granting that he were so, and a little hasty, stern, and positive, those were his sole faults (if, indeed, that can be called a fault which in no shape degrades the individual's own character; but is only apt to oppress and overstrain the weaker nature of his neighbours). Afterwards come his good qualities. About these there is nothing dubious. Where can we find justice, firmness, independence, earnestness, sincerity, fuller and purer than in him?

"But this is not all, and I am glad of it. Besides high intellect and stainless rectitude, his letters and his life attest his possession of the most true-hearted affection. WITHOUT this, however one might admire, we could not love him; but WITH it I think we love him much. A hundred such men---fifty---nay, ten or five such righteous men might save any country; might victoriously champion any cause.

"I was struck, too, by the almost unbroken happiness of his life; a happiness resulting chiefly, no doubt, from the right use to which he put that health and strength which God had given him, but also owing partly to a singular exemption from those deep and bitter griefs which most human beings are called on to endure. His wife was what he wished; his children were healthy and promising; his own health was excellent; his undertakings were crowned with success; even death was kind,---for, however sharp the pains of his last hour, they were but brief. God's blessing seems to have accompanied him from the cradle to the grave. One feels thankful to know that it has been permitted to any man to live such a life.

"When I was in Westmoreland last August, I spent an evening at Fox How, where Mrs. Arnold and her daughters still reside. It was twilight as I drove to the place, and almost dark ere I reached it; still I could perceive that the situation was lovely. The house looked like a nest half buried in flowers and creepers: and, dusk as it was, I could FEEL that the valley and the hills round were beautiful as imagination could dream."

If I say again what I have said already before, it is only to impress and re-impress upon my readers the dreary monotony of her life at this time. The dark, bleak season of the year brought back the long evenings, which tried her severely: all the more so, because her weak eyesight rendered her incapable of following any occupation but knitting by candle-light. For her father's sake, as well as for her own, she found it necessary to make some exertion to ward off settled depression of spirits. She accordingly accepted an invitation to spend a week or ten days with Miss Martineau at Ambleside. She also proposed to come to Manchester and see me, on her way to Westmoreland. But, unfortunately, I was from home, and unable to receive her. The friends with whom I was staying in the South of England (hearing me express my regret that I could not accept her friendly proposal, and aware of the sad state of health and spirits which made some change necessary for her) wrote to desire that she would come and spend a week or two with me at their house. She acknowledged this invitation in a letter to me, dated---

"Dec. 13th, 1850.

"My dear Mrs. Gaskell,---Miss ------'s kindness and yours is such that I am placed in the dilemma of not knowing how adequately to express my sense of it. THIS I know, however, very well-that if I COULD go and be with you for a week or two in such a quiet south-country house, and with such kind people as you describe, I should like it much. I find the proposal marvellously to my taste; it is the pleasantest, gentlest, sweetest, temptation possible; but, delectable as it is, its solicitations are by no means to be yielded to without the sanction of reason, and therefore I desire for the present to be silent, and to stand back till I have been to Miss Martineau's, and returned home, and considered well whether it is a scheme as right as agreeable.

"Meantime, the mere thought does me good."

On the 10th of December, the second edition of "Wuthering Heights" was published. She sent a copy of it to Mr. Dobell, with the following letter:---

To MR. DOBELL.

"Haworth, near Keighley, Yorkshire,

"Dec. 8th, 1850.

"I offer this little book to my critic in the 'Palladium,' and he must believe it accompanied by a tribute of the sincerest gratitude; not so much for anything he has said of myself, as for the noble justice he has rendered to one dear to me as myself---perhaps dearer; and perhaps one kind word spoken for her awakens a deeper, tenderer, sentiment of thankfulness than eulogies heaped on my own head. As you will see when you have read the biographical notice, my sister cannot thank you herself; she is gone out of your sphere and mine, and human blame and praise are nothing to her now. But to me, for her sake, they are something still; it revived me for many a day to find that, dead as she was, the work of her genius had at last met with worthy appreciation.

"Tell me, when you have read the introduction, whether any doubts still linger in your mind respecting the authorship of 'Wuthering Heights,' 'Wildfell Hall,' etc. Your mistrust did me some injustice; it proved a general conception of character such as I should be sorry to call mine; but these false ideas will naturally arise when we only judge an author from his works. In fairness, I must also disclaim the flattering side of the portrait. I am no 'young Penthesilea mediis in millibus,' but a plain country parson's daughter.

"Once more I thank you, and that with a full heart.

"**C. BRONTË.**"

CHAPTER IX.

Immediately after the republication of her sisters' book she went to Miss Martineau's.

"I can write to you now, dear E------, for I am away from home) and relieved, temporarily, at least, by change of air and scene, from the heavy burden of depression which, I confess, has for nearly three months been sinking me to the earth. I never shall forget last autumn! Some days and nights have been cruel; but now, having once told you this, I need say no more on the subject. My loathing of solitude grew extreme; my recollection of my sisters intolerably poignant. I am better now. I am at Miss Martineau's for a week. Her house is very pleasant, both within and without; arranged at; all points with admirable neatness and comfort. Her visitors enjoy the most perfect liberty; what she claims for herself she allows them. I rise at my own hour, breakfast alone (she is up at five, takes a cold bath, and a walk by starlight, and has finished breakfast and got to her work by seven o'clock). I pass the morning in the drawing-room---she, in her study. At two o'clock we meet---work, talk, and walk together till five, her dinner-hour, spend the evening together, when she converses fluently and abundantly, and with the most complete frankness. I go to my own room soon after ten,---she sits up writing letters till twelve. She appears exhaustless in strength and spirits, and indefatigable in the faculty of labour. She is a great and a good woman; of course not without peculiarities, but I have seen none as yet that annoy me. She is both hard and warm-hearted, abrupt and affectionate, liberal and despotic. I believe she is not at all conscious of her own absolutism. When I tell her of it, she denies the charge warmly; then I laugh at her. I believe she almost rules Ambleside. Some of the gentry dislike her, but the lower orders have a great regard for her. . . . I thought I should like to spend two or three days with you before going home, so, if it is not inconvenient to you, I will (D. V.) come on Monday and stay till Thursday. . . . I have truly enjoyed my visit here. I have seen a good many people, and all have been so marvellously kind; not the least so, the family of Dr. Arnold. Miss Martineau I relish inexpressibly."

Miss Brontë paid the visit she here proposes to her friend, but only remained two or three days. She then returned home, and immediately began to suffer from her old enemy, sickly and depressing headache. This was all the more trying to bear, as she was obliged to take an active share in the household work,---one servant being ill in bed, and the other, Tabby, aged upwards of eighty.

This visit to Ambleside did Miss Brontë much good, and gave her a stock of pleasant recollections, and fresh interests, to dwell upon in her solitary life. There are many references in her letters to Miss Martineau's character and kindness.

"She is certainly a woman of wonderful endowments, both intellectual and physical; and though I share few of her opinions, and regard her as fallible on certain points of judgment, I must still award her my sincerest esteem. The manner in which she combines the highest mental culture with the nicest discharge of feminine duties filled me with admiration; while her affectionate kindness earned my gratitude." "I think her good and noble qualities far outweigh her defects. It is my habit to consider the individual apart from his (or her) reputation, practice independent of theory, natural disposition isolated from acquired opinions. Harriet Martineau's person, practice, and character, inspire me with the truest affection and respect."You ask me whether Miss Martineau made me a convert to mesmerism? Scarcely; yet I heard miracles of its efficacy, and could hardly discredit the whole of what was told me. I even underwent a personal experiment; and though the result was not absolutely clear, it was inferred that in time I should prove an excellent subject. The question of mesmerism will be discussed with little reserve, I believe, in a forthcoming work of Miss Martineau's; and I have some painful anticipations of the manner in which other subjects, offering less legitimate ground for speculation, will be handled."

"Your last letter evinced such a sincere and discriminating admiration for Dr. Arnold, that perhaps you will not be wholly uninterested in hearing that, during my late visit to Miss Martineau, I saw much more of Fox How and its inmates, and daily admired, in the widow and children of one of the greatest and best men of his time, the possession of qualities the most estimable and endearing. Of my kind hostess herself, I cannot speak in terms too high. Without being able to share all her opinions, philosophical, political, or religious,---without adopting her theories,---I yet find a worth and greatness in herself, and a consistency, benevolence, perseverance in her practice, such as wins the sincerest esteem and affection. She is not a person to be judged by her writings alone, but rather by her own deeds and life, than which nothing can be more exemplary or nobler. She seems to me the benefactress of Ambleside, yet takes no sort of credit to herself for her active and indefatigable philanthropy. The government of her household is admirably administered: all she does is well done, from the writing of a history down to the quietest female occupation. No sort of carelessness or neglect is allowed under her rule, and yet she is not over-strict, nor too rigidly exacting: her servants and her poor neighbours love as well as respect her.

"I must not, however, fall into the error of talking too much about her merely because my own mind is just now deeply impressed with what I have seen of her intellectual power and moral worth. Faults she has; but to me they appear very trivial weighed in the balance against her excellences."

"Your account of Mr. A------ tallies exactly with Miss M------'s. She, too, said that placidity and mildness (rather than originality and power) were his external characteristics. She described him as a combination of the antique Greek sage with the European modern man of science. Perhaps it was mere perversity in me to get the notion that torpid veins, and a cold, slow-beating heart, lay under his marble outside. But he is a materialist: he serenely denies us our hope of immortality, and quietly blots from man's future Heaven and the Life to come. That is why a savour of bitterness seasoned my feeling towards him.

"All you say of Mr. Thackeray is most graphic and characteristic. He stirs in me both sorrow and anger. Why should he lead so harassing a life? Why should his mocking tongue so perversely deny the better feelings of his better moods?"

For some time, whenever she was well enough in health and spirits, she had been employing herself upon Villette; but she was frequently unable to write, and was both grieved and angry with herself for her inability. In February, she writes as follows to Mr. Smith:---

"Something you say about going to London; but the words are dreamy, and fortunately I am not obliged to hear or answer them. London and summer are many months away: our moors are all white with snow just now, and little redbreasts come every morning to the window for crumbs. One can lay no plans three or four months beforehand. Besides, I don't deserve to go to London; nobody merits a change or a treat less. I secretly think, on the contrary, I ought to be put in prison, and kept on bread and water in solitary confinement---without even a letter from Cornhill---till I had written a book. One of two things would certainly result from such a mode of treatment pursued for twelve months; either I should come out at the end of that time with a three-volume MS. in my hand, or else with a condition of intellect that would exempt me ever after from literary efforts and expectations."

Meanwhile, she was disturbed and distressed by the publication of Miss Martineau's "Letters," etc.; they came down with a peculiar force and heaviness upon a heart that looked, with fond and earnest faith, to a future life as to the meeting-place with those who were "loved and lost awhile."

"Feb. 11th, 1851.

"My dear Sir,---Have you yet read Miss Martineau's and Mr. Atkinson's new work, 'Letters on the Nature and Development of Man'? If you have not, it would be worth your while to do so.

"Of the impression this book has made on me, I will not now say much. It is the first exposition of avowed atheism and materialism I have ever read; the first unequivocal declaration of disbelief in the existence of a God or a future life I have ever seen. In judging of such exposition and declaration, one would wish entirely to put aside the sort of instinctive horror they awaken, and to consider them in an impartial spirit and collected mood. This I find it difficult to do. The strangest thing is, that we are called on to rejoice over this hopeless blank---to receive this bitter bereavement as great gain---to welcome this unutterable desolation as a state of pleasant freedom. Who COULD do this if he would? Who WOULD do it if he could?

"Sincerely, for my own part, do I wish to find and know the Truth; but if this be Truth, well may she guard herself with mysteries, and cover herself with a veil. If this be Truth, man or woman who beholds her can but curse the day he or she was born. I said, however, I would not dwell on what I thought; I wish to hear, rather, what some other person thinks,---some one whose feelings are unapt to bias his judgment. Read the book, then, in an unprejudiced spirit, and candidly say what you think of it. I mean, of course, if you have time---NOT OTHERWISE."

And yet she could not bear the contemptuous tone in which this work was spoken of by many critics; it made her more indignant than almost any other circumstance during my acquaintance with her. Much as she regretted the publication of the book, she could not see that it had given any one a right to sneer at an action, certainly prompted by no worldly motive, and which was but one error---the gravity of which she admitted---in the conduct of a person who had, all her life long, been striving, by deep thought and noble words, to serve her kind.

"Your remarks on Miss Martineau and her book pleased me greatly, from their tone and spirit. I have even taken the liberty of transcribing for her benefit one or two phrases, because I know they will cheer her; she likes sympathy and appreciation (as all people do who deserve them); and most fully do I agree with you in the dislike you express of that hard, contemptuous tone in which her work is spoken of by many critics."

Before I return from the literary opinions of the author to the domestic interests of the woman, I must copy out what she felt and thought about "The Stones of Venice".

"'The Stones of Venice' seem nobly laid and chiselled. How grandly the quarry of vast marbles is disclosed! Mr. Ruskin seems to me one of the few genuine writers, as distinguished from book-makers, of this age. His earnestness even amuses me in certain passages; for I cannot help laughing to think how utilitarians will fume and fret over his deep, serious (and as THEY will think), fanatical reverence for Art. That pure and severe mind you ascribed to him speaks in every line. He writes like a consecrated Priest of the Abstract and Ideal.

"I shall bring with me 'The Stones of Venice'; all the foundations of marble and of granite, together with the mighty quarry out of which they were hewn; and, into the bargain, a small assortment of crotchets and dicta---the private property of one John Ruskin, Esq."

As spring drew on, the depression of spirits to which she was subject began to grasp her again, and "to crush her with a day- and night-mare." She became afraid of sinking as low as she had done in the autumn; and to avoid this, she prevailed on her old friend and schoolfellow to come and stay with her for a few weeks in March. She found great benefit from this companionship,---both from the congenial society in itself, and from the self-restraint of thought imposed by the necessity of entertaining her and looking after her comfort. On this occasion, Miss Brontë said, "It will not do to get into the habit offrom home, and thus temporarily evading an running away oppression instead of facing, wrestling with and conquering it or being conquered by it."

I shall now make an extract from one of her letters, which is purposely displaced as to time. I quote it because it relates to a third offer of marriage which she had, and because I find that some are apt to imagine, from the extraordinary power with which she represented the passion of love in her novels, that she herself was easily susceptible of it.

"Could I ever feel enough for ------, to accept of him as a husband? Friendship---gratitude--- esteem---I have; but each moment he came near me, and that I could see his eyes fastened on me, my veins ran ice. Now that he is away, I feel far more gently towards him, it is only close by that I grow rigid, stiffening with a strange mixture of apprehension and anger, which nothing softens but his retreat, and a perfect subduing of his manner. I did not want to be proud, nor intend to be proud, but I was forced to be so. Most true it is, that we are over-ruled by One above us; that in His hands our very will is as clay in the hands of the potter."

I have now named all the offers of marriage she ever received, until that was made which she finally accepted. The gentle-man referred to in this letter retained so much regard for her as to be her friend to the end of her life; a circumstance to his credit and to hers.

Before her friend E------ took her departure, Mr. Brontë caught cold, and continued for some weeks much out of health, with an attack of bronchitis. His spirits, too, became much depressed; and all his daughter's efforts were directed towards cheering him.

When he grew better, and had regained his previous strength, she resolved to avail herself of an invitation which she had received some time before, to pay a visit in London. This year, 1851, was, as every one remembers, the time of the great Exhibition; but even with that attraction in prospect, she did not intend to stay there long; and, as usual, she made an agreement with her friends, before finally accepting their offered hospitality, that her sojourn at their house was to be as quiet as ever, since any other way of proceeding disagreed with her both mentally and physically. She never looked excited except for a moment, when something in conversation called her out; but she often felt so, even about comparative trifles, and the exhaustion of reaction was sure to follow. Under such circumstances, she always became extremely thin and haggard; yet she averred that the change invariably did her good afterwards.

Her preparations in the way of dress for this visit, in the gay time of that gay season, were singularly in accordance with her feminine taste; quietly anxious to satisfy her love for modest, dainty, neat attire, and not regardless of the becoming, yet remembering consistency, both with her general appearance and with her means, in every selection she made.

"By the bye, I meant to ask you when you went to Leeds, to do a small errand for me, but fear your hands will be too full of business. It was merely this: in case you chanced to be in any shop where the lace cloaks, both black and white, of which I spoke, were sold, to ask their price. I suppose they would hardly like to send a few to Haworth to be looked at; indeed, if they cost very much, it would be useless, but if they are reasonable and they would send them, I should like to see them; and also some chemisettes of small size (the full woman's size don't fit me), both of simple style for every day and good quality for best.". . . ."It appears I could not rest satisfied when I was well off. I told you I had taken one of the black lace mantles, but when I came to try it with the black satin dress, with which I should chiefly want to wear it, I found the effect was far from good; the beauty of the lace was lost, and it looked somewhat brown and rusty; I wrote to Mr. ------, requesting him to change it for a WHITE mantle of the same price; he was extremely courteous, and sent to London for one, which I have got this morning. The price is less, being but 1 pound 14s.; it is pretty, neat and light, looks well on black; and upon reasoning the matter over, I came to the philosophic conclusion, that it would be no shame for a person of my means to wear a cheaper thing; so I think I shall take it, and if you ever see it and call it 'trumpery' so much the worse."

"Do you know that I was in Leeds on the very same day with you---last Wednesday? I had thought of telling you where I was going, and having your help and company in buying a bonnet, etc., but then I reflected this would merely be making a selfish use of you, so I determined to manage or mismanage the matter alone. I went to Hurst and Hall's for the bonnet, and got one which seemed grave and quiet there amongst all the splendours; but now it looks infinitely too gay with its pink lining. I saw some beautiful silks of pale sweet colours, but had not the spirit nor the means to launch out at the rate of five shillings per yard, and went and bought a black silk at three shillings after all. I rather regret this, because papa says he would have lent me a sovereign if he had known. I believe, if you had been there, you would have forced me to get into debt. . . . I really can no more come to B------ before I go to London than I can fly. I have quantities of sewing to do, as well as household matters to arrange, before I leave, as they will clean, etc., in my absence. Besides, I am grievously afflicted with headache, which I trust to change of air for relieving; but meantime, as it proceeds from the stomach, it makes me very thin and grey; neither you nor anybody else would fatten me up or put me into good condition for the visit; it is fated otherwise. No matter. Calm your passion; yet I am glad to see it. Such spirit seems to prove health. Good-bye, in haste.

"Your poor mother is like Tabby, Martha and Papa; all these fancy I am somehow, by some mysterious process, to be married in London, or to engage myself to matrimony. How I smile internally! How groundless and improbable is the idea! Papa seriously told me yesterday, that if I married and left him he should give up housekeeping and go into lodgings!"

I copy the following, for the sake of the few words describing the appearance of the heathery moors in late summer.

TO SYDNEY DOBELL, ESQ.

"May 24th, 1851.

"My dear Sir,---I hasten to send Mrs. Dobell the autograph. It was the word 'Album' that frightened me I thought she wished me to write a sonnet on purpose for it, which I could not do.

"Your proposal respecting a journey to Switzerland is deeply kind; it draws me with the force of a mighty Temptation, but the stern Impossible holds me back. No! I cannot go to Switzerland this summer.

"Why did the editor of the 'Eclectic' erase that most powerful and pictorial passage? He could not be insensible to its beauty; perhaps he thought it profane. Poor man!

"I know nothing of such an orchard-country as you describe. I have never seen such a region. Our hills only confess the coming of summer by growing green with young fern and moss, in secret little hollows. Their bloom is reserved for autumn; then they burn with a kind of dark glow, different, doubtless, from the blush of garden blossoms. About the close of next month, I expect to go to London, to pay a brief and quiet visit. I fear chance will not be so propitious as to bring you to town while I am there; otherwise, how glad I should be if you would call. With kind regards to Mrs. Dobell,---Believe me, sincerely yours,

C. BRONTË."

Her next letter is dated from London.

"June 2nd.

"I came here on Wednesday, being summoned a day sooner than I expected, in order to be in time for Thackeray's second lecture, which was delivered on Thursday afternoon. This, as you may suppose, was a genuine treat to me, and I was glad not to miss it. It was given in Willis' Rooms, where the Almacks balls are held---a great painted and gilded saloon with long sofas for benches. The audience was said to be the cream of London society, and it looked so. I did not at all expect the great lecturer would know me or notice me under these circumstances, with admiring duchesses and countesses seated in rows before him; but he met me as I entered---shook hands---took me to his mother, whom I had not before seen, and introduced me. She is a fine, handsome, young-looking old lady; was very gracious, and called with one of her grand-daughters next day.

"Thackeray called too, separately. I had a long talk with him, and I think he knows me now a little better than he did: but of this I cannot yet be sure; he is a great and strange man. There is quite a furor for his lectures. They are a sort of essays, characterised by his own peculiar originality and power, and delivered with a finished taste and ease, which is felt, but cannot be described. Just before the lecture began, somebody came behind me, leaned over and said,

'Permit me, as a Yorkshireman, to introduce myself.' I turned round---saw a strange, not handsome, face, which puzzled me for half a minute, and then I said, 'You are Lord Carlisle.' He nodded and smiled; he talked a few minutes very pleasantly and courteously.

"Afterwards came another man with the same plea, that he was a Yorkshireman, and this turned out to be Mr. Monckton Milnes. Then came Dr. Forbes, whom I was sincerely glad to see. On Friday, I went to the Crystal Palace; it is a marvellous, stirring, bewildering sight---a mixture of a genii palace, and a mighty bazaar, but it is not much in my way; I liked the lecture better. On Saturday I saw the Exhibition at Somerset House; about half a dozen of the pictures are good and interesting, the rest of little worth. Sunday---yesterday---was a day to be marked with a white stone; through most of the day I was very happy, without being tired or over-excited. In the afternoon, I went to hear D'Aubigne, the great Protestant French preacher; it was pleasant---half sweet, half sad---and strangely suggestive to hear the French language once more. For health, I have so far got on very fairly, considering that I came here far from well."

The lady, who accompanied Miss Brontë to the lecture at Thackeray's alluded to, says that, soon after they had taken their places, she was aware that he was pointing out her companion to several of his friends, but she hoped that Miss Brontë herself would not perceive it. After some time, however, during which many heads had been turned round, and many glasses put up, in order to look at the author of "Jane Eyre", Miss Brontë said, "I am afraid Mr. Thackeray has been playing me a trick;" but she soon became too much absorbed in the lecture to notice the attention which was being paid to her, except when it was directly offered, as in the case of Lord Carlisle and Mr. Monckton Milnes. When the lecture was ended, Mr. Thackeray came down from the platform, and making his way towards her, asked her for her opinion. This she mentioned to me not many days afterwards, adding remarks almost identical with those which I subsequently read in 'Villette,' where a similar action on the part of M. Paul Emanuel is related.

"As our party left the Hall, he stood at the entrance; he saw and knew me, and lifted his hat; he offered his hand in passing, and uttered the words 'Qu'en dites-vous?'---question eminently characteristic, and reminding me, even in this his moment of triumph, of that inquisitive restlessness, that absence of what I considered desirable self-control, which were amongst his faults. He should not have cared just then to ask what I thought, or what anybody thought; but he DID care, and he was too natural to conceal, too impulsive to repress his wish. Well! if I blamed his over-eagerness, I liked his naivete. I would have praised him; I had plenty of praise in my heart; but alas I no words on my lips. Who HAS words at the right moment? I stammered some lame expressions; but was truly glad when other people, coming up with profuse congratulations, covered my deficiency by their redundancy."

As they were preparing to leave the room, her companion saw with dismay that many of the audience were forming themselves into two lines, on each side of the aisle down which they had to pass before reaching the door. Aware that any delay would only make the ordeal more trying, her friend took Miss Brontë's arm in hers, and they went along the avenue of eager and admiring faces. During this passage through the "cream of society," Miss Brontë's hand trembled to such a degree, that her companion feared lest she should turn faint and be unable to proceed; and she dared not express her sympathy or try to give her strength by any touch or word, lest it might bring on the crisis she dreaded.

Surely, such thoughtless manifestation of curiosity is a blot on the scutcheon of true politeness! The rest of the account of this, her longest visit to London, shall be told in her own words.

"I sit down to write to you this morning in an inexpressibly flat state; having spent the whole of yesterday and the day before in a gradually increasing headache, which grew at last rampant and violent, ended with excessive sickness, and this morning I am quite weak and washy. I hoped to leave my headaches behind me at Haworth; but it seems I brought them carefully packed in my trunk, and very much have they been in my way since I came. . . . Since I wrote last, I have seen various things worth describing; Rachel, the great French actress, amongst the number. But to-day I really have no pith for the task. I can only wish you good-bye with all my heart."

"I cannot boast that London has agreed with me well this time; the oppression of frequent headache, sickness, and a low tone of spirits, has poisoned many moments which might otherwise have been pleasant. Sometimes I have felt this hard, and been tempted to murmur at Fate, which compels me to comparative silence and solitude for eleven months in the year, and in the twelfth, while offering social enjoyment, takes away the vigour and cheerfulness which should turn it to account. But circumstances are ordered for us, and we must submit."

"Your letter would have been answered yesterday, but I was already gone out before post time, and was out all day. People are very kind, and perhaps I shall be glad of what I have seen afterwards, but it is often a little trying at the time. On Thursday, the Marquis of Westminster asked me to a great party, to which I was to go with Mrs. D------, a beautiful, and, I think, a kind woman too; but this I resolutely declined. On Friday I dined at the ------'s, and met Mrs. D------ and Mr. Monckton Milnes. On Saturday I went to hear and see Rachel; a wonderful sight---terrible as if the earth had cracked deep at your feet, and revealed a glimpse of hell. I shall never forget it. She made me shudder to the marrow of my bones; in her some fiend has certainly taken up an incarnate home. She is not a woman; she is a snake; she is the ------. On Sunday I went to the Spanish Ambassador's Chapel, where Cardinal Wiseman, in his archiepiscopal robes and mitre, held a confirmation. The whole scene was impiously theatrical. Yesterday (Monday) I was sent for at ten to breakfast with Mr. Rogers, the patriarch-poet. Mrs. D------ and Lord Glenelg were there; no one else:this certainly proved a most calm, refined, and intellectual treat. After breakfast, Sir David Brewster came to take us to the Crystal Palace. I had rather dreaded this, for Sir David is a man of profoundest science, and I feared it would be impossible to understand his explanations of the mechanism, etc.; indeed, I hardly knew how to ask him questions. I was spared all trouble without being questioned, he gave information in the kindest and simplest manner. After two hours spent at the Exhibition, and where, as you may suppose, I was VERY tired, we had to go to Lord Westminster's, and spend two hours more in looking at the collection of pictures in his splendid gallery."

To another friend she writes:---

"------may have told you that I have spent a month in London this summer. When you come, you shall ask what questions you like on that point, and I will answer to the best of my stammering ability. Do not press me much on the subject of the 'Crystal Palace.' I went there five times, and certainly saw some interesting things, and the 'coup d'oeil' is striking and bewildering enough; but I never was able to get any raptures on the subject, and each renewed visit was made under coercion rather than my own free will. It is an excessively bustling place; and, after all, its wonders appeal too exclusively to the eye, and rarely touch the heart or head. I make an exception to the last assertion, in favour of those who possess a large range of scientific knowledge. Once I went with Sir David Brewster, and perceived that he looked on objects with other eyes than mine."

Miss Brontë returned from London by Manchester, and paid us a visit of a couple of days at the end of June. The weather was so intensely hot, and she herself so much fatigued with her London sight-seeing, that we did little but sit in-doors, with open windows, and talk. The only thing she made a point of exerting herself to procure was a present for Tabby. It was to be a shawl, or rather a large handkerchief, such as she could pin across her neck and shoulders, in the old-fashioned country manner. Miss Brontë took great pains in seeking out one which she thought would please the old woman. On her arrival at home, she addressed the following letter to the friend with whom she had been staying in London:---

"Haworth, July 1st, 1851.

"My dear Mrs. Smith,---Once more I am at home, where, I am thankful to say, I found my father very well. The journey to Manchester was a little hot and dusty, but otherwise pleasant enough. The two stout gentlemen, who filled a portion of the carriage when I got in, quitted it at Rugby, and two other ladies and myself had it to ourselves the rest of the way. The visit to Mrs. Gaskell formed a cheering break in the journey. Haworth Parsonage is rather a contrast, yet even Haworth Parsonage does not look gloomy in this bright summer weather; it is somewhat still, but with the windows open I can hear a bird or two singing on certain thorn-trees in the garden. My father and the servants think me looking better than when I felt home, and I certainly feel better myself for the change. You are too much like your son to render it advisable I should say much about your kindness during my visit. However, one cannot help (like Captain Cuttle) making a note of these matters. Papa says I am to thank you in his name, and offer you his respects, which I do accordingly.---With truest regards to all your circle, believe me very sincerely yours,

C. BRONTË."

"July 8th, 1851.

"My dear Sir,---Thackeray's last lecture must, I think, have been his best. What he says about Sterne is true. His observations on literary men, and their social obligations and individual duties, seem to me also true and full of mental and moral vigour. . . . The International Copyright Meeting seems to have had but a barren result, judging from the report in the Literary Gazette. I cannot see that Sir E. Bulwer and the rest DID anything; nor can I well see what it is in their power to do. The argument brought forward about the damage accruing to American national literature from the present piratical system, is a good and sound argument; but I am afraid the publishers---honest men---are not yet mentally prepared to give such reasoning due weight. I should think, that which refers to the injury inflicted upon themselves, by an oppressive competition in piracy, would influence them more; but, I suppose, all established matters, be they good or evil, are difficult to change. About the 'Phrenological Character' I must not say a word. Of your own accord, you have found the safest point from which to view it: I will not say 'look higher!' I think you see the matter as it is desirable we should all see what relates to ourselves. If I had a right to whisper a word of counsel, it should be merely this: whatever your present self may be, resolve with all your strength of resolution, never to degenerate thence. Be jealous of a shadow of falling off. Determine rather to look above that standard, and to strive beyond it. Everybody appreciates certain social properties, and likes his neighbour for possessing them; but perhaps few dwell upon a friend's capacity for the intellectual, or care how this might expand, if there were but facilities allowed for cultivation, and space given for growth. It seems to me that, even should such space and facilities be denied by stringent circumstances and a rigid fate, still it should do you good fully to know, and tenaciously to remember, that you have such a capacity. When other people overwhelm you with acquired knowledge, such as you have not had opportunity, perhaps not application, to gain---derive not pride, but support from the thought. If no new books had ever been written, some of these minds would themselves have remained blank pages: they only take an impression; they were not born with a record of thought on the brain, or an instinct of sensation on the heart. If I had never seen a printed volume, Nature would have offered my perceptions a varying picture of a continuous narrative, which, without any other teacher than herself, would have schooled me to knowledge, unsophisticated, but genuine.

"Before I received your last, I had made up my mind to tell you that I should expect no letter for three months to come (intending afterwards to extend this abstinence to six months, for I am jealous of becoming dependent on this indulgence: you doubtless cannot see why, because you do not live my life). Nor shall I now expect a letter; but since you say that you would like to write now and then, I cannot say 'never write,' without imposing on my real wishes a falsehood which they reject, and doing to them a violence, to which they entirely refuse to submit. I can only observe that when it pleases you to write, whether seriously or for a little amusement, your notes, if they come to me, will come where they are welcome. Tell------I will try to cultivate good spirits, as assiduously as she cultivates her geraniums."

CHAPTER X.

Soon after she returned home, her friend paid her a visit. While she stayed at Haworth, Miss Brontë wrote the letter from which the following extract is taken. The strong sense and right feeling displayed in it on the subject of friendship, sufficiently account for the constancy of affection which Miss Brontë earned from all those who once became her friends.

To W. S. WILLIAMS, ESQ.

"July 21th, 1851.

". . . I could not help wondering whether Cornhill will ever change for me, as Oxford has changed for you. I have some pleasant associations connected with it now---will these alter their character some day?

"Perhaps they may---though I have faith to the contrary, because, I THINK, I do not exaggerate my partialities; I THINK I take faults along with excellences---blemishes together with beauties. And, besides, in the matter of friendship, I have observed that disappointment here arises chiefly, NOT from liking our friends too well, or thinking of them too highly, but rather from an over-estimate of THEIR liking for and opinion of US; and that if we guard ourselves with sufficient scrupulousness of care from error in this direction, and can be content, and even happy to give more affection than we receive---can make just comparison of circumstances, and be severely accurate in drawing inferences thence, and never let self-love blind our eyes---I think we may manage to get through life with consistency and constancy, unembittered by that misanthropy which springs from revulsions of feeling. All this sounds a little metaphysical, but it is good sense if you consider it. The moral of it is, that if we would build on a sure foundation in friendship, we must love our friends for THEIR sakes rather than for OUR OWN; we must look at their truth to THEMSELVES, full as much as their truth to US. In the latter case, every wound to self-love would be a cause of coldness; in the former, only some painful change in the friend's character and disposition---some fearful breach in his allegiance to his better self---could alienate the heart.

"How interesting your old maiden-cousin's gossip about your parents must have been to you; and how gratifying to find that the reminiscence turned on none but pleasant facts and characteristics! Life must, indeed, be slow in that little decaying hamlet amongst the chalk hills. After all, depend upon it, it is better to be worn out with work in a thronged community, than to perish of inaction in a stagnant solitude: take this truth into consideration whenever you get tired of work and bustle."

I received a letter from her a little later than this; and though there is reference throughout to what I must have said in writing to her, all that it called forth in reply is so peculiarly characteristic, that I cannot prevail upon myself to pass it over without a few extracts:---

"Haworth, Aug. 6th, 1851.

"My dear Mrs. Gaskell,---I was too much pleased with your letter, when I got it at last, to feel disposed to murmur now about the delay.

"About a fortnight ago, I received a letter from Miss Martineau; also a long letter, and treating precisely the same subjects on which yours dwelt, viz., the Exhibition and Thackeray's last lecture. It was interesting mentally to place the two documents side by side---to study the two aspects of mind---to view, alternately, the same scene through two mediums. Full striking was the difference; and the more striking because it was not the rough contrast of good and evil, but the more subtle opposition, the more delicate diversity of different kinds of good. The excellences of one nature resembled (I thought) that of some sovereign medicine---harsh, perhaps, to the taste, but potent to invigorate; the good of the other seemed more akin to the nourishing efficacy of our daily bread. It is not bitter; it is not lusciously sweet: it pleases, without flattering the palate; it sustains, without forcing the strength.

"I very much agree with you in all you say. For the sake of variety, I could almost wish that the concord of opinion were less complete.

"To begin with Trafalgar Square. My taste goes with yours and Meta's completely on this point. I have always thought it a fine site (and SIGHT also). The view from the summit of those steps has ever struck me as grand and imposing---Nelson Column included the fountains I could dispense with. With respect, also, to the Crystal Palace, my thoughts are precisely yours.

"Then I feel sure you speak justly of Thackeray's lecture. You do well to set aside odious comparisons, and to wax impatient of that trite twaddle about 'nothing newness'---a jargon which simply proves, in those who habitually use it, a coarse and feeble faculty of appreciation; an inability to discern the relative value of ORIGINALITY and NOVELTY; a lack of that refined perception which, dispensing with the stimulus of an ever-new subject, can derive sufficiency of pleasure from freshness of treatment. To such critics, the prime of a summer morning would bring no delight; wholly occupied with railing at their cook for not having provided a novel and piquant breakfast-dish, they would remain insensible to such influences as lie in sunrise, dew, and breeze: therein would be 'nothing new.'

"Is it Mr. ------'s family experience which has influenced your feelings about the Catholics? I own, I cannot be sorry for this commencing change. Good people---VERY good people---I doubt not, there are amongst the Romanists, but the system is not one which would have such sympathy as YOURS. Look at Popery taking off the mask in Naples!

"I have read the 'Saints' Tragedy.' As a 'work of art' it seems to me far superior to either 'Alton Locke' or 'Yeast.' Faulty it may be, crude and unequal, yet there are portions where some of the deep chords of human nature are swept with a hand which is strong even while it falters. We see throughout (I THINK) that Elizabeth has not, and never had, a mind perfectly sane. From the time that she was what she herself, in the exaggeration of her humility, calls 'an idiot girl,' to the hour when she lay moaning in visions on her dying bed, a slight craze runs through her whole existence. This is good: this is true. A sound mind, a healthy intellect, would have dashed the priest-power to the wall; would have defended her natural affections from his grasp, as a lioness defends her young; would have been as true to husband and children, as your leal-hearted little Maggie was to her Frank. Only a mind weak with some fatal flaw COULD have been influenced as was this poor saint's. But what anguish what struggles! Seldom do I cry over books; but here, my eyes rained as I read. When Elizabeth turns her face to the wall---I stopped---there needed no more.

"Deep truths are touched on in this tragedy---touched on, not fully elicited; truths that stir a peculiar pity---a compassion hot with wrath, and bitter with pain. This is no poet's dream: we know that such things HAVE been done; that minds HAVE been thus subjugated, and lives thus laid waste.

"Remember me kindly and respectfully to Mr. Gaskell, and though I have not seen Marianne, I must beg to include her in the love I send the others. Could you manage to convey a small kiss to that dear, but dangerous little person, Julia? She surreptitiously possessed herself of a minute fraction of my heart, which has been missing, ever since I saw her.---Believe me, sincerely and affectionately yours,

C. BRONTË."

The reference which she makes at the end of this letter is to my youngest little girl, between whom and her a strong mutual attraction existed. The child would steal her little hand into Miss Brontë's scarcely larger one, and each took pleasure in this apparently unobserved caress. Yet once when I told Julia to take and show her the way to some room in the house, Miss Brontë shrunk back: "Do not BID her do anything for me," she said; "it has been so sweet hitherto to have her rendering her little kindnesses SPONTANEOUSLY."

As illustrating her feelings with regard to children, I may give what she says ill another of her letters to me.

"Whenever I see Florence and Julia again, I shall feel like a fond but bashful suitor, who views at a distance the fair personage to whom, in his clownish awe, he dare not risk a near approach. Such is the clearest idea I can give you of my feeling towards children I like, but to whom I am a stranger;---and to what children am I not a stranger? They seem to me little wonders; their talk, their ways are all matter of half-admiring, half-puzzled speculation."

The following is part of a long letter which I received from her, dated September 20th, 1851:---

". . . Beautiful are those sentences out of James Martineau's sermons; some of them gems most pure and genuine; ideas deeply conceived, finely expressed. I should like much to see his review of his sister's book. Of all the articles respecting which you question me, I have seen none, except that notable one in the 'Westminster' on the Emancipation of Women. But why are you and I to think (perhaps I should rather say to FEEL) so exactly alike on some points that there can be no discussion between us? Your words on this paper express my thoughts. Well-argued it is,---clear, logical,---but vast is the hiatus of omission; harsh the consequent jar on every finer chord of the soul. What is this hiatus? I think I know; and, knowing, I will venture to say. I think the writer forgets there is such a thing as self-sacrificing love and disinterested devotion. When I first read the paper, I thought it was the work of a powerful-minded, clear-headed woman, who had a hard, jealous heart, muscles of iron, and nerves of bend[*] leather; of a woman who longed for power, and had never felt affection. To many women affection is sweet, and power conquered indifferent---though we all like influence won. I believe J. S. Mill would make a hard, dry, dismal world of it; and yet he speaks admirable sense through a great portion of his article---especially when he says, that if there be a natural unfitness in women for men's employment, there is no need to make laws on the subject; leave all careers open; let them try; those who ought to succeed will succeed, or, at east, will have a fair chance---the incapable will fall back into their right place. He likewise disposes of the 'maternity' question very neatly. In short, J. S. Mill's head is, I dare say, very good, but I feel disposed to scorn his heart. You are right when you say that there is a large margin in human nature over which the logicians have no dominion; glad am I that it is so. [*] "Bend," in Yorkshire, is strong ox leather.

'I send by this post Ruskin's 'Stones of Venice,' and I hope you and Meta will find passages in it that will please you. Some parts would be dry and technical were it not for the character, the marked individuality which pervades every page. I wish Marianne had come to speak to me at the lecture; it would have given me such pleasure. What you say of that small sprite Julia, amuses me much. I believe you don't know that she has a great deal of her mama's nature (modified) in her; yet I think you will find she has as she grows up.

'Will it not be a great mistake, if Mr. Thackeray should deliver his lectures at Manchester under such circumstances and conditions as will exclude people like you and Mr. Gaskell from the number of his audience? I thought his London-plan too narrow. Charles Dickens would not thus limit his sphere of action.

'You charge me to write about myself. What can I say on that precious topic? My health is pretty good. My spirits are not always alike. Nothing happens to me. I hope and expect little in this world, and am thankful that I do not despond and suffer more. Thank you for inquiring after our old servant; she is pretty well; the little shawl, etc., pleased her much. Papa likewise, I am glad to say, is pretty well; with his and my kindest regards to you and Mr. Gaskell--- Believe me sincerely and affectionately yours,

C. BRONTË."

Before the autumn was far advanced, the usual effects of her solitary life, and of the unhealthy situation of Haworth Parsonage, began to appear in the form of sick headaches, and miserable, starting, wakeful nights. She does not dwell on this in her letters; but there is an absence of all cheerfulness of tone, and an occasional sentence forced out of her, which imply far more than many words could say. There was illness all through the Parsonage household---taking its accustomed forms of lingering influenza and low fever; she herself was outwardly the strongest of the family, and all domestic exertion fell for a time upon her shoulders.

TO W. S. WILLIAMS, ESQ.

'Sept. 26th.
'As I laid down your letter, after reading with interest the graphic account it gives of a very striking scene, I could not help feeling with renewed force a truth, trite enough, yet ever impressive; viz., that it is good to be attracted out of ourselves---to be forced to take a near view of the sufferings, the privations, the efforts, the difficulties of others. If we ourselves live in fulness of content, it is well to be reminded that thousands of our fellow-creatures undergo a different lot; it is well to have sleepy sympathies excited, and lethargic selfishness shaken up. If, on the other hand, we be contending with the special grief,---the intimate trial,---the peculiar bitterness with which God has seen fit to mingle our own cup of existence,---it is very

good to know that our overcast lot is not singular; it stills the repining word and thought,---it rouses the flagging strength, to have it vividly set before us that there are countless afflictions in the world, each perhaps rivalling---some surpassing---the private pain over which we are too prone exclusively to sorrow.

"All those crowded emigrants had their troubles,---their untoward causes of banishment; you, the looker-on, had 'your wishes and regrets,'---your anxieties, alloying your home happiness and domestic bliss; and the parallel might be pursued further, and still it would be true,---still the same; a thorn in the flesh for each; some burden, some conflict for all.

"How far this state of things is susceptible of amelioration from changes in public institutions,---alterations in national habits,---may and ought to be earnestly considered: but this is a problem not easily solved. The evils, as you point them out, are great, real, and most obvious; the remedy is obscure and vague; yet for such difficulties as spring from over-competition, emigration must be good; the new life in a new country must give a new lease of hope; the wider field, less thickly peopled, must open a new path for endeavour. But I always think great physical powers of exertion and endurance ought to accompany such a step. . . . I am truly glad to hear that an ORIGINAL writer has fallen in your way. Originality is the pearl of great price in literature,---the rarest, the most precious claim by which an author can be recommended. Are not your publishing prospects for the coming season tolerably rich and satisfactory? You inquire after 'Currer Bell.' It seems to me that the absence of his name from your list of announcements will leave no blank, and that he may at least spare himself the disquietude of thinking he is wanted when it is certainly not his lot to appear.

"Perhaps Currer Bell has his secret moan about these matters; but if so, he will keep it to himself. It is an affair about which no words need be wasted, for no words can make a change: it is between him and his position, his faculties and his fate."

My husband and I were anxious that she should pay us a visit before the winter had set completely in; and she thus wrote, declining our invitation:---

"Nov. 6th.

"If anybody would tempt me from home, you would; but, just now, from home I must not, will not go. I feel greatly better at present than I did three weeks ago. For a month or six weeks about the equinox (autumnal or vernal) is a period of the year which, I have noticed, strangely tries me. Sometimes the strain falls on the mental, sometimes on the physical part of me; I am ill with neuralgic headache, or I am ground to the dust with deep dejection of spirits (not, however, such dejection but I can keep it to myself). That weary time has, I think and trust, got over for this year. It was the anniversary of my poor brother's death, and of my sister's failing health: I need say no more.

"As to running away from home every time I have a battle of this sort to fight, it would not do besides, the 'weird' would follow. As to shaking it off, that cannot be. I have declined to go to Mrs. ------, to Miss Martineau, and now I decline to go to you. But listen do not think that I throw your kindness away; or that it fails of doing the good you desire. On the contrary, the feeling expressed in your letter,---proved by your invitation---goes RIGHT HOME where you would have it to go, and heals as you would have it to heal.

"Your description of Frederika Bremer tallies exactly with one I read somewhere, in I know not what book. I laughed out when I got to the mention of Frederika's special accomplishment, given by you with a distinct simplicity that, to my taste, is what the French would call 'impayable.' Where do you find the foreigner who is without some little drawback of this description? It is a pity."

A visit from Miss Wooler at this period did Miss Brontë much good for the time. She speaks of her guest's company as being very pleasant,"like good wine," both to her father and to herself. But Miss Wooler could not remain with her long; and then again the monotony of her life returned upon her in all its force; the only events of her days and weeks consisting in the small changes which occasional letters brought. It must be remembered that her health was often such as to prevent her stirring out of the house in inclement or wintry weather. She was liable to sore throat, and depressing pain at the chest, and difficulty of breathing, on the least exposure to cold.

A letter from her late visitor touched and gratified her much; it was simply expressive of gratitude for attention and kindness shown to her, but it wound up by saying that she had not for many years experienced so much enjoyment as during the ten days passed at Haworth. This little sentence called out a wholesome sensation of modest pleasure in Miss Brontë's mind; and she says, "it did me good."

I find, in a letter to a distant friend, written about this time, a retrospect of her visit to London. It is too ample to be considered as a mere repetition of what she had said before; and, besides, it shows that her first impressions of what she saw and heard were not crude and transitory, but stood the tests of time and after-thought.

"I spent a few weeks in town last summer, as you have heard; and was much interested by many things I heard and saw there. What now chiefly dwells in my memory are Mr. Thackeray's lectures, Mademoiselle Rachel's acting, D'Aubigne's, Melville's, and Maurice's preaching, and the Crystal Palace.

"Mr. Thackeray's lectures you will have seen mentioned and commented on in the papers; they were very interesting. I could not always coincide with the sentiments expressed, or the opinions broached; but I admired the gentlemanlike ease, the quiet humour, the taste, the talent, the simplicity, and the originality of the lecturer.

"Rachel's acting transfixed me with wonder, enchained me with interest, and thrilled me with horror. The tremendous force with which she expresses the very worst passions in their strongest essence forms an exhibition as exciting as the bull fights of Spain, and the gladiatorial combats of old Rome, and (it seemed to me) not one whit more moral than these poisoned stimulants to popular ferocity. It is scarcely human nature that she shows you; it is something wilder and worse; the feelings and fury of a fiend. The great gift of genius she undoubtedly has; but, I fear, she rather abuses it than turns it to good account.

"With all the three preachers I was greatly pleased. Melville seemed to me the most eloquent, Maurice the most in earnest; had I the choice, it is Maurice whose ministry I should frequent.

"On the Crystal Palace I need not comment. You must already have heard too much of it. It struck me at the first with only a vague sort of wonder and admiration; but having one day the privilege of going over it in company with an eminent countryman of yours, Sir David Brewster, and hearing, in his friendly Scotch accent, his lucid explanation of many things that had been to me before a sealed book, I began a little better to comprehend it, or at least a small part of it: whether its final results will equal expectation, I know not."

Her increasing indisposition subdued her at last, in spite of all her efforts of reason and will. She tried to forget oppressive recollections in writing. Her publishers were importunate for a new book from her pen. "Villette" was begun, but she lacked power to continue it.

"It is not at all likely" (she says) "that my book will be ready at the time you mention. If my health is spared, I shall get on with it as fast as is consistent with its being done, if not WELL, yet as well as I can do it. NOT ONE WHIT FASTER. When the mood leaves me (it has left me now, without vouchsafing so much as a word or a message when it will return) I put by the MS. and wait till it comes back again. God knows, I sometimes have to wait long---VERY long it seems to me. Meantime, if I might make a request to you, it would be this. Please to say nothing about my book till it is written, and in your hands. You may not like it. I am not myself elated with it as far as it is gone, and authors, you need not be told, are always tenderly indulgent, even blindly partial to their own. Even if it should turn out reasonably well, still I regard it as ruin to the prosperity of an ephemeral book like a novel, to be much talked of beforehand, as if it were something great. People are apt to conceive, or at least to profess, exaggerated expectation, such as no performance can realise; then ensue disappointment and the due revenge, detraction, and failure. If when I write, I were to think of the critics who, I know, are waiting for Currer Bell, ready 'to break all his bones or ever he comes to the bottom of the den,' my hand would fall paralysed on my desk. However, I can but do my best, and then muffle my head in the mantle of Patience, and sit down at her feet and wait."

The "mood" here spoken of did not go off; it had a physical origin. Indigestion, nausea, headache, sleeplessness,---all combined to produce miserable depression of spirits. A little event which occurred about this time, did not tend to cheer her. It was the death of poor old faithful Keeper, Emily's dog. He had come to the Parsonage in the fierce strength of his youth. Sullen and ferocious he had met with his master in the indomitable Emily. Like most dogs of his kind, he feared, respected, and deeply loved her who subdued him. He had mourned her with the pathetic fidelity of his nature, falling into old age after her death. And now, her surviving sister wrote: "Poor old Keeper died last Monday morning, after being ill one night; he went gently to sleep; we laid his old faithful head in the garden. Flossy (the 'fat curly-haired dog') is dull, and misses him. There was something very sad in losing the old dog; yet I am glad he met a natural fate. People kept hinting he ought to be put away, which neither papa nor I liked to think of."

When Miss Brontë wrote this, on December 8th, she was suffering from a bad cold, and pain in her side. Her illness increased, and on December 17th, she---so patient, silent, and enduring of suffering---so afraid of any unselfish taxing of others---had to call to her friend for help:

"I cannot at present go to see you, but I would be grateful if you could come and see me, even were it only for a few days. To speak truth, I have put on but a poor time of it during this month past. I kept hoping to be better, but was at last obliged to have recourse to a medical man. Sometimes I have felt very weak and low, and longed much for society, but could not persuade myself to commit the selfish act of asking you merely for my own relief. The doctor speaks encouragingly, but as yet I get no better. As the illness has been coming on for a long time, it cannot, I suppose, be expected to disappear all at once. I am not confined to bed, but I am weak,---have had no appetite for about three weeks---and my nights are very bad. I am well aware myself that extreme and continuous depression of spirits has had much to do with the origin of the illness; and I know a little cheerful society would do me more good than gallons of medicine. If you CAN come, come on Friday. Write to-morrow and say whether this be possible, and what time you will be at Keighley, that I may send the gig. I do not ask you to stay long; a few days is all I request."

Of course, her friend went; and a certain amount of benefit was derived from her society, always so grateful to Miss Brontë. But the evil was now too deep-rooted to be more than palliated for a time by "the little cheerful society" for which she so touchingly besought.

A relapse came on before long. She was very ill, and the remedies employed took an unusual effect on her peculiar sensitiveness of constitution. Mr. Brontë was miserably anxious about the state of his only remaining child, for she was reduced to the last degree of weakness, as she had been unable to swallow food for above a week before. She rallied, and derived her sole sustenance from half-a-tea-cup of liquid, administered by tea-spoonfuls, in the course of the day. Yet she kept out of bed, for her father's sake, and struggled in solitary patience through her worst hours.

When she was recovering, her spirits needed support, and then she yielded to her friend's entreaty that she would visit her. All the time that Miss Brontë's illness had lasted, Miss ------ had been desirous of coming to her; but she refused to avail herself of this kindness, saying, that "it was enough to burden herself; that it would be misery to annoy another;" and, even at her worst time, she tells her friend, with humorous glee, how coolly she had managed to capture one of Miss ------'s letters to Mr. Brontë, which she suspected was of a kind to aggravate his alarm about his daughter's state, "and at once conjecturing its tenor, made its contents her own."

Happily for all parties, Mr. Brontë was wonderfully well this winter; good sleep, good spirits, and an excellent steady appetite, all seemed to mark vigour; and in such a state of health, Charlotte could leave him to spend a week with her friend, without any great anxiety.

She benefited greatly by the kind attentions and cheerful society of the family with whom she went to stay. They did not care for her in the least as "Currer Bell," but had known and loved her for years as Charlotte Brontë. To them her invalid weakness was only a fresh claim upon their tender regard, from the solitary woman, whom they had first known as a little, motherless school-girl.

Miss Brontë wrote to me about this time, and told me something of what she had suffered.

"Feb. 6th, 1852.

"Certainly, the past winter has been to me a strange time; had I the prospect before me of living it over again, my prayer must necessarily be, 'Let this cup pass from me.' That depression of spirits, which I thought was gone by when I wrote last, came back again with a heavy recoil; internal congestion ensued, and then inflammation. I had severe pain in my right side, frequent burning and aching in my chest; sleep almost forsook me, or would never come, except accompanied by ghastly dreams; appetite vanished, and slow fever was my continual companion. It was some time before I could bring myself to have recourse to medical advice. I thought my lungs were affected, and could feel no confidence in the power of medicine. When, at last, however, a doctor was consulted, he declared my lungs and chest sound, and ascribed all my sufferings to derangement of the liver, on which organ it seems the inflammation had fallen. This information was a great relief to my dear father, as well as to myself; but I had subsequently rather sharp medical discipline to undergo, and was much reduced. Though not yet well, it is with deep thankfulness that I can say, I am GREATLY BETTER. My sleep, appetite, and strength seem all returning."

It was a great interest to her to be allowed an early reading of Esmond; and she expressed her

thoughts on the subject, in a criticising letter to Mr. Smith, who had given her this privilege.
"Feb. 14th, 1852.

"My dear Sir,---It has been a great delight to me to read Mr. Thackeray's work; and I so seldom now express my sense of kindness that, for once, you must permit me, without rebuke, to thank you for a pleasure so rare and special. Yet I am not going to praise either Mr. Thackeray or his book. I have read, enjoyed, been interested, and, after all, feel full as much ire and sorrow as gratitude and admiration. And still one can never lay down a book of his without the last two feelings having their part, be the subject or treatment what it may. In the first half of the book, what chiefly struck me was the wonderful manner in which the writer throws himself into the spirit and letters of the times whereof he treats; the allusions, the illustrations, the style, all seem to me so masterly in their exact keeping, their harmonious consistency, their nice, natural truth, their pure exemption from exaggeration. No second-rate imitator can write in that way; no coarse scene-painter can charm us with an allusion so delicate and perfect. But what bitter satire, what relentless dissection of diseased subjects! Well, and this, too, is right, or would be right, if the savage surgeon did not seem so fiercely pleased with his work. Thackeray likes to dissect an ulcer or an aneurism; he has pleasure in putting his cruel knife or probe into quivering, living flesh. Thackeray would not like all the world to be good; no great satirist would like society to be perfect.

"As usual, he is unjust to women; quite unjust. There is hardly any punishment he does not deserve for making Lady Castlewood peep through a keyhole, listen at a door, and be jealous of a boy and a milkmaid. Many other things I noticed that, for my part, grieved and exasperated me as I read; but then, again, came passages so true, so deeply thought, so tenderly felt, one could not help forgiving and admiring.
* * * * *

But I wish he could be told not to care much for dwelling on the political or religious intrigues of the times. Thackeray, in his heart, does not value political or religious intrigues of any age or date. He likes to show us human nature at home, as he himself daily sees it; his wonderful observant faculty likes to be in action. In him this faculty is a sort of captain and leader; and if ever any passage in his writings lacks interest, it is when this master-faculty is for a time thrust into a subordinate position. I think such is the case in the former half of the present volume. Towards the middle, he throws off restraint, becomes himself, and is strong to the close. Everything now depends on the second and third volumes. If, in pith and interest, they fall short of the first, a true success cannot ensue. If the continuation be an improvement upon the commencement, if the stream gather force as it rolls, Thackeray will triumph. Some people have been in the habit of terming him the second writer of the day; it just depends on himself whether or not these critics shall be justified in their award. He need not be the second. God made him second to no man. If I were he, I would show myself as I am, not as critics report me; at any rate, I would do my best. Mr. Thackeray is easy and indolent, and seldom cares to do his best. Thank you once more; and believe me yours sincerely,

C. BRONTË."

Miss Brontë's health continued such, that she could not apply herself to writing as she wished, for many weeks after the serious attack from which she had suffered. There was not very much to cheer her in the few events that touched her interests during this time. She heard in March of the death of a friend's relation in the Colonies; and we see something of what was the corroding dread at her heart.

"The news of E------'s death came to me last week in a letter from M ------; a long letter, which wrung my heart so, in its simple, strong, truthful emotion, I have only ventured to read it once. It ripped up half-scarred wounds with terrible force. The death-bed was just the same,---breath failing, etc. She fears she shall now, in her dreary solitude, become a 'stern, harsh, selfish woman.' This fear struck home; again and again have I felt it for myself, and what is MY position to M------'s? May God help her, as God only can help!"

Again and again, her friend urged her to leave home; nor were various invitations wanting to enable her to do this, when these constitutional accesses of low spirits preyed too much upon her in her solitude. But she would not allow herself any such indulgence, unless it became absolutely necessary from the state of her health. She dreaded the perpetual recourse to such stimulants as change of scene and society, because of the reaction that was sure to follow. As far as she could see, her life was ordained to be lonely, and she must subdue her nature to her life, and, if possible, bring the two into harmony. When she could employ herself in fiction, all was comparatively well. The characters were her companions in the quiet hours, which she spent utterly alone, unable often to stir out of doors for many days together. The interests of the persons in her novels supplied the lack of interest in her own life; and Memory and Imagination found their appropriate work, and ceased to prey upon her vitals. But too frequently she could not write, could not see her people, nor hear them speak; a great mist of head-ache had blotted them out; they were non-existent to her.

This was the case all through the present spring; and anxious as her publishers were for its completion, Villette stood still. Even her letters to her friend are scarce and brief. Here and there I find a sentence in them which can be extracted, and which is worth preserving.

"M------'s letter is very interesting; it shows a mind one cannot but truly admire. Compare its serene trusting strength, with poor ------'s vacillating dependence. When the latter was in her first burst of happiness, I never remember the feeling finding vent in expressions of gratitude to God. There was always a continued claim upon your sympathy in the mistrust and doubt she felt of her own bliss. M------ believes; her faith is grateful and at peace; yet while happy in herself, how thoughtful she is for others!"

"March 23rd, 1852.

"You say, dear E------, that you often wish I would chat on paper, as you do. How can I? Where are my materials? Is my life fertile in subjects of chat? What callers do I see? What visits do I pay? No, you must chat, and I must listen, and say 'Yes,' and 'No,' and 'Thank you!' for five minutes' recreation.

* * * * *

"I am amused at the interest you take in politics. Don't expect to rouse me; to me, all ministries and all oppositions seem to be pretty much alike. D'Israeli was factious as leader of the Opposition; Lord John Russell is going to be factious, now that he has stepped into D'Israeli's shoes. Lord Derby's 'Christian love and spirit,' is worth three half-pence farthing."

To W. S. WILLIAMS, ESQ.

"March 25th, 1852.

"My dear Sir,---Mr. Smith intimated a short time since, that he had some thoughts of publishing a reprint of Shirley. Having revised the work, I now enclose the errata. I have likewise sent off to-day, per rail, a return-box of Cornhill books.

"I have lately read with great pleasure, 'The Two Families.' This work, it seems, should have reached me in January; but owing to a mistake, it was detained at the Dead Letter Office, and lay there nearly two months. I liked the commencement very much; the close seemed to me scarcely equal to 'Rose Douglas.' I thought the authoress committed a mistake in shifting the main interest from the two personages on whom it first rests---viz., Ben Wilson and Mary---to other characters of quite inferior conception. Had she made Ben and Mary her hero and heroine, and continued the development of their fortunes and characters in the same truthful natural vein in which she commences it, an excellent, even an original, book might have been the result. As for Lilias and Ronald, they are mere romantic figments, with nothing of the genuine Scottish peasant about them; they do not even speak the Caledonian dialect; they palaver like a fine lady and gentleman.

"I ought long since to have acknowledged the gratification with which I read Miss Kavanagh's 'Women of Christianity.' Her charity and (on the whole) her impartiality are very beautiful. She touches, indeed, with too gentle a hand the theme of Elizabeth of Hungary; and, in her own mind, she evidently misconstrues the fact of Protestant charities SEEMING to be fewer than Catholic. She forgets, or does not know, that Protestantism is a quieter creed than Romanism; as it does not clothe its priesthood in scarlet, so neither does it set up its good women for saints, canonise their names, and proclaim their good works. In the records of man, their almsgiving will not perhaps be found registered, but Heaven has its account as well as earth.

"With kind regards to yourself and family, who, I trust, have all safely weathered the rough winter lately past, as well as the east winds, which are still nipping our spring in Yorkshire,---I am, my dear Sir, yours sincerely,

C. BRONTË."

"April 3rd, 1852.

"My dear Sir,---The box arrived quite safely, and I very much thank you for the contents, which are most kindly selected.

"As you wished me to say what I thought of 'The School for Fathers,' I hastened to read it. The book seems to me clever, interesting, very amusing, and likely to please generally. There is a merit in the choice of ground, which is not yet too hackneyed; the comparative freshness of subject, character, and epoch give the tale a certain attractiveness. There is also, I think, a graphic rendering of situations, and a lively talent for describing whatever is visible and tangible---what the eye meets on the surface of things. The humour appears to me such as would answer well on the stage; most of the scenes seem to demand dramatic accessories to give them their full effect. But I think one cannot with justice bestow higher praise than this. To speak candidly, I felt, in reading the tale, a wondrous hollowness in the moral and sentiment; a strange dilettante shallowness in the purpose and feeling. After all, 'Jack' is not much better than a 'Tony Lumpkin,' and there is no very great breadth of choice between the clown he IS and the fop his father would have made him. The grossly material life of the old English fox-hunter, and the frivolous existence of the fine gentleman present extremes, each in its way so repugnant, that one feels half inclined to smile when called upon to sentimentalise over the lot of a youth forced to pass from the one to the other; torn from the stables, to be ushered perhaps into the ball-room. Jack dies mournfully indeed, and you are sorry for the poor fellow's untimely end; but you cannot forget that, if he had not been thrust into the way of Colonel Penruddock's weapon, he might possibly have broken his neck in a fox-hunt. The character of Sir Thomas Warren is excellent; consistent throughout. That of Mr. Addison not bad, but sketchy, a mere outline---wanting colour and finish. The man's portrait is there, and his costume, and fragmentary anecdotes of his life; but where is the man's nature---soul and self? I say nothing about the female characters---not one word; only that Lydia seems to me like a pretty little actress, prettily dressed gracefully appearing and disappearing, and reappearing in a genteel comedy, assuming the proper sentiments of her part with all due tact and naivete, and---that is all.

"Your description of the model man of business is true enough, I doubt not; but we will not fear that society will ever be brought quite to this standard; human nature (bad as it is) has, after all, elements that forbid it. But the very tendency to such a consummation---the marked tendency, I fear, of the day---produces, no doubt, cruel suffering. Yet, when the evil of competition passes a certain limit, must it not in time work its own cure? I suppose it will, but then through some convulsed crisis, shattering all around it like an earthquake. Meantime, for how many is life made a struggle; enjoyment and rest curtailed; labour terribly enhanced beyond almost what nature can bear I often think that this world would be the most terrible of enigmas, were it not for the firm belief that there is a world to come, where conscientious effort and patient pain will meet their reward.---Believe me, my dear Sir, sincerely yours,

C. BRONTË."

A letter to her old Brussels schoolfellow gives a short retrospect of the dreary winter she had passed through.

"Haworth, April 12th, 1852.

". . . I struggled through the winter, and the early part of the spring, often with great difficulty. My friend stayed with me a few days in the early part of January; she could not be spared longer. I was better during her visit, but had a relapse soon after she left me, which reduced my strength very much. It cannot be denied that the solitude of my position fearfully aggravated its other evils. Some long stormy days and nights there were, when I felt such a craving for support and companionship as I cannot express. Sleepless, I lay awake night after night, weak and unable to occupy myself. I sat in my chair day after day, the saddest memories my only company. It was a time I shall never forget; but God sent it, and it must have been for the best.

"I am better now; and very grateful do I feel for the restoration of tolerable health; but, as if there was always to be some affliction, papa, who enjoyed wonderful health during the whole winter, is ailing with his spring attack of bronchitis. I earnestly trust it may pass over in the comparatively ameliorated form in which it has hitherto shown itself.

"Let me not forget to answer your question about the cataract. Tell your papa that MY father was seventy at the time he underwent an operation; he was most reluctant to try the experiment; could not believe that, at his age, and with his want of robust strength, it would succeed. I was obliged to be very decided in the matter, and to act entirely on my own responsibility. Nearly six years have now elapsed since the cataract was extracted (it was not merely depressed); he has never once during that time regretted the step, and a day seldom passes that he does not express gratitude and pleasure at the restoration of that inestimable privilege of vision whose loss he once knew."

I had given Miss Brontë; in one of my letters, an outline of the story on which I was then engaged, and in reply she says:---

"The sketch you give of your work (respecting which I am, of course, dumb) seems to me very noble; and its purpose may be as useful in practical result as it is high and just in theoretical tendency. Such a book may restore hope and energy to many who thought they had forfeited their right to both; and open a clear course for honourable effort to some who deemed that they and all honour had parted company in this world.

"Yet---hear my protest!

"Why should she die? Why are we to shut up the book weeping?

"My heart fails me already at the thought of the pang it will have to undergo. And yet you must follow the impulse of your own inspiration. If THAT commands the slaying of the victim, no bystander has a right to put out his hand to stay the sacrificial knife: but I hold you a stern priestess in these matters."

As the milder weather came on, her health improved, and her power of writing increased. She set herself with redoubled vigour to the work before her; and denied herself pleasure for the purpose of steady labour. Hence she writes to her friend:---

"May 11th.

"Dear E------, ---I must adhere to my resolution of neither visiting nor being visited at present. Stay you quietly at B., till you go to S., as I shall stay at Haworth; as sincere a farewell can be taken with the heart as with the lips, and perhaps less painful. I am glad the weather is changed; the return of the south-west wind suits me; but I hope you have no cause to regret the departure of your favourite east wind. What you say about ------ does not surprise me; I have had many little notes (whereof I answer about one in three) breathing the same spirit,---self and child the sole all-absorbing topics, on which the changes are rung even to weariness. But I suppose one must not heed it, or think the case singular. Nor, I am afraid, must one expect her to improve. I read in a French book lately, a sentence to this effect, that 'marriage might be defined as the state of two-fold selfishness.' Let the single therefore take comfort. Thank you for Mary's letter. She DOES seem most happy; and I cannot tell you how much more real, lasting, and better-warranted her happiness seems than ever ------'s did. I think so much of it is in herself, and her own serene, pure, trusting, religious nature. ------'s always gives me the idea of a vacillating, unsteady rapture, entirely dependent on circumstances with all their fluctuations. If Mary lives to be a mother, you will then see a greater difference.

"I wish you, dear E., all health and enjoyment in your visit; and, as far as one can judge at present, there seems a fair prospect of the wish being realised.---Yours sincerely,

"C. BRONTË."

CHAPTER XI.

The reader will remember that Anne Brontë had been interred in the churchyard of the Old Church at Scarborough. Charlotte had left directions for a tombstone to be placed over her; but many a time during the solitude of the past winter, her sad, anxious thoughts had revisited the scene of that last great sorrow, and she had wondered whether all decent services had been rendered to the memory of the dead, until at last she came to a silent resolution to go and see for herself whether the stone and inscription were in a satisfactory state of preservation.

"Cliffe House, Filey, June 6th, 1852.

"Dear E------, ---I am at Filey utterly alone. Do not be angry, the step is right. I considered it, and resolved on it with due deliberation. Change of air was necessary; there were reasons why I should NOT go to the south, and why I should come here. On Friday I went to Scarborough, visited the churchyard and stone. It must be refaced and relettered; there are five errors. I gave the necessary directions. THAT duty, then, is done; long has it lain heavy on my mind; and that was a pilgrimage I felt I could only make alone.

"I am in our old lodgings at Mrs. Smith's; not, however, in the same rooms, but in less expensive apartments. They seemed glad to see me, remembered you and me very well, and, seemingly, with great good will. The daughter who used to wait on us is just married. Filey seems to me much altered; more lodging-houses---some of them very handsome---have been built; the sea has all its old grandeur. I walk on the sands a good deal, and try NOT to feel desolate and melancholy. How sorely my heart longs for you, I need not say. I have bathed once; it seemed to do me good. I may, perhaps, stay here a fortnight. There are as yet scarcely any visitors. A Lady Wenlock is staying at the large house of which you used so vigilantly to observe the inmates. One day I set out with intent to trudge to Filey Bridge, but was frightened back by two cows. I mean to try again some morning. I left papa well. I have been a good deal troubled with headache, and with some pain in the side since I came here, but I feel that this has been owing to the cold wind, for very cold has it been till lately; at present I feel better. Shall I send the papers to you as usual. Write again directly, and tell me this, and anything and everything else that comes into your mind.---Believe me, yours faithfully,

"C. BRONTË."

"Filey, June 16th, 1852.

"Dear E------, ---Be quite easy about me. I really think I am better for my stay at Filey; that I have derived more benefit from it than I dared to anticipate. I believe, could I stay here two months, and enjoy something like social cheerfulness as well as exercise and good air, my health would be quite renewed. This, however, cannot possibly be; but I am most thankful for the good received. I stay here another week.

"I return ------'s letter. I am sorry for her: I believe she suffers; but I do not much like her style of expressing herself. . . . Grief as well as joy manifests itself in most different ways in different people; and I doubt not she is sincere and in earnest when she talks of her 'precious, sainted father;' but I could wish she used simpler language."

Soon after her return from Filey, she was alarmed by a very serious and sharp attack of illness with which Mr. Brontë was seized. There was some fear, for a few days, that his sight was permanently lost, and his spirits sank painfully under this dread.

"This prostration of spirits," writes his daughter, "which accompanies anything like a relapse is almost the most difficult point to manage. Dear E------, you are tenderly kind in offering your society; but rest very tranquil where you are; be fully assured that it is not now, nor under present circumstances, that I feel the lack either of society or occupation; my time is pretty well filled up, and my thoughts appropriated. . . . I cannot permit myself to comment much on the chief contents of your last; advice is not necessary: as far as I can judge, you seem hitherto enabled to take these trials in a good and wise spirit. I can only pray that such combined strength and resignation may be continued to you. Submission, courage, exertion, when practicable---these seem to be the weapons with which we must fight life's long battle."

I suppose that, during the very time when her thoughts were thus fully occupied with anxiety for her father, she received some letter from her publishers, making inquiry as to the progress of the work which they knew she had in hand, as I find the following letter to Mr. Williams, bearing reference to some of Messrs. Smith and Elder's proposed arrangements.

"To W. S. WILLIAMS, ESQ.

"July 28th, 1852.

"My dear Sir,---Is it in contemplation to publish the new edition of 'Shirley' soon? Would it not be better to defer it for a time? In reference to a part of your letter, permit me to express this wish,---and I trust in doing so, I shall not be regarded as stepping out of my position as an author, and encroaching on the arrangements of business,---viz.: that no announcement of a new work by the author of 'Jane Eyre' shall be made till the MS. of such work is actually in my publisher's hands. Perhaps we are none of us justified in speaking very decidedly where the future is concerned; but for some too much caution in such calculations can scarcely be observed: amongst this number I must class myself. Nor, in doing so, can I assume an apologetic tone. He does right who does his best.

"Last autumn I got on for a time quickly. I ventured to look forward to spring as the period of publication: my health gave way; I passed such a winter as, having been once experienced, will never be forgotten. The spring proved little better than a protraction of trial. The warm weather and a visit to the sea have done me much good physically; but as yet I have recovered neither elasticity of animal spirits, nor flow of the power of composition. And if it were otherwise, the difference would be of no avail; my time and thoughts are at present taken up with close attendance on my father, whose health is just now in a very critical state, the heat of the weather having produced determination of blood to the head.---I am, yours sincerely,

C. BRONTË."

Before the end of August, Mr. Brontë's convalescence became quite established, and he was anxious to resume his duties for some time before his careful daughter would permit him.

On September the 14th the "great duke" died. He had been, as we have seen, her hero from childhood; but I find no further reference to him at this time than what is given in the following extract from a letter to her friend:---

"I do hope and believe the changes you have been having this summer will do you permanent good, notwithstanding the pain with which they have been too often mingled. Yet I feel glad that you are soon coming home; and I really must not trust myself to say how much I wish the time were come when, without let or hindrance, I could once more welcome you to Haworth. But oh I don't get on; I feel fretted---incapable---sometimes very low. However, at present, the subject must not be dwelt upon; it presses me too hardly---nearly---and painfully. Less than ever can I taste or know pleasure till this work is wound up. And yet I often sit up in bed at night, thinking of and wishing for you. Thank you for the Times; what it said on the mighty and mournful subject was well said. All at once the whole nation seems to take a just view of that great character. There was a review too of an American book, which I was glad to see. Read 'Uncle Tom's Cabin': probably, though, you have read it.

"Papa's health continues satisfactory, thank God! As for me, my wretched liver has been disordered again of late, but I hope it is now going to be on better behaviour; it hinders me in working---depresses both power and tone of feeling. I must expect this derangement from time to time."

Haworth was in an unhealthy state, as usual; and both Miss Brontë and Tabby suffered severely from the prevailing epidemics. The former was long in shaking off the effects of this illness. In vain she resolved against allowing herself any society or change of scene until she had accomplished her labour. She was too ill to write; and with illness came on the old heaviness of heart, recollections of the past, and anticipations of the future. At last Mr. Brontë expressed so strong a wish that her friend should be asked to visit her, and she felt some little refreshment so absolutely necessary, that on October the 9th she begged her to come to Haworth, just for a single week.

"I thought I would persist in denying myself till I had done my work, but I find it won't do; the matter refuses to progress, and this excessive solitude presses too heavily; so let me see your dear face, E., just for one reviving week."

But she would only accept of the company of her friend for the exact time specified. She thus writes to Miss Wooler on October the 21st:---

"E------ has only been my companion one little week. I would not have her any longer, for I am disgusted with myself and my delays; and consider it was a weak yielding to temptation in me to send for her at all; but in truth, my spirits were getting low---prostrate sometimes---and she has done me inexpressible good. I wonder when I shall see you at Haworth again; both my father and the servants have again and again insinuated a distinct wish that you should be requested to come in the course of the summer and autumn, but I have always turned rather a deaf ear; 'not yet,' was my thought, 'I want first to be free;' work first, then pleasure."

Miss ------'s visit had done her much good. Pleasant companionship during the day produced, for the time, the unusual blessing of calm repose at night; and after her friend's departure she was well enough to "fall to business," and write away, almost incessantly, at her story of Villette, now drawing to a conclusion. The following letter to Mr. Smith, seems to have accompanied the first part of the MS.

"Oct. 30th, 1852.

"My dear Sir,---You must notify honestly what you think of 'Villette' when you have read it. I can hardly tell you how I hunger to hear some opinion besides my own, and how I have sometimes desponded, and almost despaired, because there was no one to whom to read a line, or of whom to ask a counsel. 'Jane Eyre' was not written under such circumstances, nor were two-thirds of 'Shirley'. I got so miserable about it, I could bear no allusion to the book. It is not finished yet; but now I hope. As to the anonymous publication, I have this to say: If the withholding of the author's name should tend materially to injure the publisher's interest, to interfere with booksellers' orders, etc., I would not press the point; but if no such detriment is contingent, I should be most thankful for the sheltering shadow of an incognito. I seem to dread the advertisements---the large-lettered 'Currer Bell's New Novel,' or 'New Work, by the Author of Jane Eyre.' These, however, I feel well enough, are the transcendentalisms of a retired wretch; so you must speak frankly. . . . I shall be glad to see 'Colonel Esmond.' My objection to the second volume lay here: I thought it contained decidedly too much history--- too little story."

In another letter, referring to "Esmond," she uses the following words:---

"The third volume seemed to me to possess the most sparkle, impetus, and interest. Of the first and second my judgment was, that parts of them were admirable; but there was the fault of containing too much History---too little story. I hold that a work of fiction ought to be a work of creation: that the REAL should be sparingly introduced in pages dedicated to the IDEAL. Plain household bread is a far more wholesome and necessary thing than cake; yet who would like to see the brown loaf placed on the table for dessert? In the second volume, the author gives us an ample supply of excellent brown bread; in his third, only such a portion as gives substance, like the crumbs of bread in a well-made, not too rich, plum-pudding."

Her letter to Mr. Smith, containing the allusion to 'Esmond,' which reminded me of the quotation just given continues:---

"You will see that 'Villette' touches on no matter of public interest. I cannot write books handling the topics of the day; it is of no use trying. Nor can I write a book for its moral. Nor can I take up a philanthropic scheme, though I honour philanthropy; and voluntarily and sincerely veil my face before such a mighty subject as that handled in Mrs. Beecher Stowe's work, 'Uncle Tom's Cabin.' To manage these great matters rightly, they must be long and practically studied---their bearings known intimately, and their evils felt genuinely; they must not be taken up as a business matter, and a trading speculation. I doubt not, Mrs. Stowe had felt the iron of slavery enter into her heart, from childhood upwards, long before she ever thought of writing books. The feeling throughout her work is sincere, and not got up. Remember to be an honest critic of 'Villette,' and tell Mr. Williams to be unsparing: not that I am likely to alter anything, but I want to know his impressions and yours."

To G. SMITH, ESQ.

"Nov. 3rd.

"My dear Sir,---I feel very grateful for your letter; it relieved me much, for I was a good deal harassed by doubts as to how 'Villette' might appear in other eyes than my own. I feel in some degree authorised to rely on your favourable impressions, because you are quite right where you hint disapprobation. You have exactly hit two points at least where I was conscious of defect;---the discrepancy, the want of perfect harmony, between Graham's boyhood and manhood,---the angular abruptness of his change of sentiment towards Miss Fanshawe. You must remember, though, that in secret he had for some time appreciated that young lady at a somewhat depressed standard---held her a LITTLE lower than the angels. But still the reader ought to have been better made to feel this preparation towards a change of mood. As to the publishing arrangement, I leave them to Cornhill. There is, undoubtedly, a certain force in what you say about the inexpediency of affecting a mystery which cannot be sustained; so you must act as you think is for the best. I submit, also, to the advertisements in large letters, but under protest, and with a kind of ostrich-longing for concealment. Most of the third volume is given to the development of the 'crabbed Professor's' character. Lucy must not marry Dr. John; he is far too youthful, handsome, bright-spirited, and sweet-tempered; he is a 'curled darling' of Nature and of Fortune, and must draw a prize in life's lottery. His wife must be young, rich, pretty; he must be made very happy indeed. If Lucy marries anybody, it must be the Professor---a man in whom there is much to forgive, much to 'put up with.' But I am not leniently disposed towards Miss FROST from the beginning, I never meant to appoint her lines in pleasant places. The conclusion of this third volume is still a matter of some anxiety: I can but do my best, however. It would speedily be finished, could I ward off certain obnoxious headaches, which, whenever I get into the spirit of my work, are apt to seize and prostrate me. . . . .

"Colonel Henry Esmond is just arrived. He looks very antique and distinguished in his Queen Anne's garb; the periwig, sword, lace, and ruffles are very well represented by the old 'Spectator' type."

In reference to a sentence towards the close of this letter, I may mention what she told me; that Mr. Brontë was anxious that her new tale should end well, as he disliked novels which left a melancholy impression upon the mind; and he requested her to make her hero and heroine (like the heroes and heroines in fairy-tales) "marry, and live very happily ever after." But the idea of M. Paul Emanuel's death at sea was stamped on her imagination till it assumed the distinct force of reality; and she could no more alter her fictitious ending than if they had been facts which she was relating. All she could do in compliance with her father's wish was so to veil the fate in oracular words, as to leave it to the character and discernment of her readers to interpret her meaning.

To W. S. WILLIAMS, ESQ.

"Nov. 6th, 1852.

"My dear Sir,---I must not delay thanking you for your kind letter, with its candid and able commentary on 'Villette.' With many of your strictures I concur. The third volume may, perhaps, do away with some of the objections; others still remain in force. I do not think the interest culminates anywhere to the degree you would wish. What climax there is does not come on till near the conclusion; and even then, I doubt whether the regular novel-reader will consider the 'agony piled sufficiently high' (as the Americans say), or the colours dashed on to the canvas with the proper amount of daring. Still, I fear, they must be satisfied with what is offered: my palette affords no brighter tints; were I to attempt to deepen the reds, or burnish the yellows, I should but botch.

"Unless I am mistaken, the emotion of the book will be found to be kept throughout in tolerable subjection. As to the name of the heroine, I can hardly express what subtlety of thought made me decide upon giving her a cold name; but, at first, I called her 'Lucy Snowe' (spelt with an 'e'); which Snowe I afterwards changed to 'Frost.' Subsequently, I rather egretted the change, and wished it 'Snowe' again. If not too late, I should like the alteration to be made now throughout the MS. A COLD name she must have; partly, perhaps, on the 'lucus a non lucendo' principle---partly on that of the 'fitness of things,' for she has about her an external coldness.

"You say that she may be thought morbid and weak, unless the history of her life be more fully given. I consider that she is both morbid and weak at times; her character sets up no pretensions to unmixed strength, and anybody living her life would necessarily become morbid. It was no impetus of healthy feeling which urged her to the confessional, for instance; it was the semi-delirium of solitary grief and sickness. If, however, the book does not express all this, there must be a great fault somewhere. I might explain away a few other points, but it would be too much like drawing a picture and then writing underneath the name of the object intended to be represented. We know what sort of a pencil that is which needs an ally in the pen.

"Thanking you again for the clearness and fulness with which you have responded to my request for a statement of impressions, I am, my dear Sir, yours very sincerely,

"C. BRONTË."

"I trust the work will be seen in MS. by no one except Mr. Smith and yourself."

"Nov. 10th, 1852.

"My dear Sir,---I only wished the publication of 'Shirley' to be delayed till 'Villette' was nearly ready; so that there can now be no objection to its being issued whenever you think fit. About putting the MS. into type, I can only say that, should I be able to proceed with the third volume at my average rate of composition, and with no more than the average amount of interruptions, I should hope to have it ready in about three weeks. I leave it to you to decide whether it would be better to delay the printing that space of time, or to commence it immediately. It would certainly be more satisfactory if you were to see the third volume before printing the first and the second; yet, if delay is likely to prove injurious, I do not think it is indispensable. I have read the third volume of 'Esmond.' I found it both entertaining and exciting to me; it seems to possess an impetus and excitement beyond the other two,---that movement and brilliancy its predecessors sometimes wanted, never fails here. In certain passages, I thought Thackeray used all his powers; their grand, serious force yielded a profound satisfaction. 'At last he puts forth his strength,' I could not help saying to myself. No character in the book strikes me as more masterly than that of Beatrix; its conception is fresh, and its delineation vivid. It is peculiar; it has impressions of a new kind---new, at least, to me. Beatrix is not, in herself, all bad. So much does she sometimes reveal of what is good and great as to suggest this feeling---you would think she was urged by a fate. You would think that some antique doom presses on her house, and that once in so many generations its brightest ornament was to become its greatest disgrace. At times, what is good in her struggles against this terrible destiny, but the Fate conquers. Beatrix cannot be an honest woman and a good man's wife. She 'tries, and she CANNOT.' Proud, beautiful, and sullied, she was born what she becomes, a king's mistress. I know not whether you have seen the notice in the Leader; I read it just after concluding the book. Can I be wrong in deeming it a notice tame, cold, and insufficient? With all its professed friendliness, it produced on me a most disheartening impression. Surely, another sort of justice than this will be rendered to 'Esmond' from other quarters. One acute remark of the critic is to the effect that Blanche Amory and Beatrix are identical---sketched from the same original! To me they are about as identical as a weazel and a royal tigress of Bengal; both the latter are quadrupeds,---both the former, women. But I must not take up either your time or my own with further remarks. Believe me yours sincerely,

"C. BRONTË."

On a Saturday, a little later in this month, Miss Brontë completed 'Villette,' and sent it off to her publishers. "I said my prayers when I had done it. Whether it is well or ill done, I don't know; D. V., I will now try and wait the issue quietly. The book, I think, will not be considered pretentious; nor is it of a character to excite hostility."

As her labour was ended, she felt at liberty to allow herself a little change. There were several friends anxious to see her and welcome her to their homes Miss Martineau, Mrs. Smith, and her own faithful E------. With the last, in the same letter as that in which she announced the completion of 'Villette,' she offered to spend a week. She began, also, to consider whether it might not be well to avail herself of Mrs. Smith's kind invitation, with a view to the convenience of being on the spot to correct the proofs.

The following letter is given, not merely on account of her own criticisms on 'Villette,' but because it shows how she had learned to magnify the meaning of trifles, as all do who live a self-contained and solitary life. Mr. Smith had been unable to write by the same post as that which brought the money for 'Villette,' and she consequently received it without a line. The friend with whom she was staying says, that she immediately fancied there was some disappointment about 'Villette,' or that some word or act of hers had given offence; and had not the Sunday intervened, and so allowed time for Mr. Smith's letter to make its appearance, she would certainly have crossed it on her way to London.

"Dec. 6th, 1852.

"My dear Sir,---The receipts have reached me safely. I received the first on Saturday, enclosed in a cover without a line, and had made up my mind to take the train on Monday, and go up to London to see what was the matter, and what had struck my publisher mute. On Sunday morning your letter came, and you have thus been spared the visitation of the unannounced and unsummoned apparition of Currer Bell in Cornhill. Inexplicable delays should be avoided when possible, for they are apt to urge those subjected to their harassment to sudden and impulsive steps. I must pronounce you right again, in your complaint of the transfer of interest in the third volume, from one set of characters to another. It is not pleasant, and it will probably be found as unwelcome to the reader, as it was, in a sense, compulsory upon the writer. The spirit of romance would have indicated another course, far more flowery and inviting; it would have fashioned a paramount hero, kept faithfully with him, and made him supremely worshipful; he should have been an idol, and not a mute, unresponding idol either; but this would have been unlike real LIFE---inconsistent with truth---at variance with probability. I greatly apprehend, however, that the weakest character in the book is the one I aimed at making the most beautiful; and, if this be the case, the fault lies in its wanting the germ of the real---in its being purely imaginary. I felt that this character lacked substance; I fear that the reader will feel the same. Union with it resembles too much the fate of Ixion, who was mated with a cloud. The childhood of Paulina is, however, I think, pretty well imagined, but her. . ." (the remainder of this interesting sentence is torn off the letter). "A brief visit to London becomes thus more practicable, and if your mother will kindly write, when she has time, and name a day after Christmas which will suit her, I shall have pleasure, papa's health permitting, in availing myself of her invitation. I wish I could come in time to correct some at least of the proofs; it would save trouble."

CHAPTER XII.

The difficulty that presented itself most strongly to me, when I first had the honour of being requested to write this biography, was how I could show what a noble, true, and tender woman Charlotte Brontë really was, without mingling up with her life too much of the personal history of her nearest and most intimate friends. After much consideration of this point, I came to the resolution of writing truly, if I wrote at all; of withholding nothing, though some things, from their very nature, could not be spoken of so fully as others.

One of the deepest interests of her life centres naturally round her marriage, and the preceding circumstances; but more than all other events (because of more recent date, and concerning another as intimately as herself), it requires delicate handling on my part, lest I intrude too roughly on what is most sacred to memory. Yet I have two reasons, which seem to me good and valid ones, for giving some particulars of the course of events which led to her few months of wedded life---that short spell of exceeding happiness. The first is my desire to call attention to the fact that Mr. Nicholls was one who had seen her almost daily for years; seen her as a daughter, a sister, a mistress and a friend. He was not a man to be attracted by any kind of literary fame. I imagine that this, by itself, would rather repel him when he saw it in the possession of a woman. He was a grave, reserved, conscientious man, with a deep sense of religion, and of his duties as one of its ministers.

In silence he had watched her, and loved her long. The love of such a man---a daily spectator of her manner of life for years---is a great testimony to her character as a woman.

How deep his affection was I scarcely dare to tell, even if I could in words. She did not know---she had hardly begun to suspect---that she was the object of any peculiar regard on his part, when, in this very December, he came one evening to tea. After tea, she returned from the study to her own sitting-room, as was her custom, leaving her father and his curate together. Presently she heard the study-door open, and expected to hear the succeeding clash of the front door. Instead, came a tap; and, "like lightning, it flashed upon me what was coming. He entered. He stood before me. What his words were you can imagine; his manner you can hardly realise, nor can I forget it. He made me, for the first time, feel what it costs a man to declare affection when he doubts response. . . . The spectacle of one, ordinarily so statue-like, thus trembling, stirred, and overcome, gave me a strange shock. I could only entreat him to leave me then, and promise a reply on the morrow. I asked if he had spoken to Papa. He said he dared not. I think I half led, half put him out of the room."

So deep, so fervent, and so enduring was the affection Miss Brontë had inspired in the heart of this good man! It is an honour to her; and, as such, I have thought it my duty to speak thus much, and quote thus fully from her letter about it. And now I pass to my second reason for dwelling on a subject which may possibly be considered by some, at first sight, of too private a nature for publication. When Mr. Nicholls had left her, Charlotte went immediately to her father and told him all. He always disapproved of marriages, and constantly talked against them. But he more than disapproved at this time; he could not bear the idea of this attachment of Mr. Nicholls to his daughter. Fearing the consequences of agitation to one so recently an invalid, she made haste to give her father a promise that, on the morrow, Mr. Nicholls should have a distinct refusal. Thus quietly and modestly did she, on whom such hard judgments had been passed by ignorant reviewers, receive this vehement, passionate declaration of love,---thus thoughtfully for her father, and unselfishly for herself, put aside all consideration of how she should reply, excepting as he wished!

The immediate result of Mr. Nicholls' declaration of attachment was, that he sent in his resignation of the curacy of Haworth; and that Miss Brontë held herself simply passive, as far as words and actions went, while she suffered acute pain from the strong expressions which her father used in speaking of Mr. Nicholls, and from the too evident distress and failure of health on the part of the latter. Under these circumstances she, more gladly than ever, availed herself of Mrs. Smith's proposal, that she should again visit them in London; and thither she accordingly went in the first week of the year 1853.

From thence I received the following letter. It is with a sad, proud pleasure I copy her words of friendship now.

"January 12th, 1853.

"It is with YOU the ball rests. I have not heard from you since I wrote last; but I thought I knew the reason of your silence, viz. application to work,---and therefore I accept it, not merely with resignation, but with satisfaction.

"I am now in London, as the date above will show; staying very quietly at my publisher's, and correcting proofs, etc. Before receiving yours, I had felt, and expressed to Mr. Smith, reluctance to come in the way of 'Ruth;' not that I think SHE would suffer from contact with 'Villette'---we know not but that the damage might be the other way; but I have ever held comparisons to be odious, and would fain that neither I nor my friends should be made subjects for the same. Mr. Smith proposes, accordingly, to defer the publication of my book till the 24th inst.; he says that will give 'Ruth' the start in the papers daily and weekly, and also will leave free to her all the February magazines. Should this delay appear to you insufficient, speak! and it shall be protracted.

"I dare say, arrange as we may, we shall not be able wholly to prevent comparisons; it is the nature of some critics to be invidious; but we need not care we can set them at defiance; they SHALL not make us foes, they SHALL not mingle with our mutual feelings one taint of jealousy there is my hand on that; I know you will give clasp for clasp.

"'Villette' has indeed no right to push itself before 'Ruth.' There is a goodness, a philanthropic purpose, a social use in the latter to which the former cannot for an instant pretend; nor can it claim precedence on the ground of surpassing power I think it much quieter than 'Jane Eyre.'
* * * * *

"I wish to see YOU, probably at least as much as you can wish to see ME, and therefore shall consider your invitation for March as an engagement; about the close of that month, then, I hope to pay you a brief visit. With kindest remembrances to Mr. Gaskell and all your precious circle, I am," etc.

This visit at Mrs. Smith's was passed more quietly than any previous one, and was consequently more in accordance with her own tastes. She saw things rather than persons; and being allowed to have her own choice of sights, she selected the "REAL in preference to the DECORATIVE side of life." She went over two prisons,---one ancient, the other modern,---

Newgate and Pentonville; over two hospitals, the Foundling and Bethlehem. She was also taken, at her own request, to see several of the great City sights; the Bank, the Exchange, Rothschild's, etc.

The power of vast yet minute organisation, always called out her respect and admiration. She appreciated it more fully than most women are able to do. All that she saw during this last visit to London impressed her deeply---so much so as to render her incapable of the immediate expression of her feelings, or of reasoning upon her impressions while they were so vivid. If she had lived, her deep heart would sooner or later have spoken out on these things.

What she saw dwelt in her thoughts, and lay heavy on her spirits. She received the utmost kindness from her hosts, and had the old, warm, and grateful regard for them. But looking back, with the knowledge of what was then the future, which Time has given, one cannot but imagine that there was a toning-down in preparation for the final farewell to these kind friends, whom she saw for the last time on a Wednesday morning in February. She met her friend E------ at Keighley, on her return, and the two proceeded to Haworth together.

"Villette"---which, if less interesting as a mere story than "Jane Eyre," displays yet more of the extraordinary genius of the author---was received with one burst of acclamation. Out of so small a circle of characters, dwelling in so dull and monotonous an area as a "pension," this wonderful tale was evolved!

See how she receives the good tidings of her success!

"Feb. 15th, 1853.

"I got a budget of no less than seven papers yesterday and to-day. The import of all the notices is such as to make my heart swell with thankfulness to Him, who takes note both of suffering, and work, and motives. Papa is pleased too. As to friends in general, I believe I can love them still, without expecting them to take any large share in this sort of gratification. The longer I live, the more plainly I see that gentle must be the strain on fragile human nature; it will not bear much."

I suspect that the touch of slight disappointment, perceptible in the last few lines, arose from her great susceptibility to an opinion she valued much,---that of Miss Martineau, who, both in an article on 'Villette' in the Daily News, and in a private letter to Miss Brontë, wounded her to the quick by expressions of censure which she believed to be unjust and unfounded, but which, if correct and true, went deeper than any merely artistic fault. An author may bring himself to believe that he can bear blame with equanimity, from whatever quarter it comes; but its force is derived altogether from the character of this. To the public, one reviewer may be the same impersonal being as another; but an author has frequently a far deeper significance to attach to opinions. They are the verdicts of those whom he respects and admires, or the mere words of those for whose judgment he cares not a jot. It is this knowledge of the individual worth of the reviewer's opinion, which makes the censures of some sink so deep, and prey so heavily upon an author's heart. And thus, in proportion to her true, firm regard for Miss Martineau, did Miss Brontë suffer under what she considered her misjudgment not merely of writing, but of character.

She had long before asked Miss Martineau to tell her whether she considered that any want of womanly delicacy or propriety was betrayed in "Jane Eyre". And on receiving Miss Martineau's assurance that she did not, Miss Brontë entreated her to declare it frankly if she thought there was any failure of this description in any future work of "Currer Bell's." The promise then given of faithful truth-speaking, Miss Martineau fulfilled when "Villette" appeared. Miss Brontë writhed under what she felt to be injustice.

This seems a fitting place to state how utterly unconscious she was of what was, by some, esteemed coarse in her writings. One day, during that visit at the Briery when I first met her, the conversation turned upon the subject of women's writing fiction; and some one remarked on the fact that, in certain instances, authoresses had much outstepped the line which men felt to be proper in works of this kind. Miss Brontë said she wondered how far this was a natural consequence of allowing the imagination to work too constantly; Sir James and Lady Kay Shuttleworth and I expressed our belief that such violations of propriety were altogether unconscious on the part of those to whom reference had been made. I remember her grave, earnest way of saying, "I trust God will take from me whatever power of invention or expression I may have, before He lets me become blind to the sense of what is fitting or unfitting to be said!"

Again, she was invariably shocked and distressed when she heard of any disapproval of "Jane Eyre" on the ground above-mentioned. Some one said to her in London, "You know, you and I, Miss Brontë, have both written naughty books!" She dwelt much on this; and, as if it weighed on her mind, took an opportunity to ask Mrs. Smith, as she would have asked a mother---if she had not been motherless from earliest childhood---whether, indeed, there was anything so wrong in "Jane Eyre."

I do not deny for myself the existence of coarseness here and there in her works, otherwise so entirely noble. I only ask those who read them to consider her life,---which has been openly laid bare before them,---and to say how it could be otherwise. She saw few men; and among these few were one or two with whom she had been acquainted since early girlhood,---who had shown her much friendliness and kindness,---through whose family she had received many pleasures,---for whose intellect she had a great respect,---but who talked before her, if not to her with as little reticence as Rochester talked to Jane Eyre. Take this in connection with her poor brother's sad life, and the out-spoken people among whom she lived,--- remember her strong feeling of the duty of representing life as it really is, not as it ought to be,---and then do her justice for all that she was, and all that she would have been (had God spared her), rather than censure her because circumstances forced her to touch pitch, as it were, and by it her hand was for a moment defiled. It was but skin-deep. Every change in her life was purifying her; it hardly could raise her. Again I cry, "If she had but lived!"

The misunderstanding with Miss Martineau on account of "Villette," was the cause of bitter regret to Miss Brontë. Her woman's nature had been touched, as she thought, with insulting misconception; and she had dearly loved the person who had thus unconsciously wounded her. It was but in the January just past that she had written as follows, in reply to a friend, the tenor of whose letter we may guess from this answer:---

"I read attentively all you say about Miss Martineau; the sincerity and constancy of your solicitude touch me very much; I should grieve to neglect or oppose your advice, and yet I do not feel it would be right to give Miss Martineau up entirely. There is in her nature much that is very noble; hundreds have forsaken her, more, I fear, in the apprehension that their fair names may suffer, if seen in connection with hers, than from any pure convictions, such as you suggest, of harm consequent on her fatal tenets. With these fair-weather friends I cannot bear to rank; and for her sin, is it not one of those of which God and not man must judge?

"To speak the truth, my dear Miss ------, I believe, if you were in my place, and knew Miss Martineau as I do,---if you had shared with me the proofs of her genuine kindliness, and had seen how she secretly suffers from abandonment,---you would be the last to give her up; you would separate the sinner from the sin, and feel as if the right lay rather in quietly adhering to her in her strait, while that adherence is unfashionable and unpopular, than in turning on her your back when the world sets the example. I believe she is one of those whom opposition and desertion make obstinate in error; while patience and tolerance touch her deeply and keenly, and incline her to ask of her own heart whether the course she has been pursuing may not possibly be a faulty course."

Kindly and faithful words! which Miss Martineau never knew of; to be repaid in words more grand and tender, when Charlotte lay deaf and cold by her dead sisters. In spite of their short sorrowful misunderstanding, they were a pair of noble women and faithful friends.

I turn to a pleasanter subject. While she was in London, Miss Brontë had seen Lawrence's portrait of Mr. Thackeray, and admired it extremely. Her first words, after she had stood before it some time in silence, were, "And there came up a Lion out of Judah!" The likeness was by this time engraved, and Mr. Smith sent her a copy of it.

To G. SMITH, ESQ.

"Haworth, Feb. 26th, 1853.

"My dear Sir,---At a late hour yesterday evening, I had the honour of receiving, at Haworth Parsonage, a distinguished guest, none other than W. M. Thackeray, Esq. Mindful of the rites of hospitality, I hung him up in state this morning. He looks superb in his beautiful, tasteful gilded gibbet. For companion he has the Duke of Wellington, (do you remember giving me that picture?) and for contrast and foil Richmond's portrait of an unworthy individual, who, in such society, must be name-less. Thackeray looks away from the latter character with a grand scorn, edifying to witness. I wonder if the giver of these gifts will ever see them on the walls where they now hang; it pleases me to fancy that one day he may. My father stood for a quarter of an hour this morning examining the great man's picture. The conclusion of his survey was, that he thought it a puzzling head; if he had known nothing previously of the original's character; he could not have read it in his features. I wonder at this. To me the broad brow seems to express intellect. Certain lines about the nose and cheek, betray the satirist and cynic; the mouth indicates a child-like simplicity---perhaps even a degree of irresoluteness, inconsistency---weakness in short, but a weakness not unamiable. The engraving seems to me very good. A certain not quite Christian expression---'not to put too fine a point upon it'---an expression of spite, most vividly marked in the original, is here softened, and perhaps a little---a very little---of the power has escaped in this ameliorating process. Did it strike you thus?"

Miss Brontë was in much better health during this winter of 1852-3, than she had been the year before.

"For my part," (she wrote to me in February) "I have thus far borne the cold weather well. I have taken long walks on the crackling snow, and felt the frosty air bracing. This winter has, for me, not been like last winter. December, January, February, '51-2, passed like a long stormy night, conscious of one painful dream) all solitary grief and sickness. The corresponding l in '52-3 have gone over my head quietly and not uncheerfully. Thank God for the change and the repose! How welcome it has been He only knows! My father too has borne the season well; and my book, and its reception thus far, have pleased and cheered him."

In March the quiet Parsonage had the honour of receiving a visit from the then Bishop of Ripon. He remained one night with Mr. Brontë. In the evening, some of the neighbouring clergy were invited to meet him at tea and supper; and during the latter meal, some of the "curates" began merrily to upbraid Miss Brontë with "putting them into a book;" and she, shrinking from thus having her character as authoress thrust upon her at her own table, and in the presence of a stranger, pleasantly appealed to the bishop as to whether it was quite fair thus to drive her, into a corner. His Lordship, I have been told, was agreeably impressed with the gentle unassuming manners of his hostess, and with the perfect propriety and consistency of the arrangements in the modest household. So much for the Bishop's recollection of his visit. Now we will turn to hers.

"March 4th.

"The Bishop has been, and is gone. He is certainly a most charming Bishop; the most benignant gentleman that ever put on lawn sleeves; yet stately too, and quite competent to check encroachments. His visit passed capitally well; and at its close, as he was going away, he expressed himself thoroughly gratified with all he had seen. The Inspector has been also in the course of the past week; so that I have had a somewhat busy time of it. If you could have been at Haworth to share the pleasures of the company, without having been inconvenienced by the little bustle of the preparation, I should have been VERY glad. But the house was a good deal put out of its way, as you may suppose; all passed, however, orderly, quietly, and well. Martha waited very nicely, and I had a person to help her in the kitchen. Papa kept up, too, fully as well as I expected, though I doubt whether he could have borne another day of it. My penalty came on in a strong headache as soon as the Bishop was gone: how thankful I was that it had patiently waited his departure. I continue stupid to-day: of course, it is the reaction consequent on several days of extra exertion and excitement. It is very well to talk of receiving a Bishop without trouble, but you MUST prepare for him."

By this time some of the Reviews had began to find fault with "Villette." Miss Brontë made her old request.

TO W. S. WILLIAMS, ESQ.

"My dear Sir,---Were a review to appear, inspired with treble their animus, PRAY do not withhold it from me. I like to see the satisfactory notices,---especially I like to carry them to my father; but I MUST see such as are UNsatisfactory and hostile; these are for my own especial edification;---it is in these I best read public feeling and opinion. To shun examination into the dangerous and disagreeable seems to me cowardly. I long always to know what really IS, and am only unnerved when kept in the dark. . . . . . .

"As to the character of 'Lucy Snowe,' my intention from the first was that she should not occupy the pedestal to which 'Jane Eyre' was raised by some injudicious admirers. She is where I meant her to be, and where no charge of self-laudation can touch her.

"The note you sent this morning from Lady Harriette St. Clair, is precisely to the same purport as Miss Muloch's request,---an application for exact and authentic information respecting the fate of M. Paul Emanuel! You see how much the ladies think of this little man, whom you none of you like. I had a letter the other day; announcing that a lady of some note, who had always determined that whenever she married, her husband should be the counterpart of 'Mr. Knightly' in Miss Austen's 'Emma,' had now changed her mind, and vowed that she would either find the duplicate of Professor Emanuel, or remain for ever single! I have sent Lady Harriette an answer so worded as to leave the matter pretty much where it was. Since the little puzzle amuses the ladies, it would be a pity to spoil their sport by giving them the key."

When Easter, with its duties arising out of sermons to be preached by strange clergymen who had afterwards to be entertained at the Parsonage,---with Mechanics' Institute Meetings, and school tea-drinkings, was over and gone; she came, at the close of April, to visit us in Manchester. We had a friend, a young lady, staying with us. Miss Brontë had expected to find us alone; and although our friend was gentle and sensible after Miss Brontë's own heart, yet her presence was enough to create a nervous tremour. I was aware that both of our guests were unusually silent; and I saw a little shiver run from time to time over Miss Brontë's frame. I could account for the modest reserve of the young lady; and the next day Miss Brontë told me how the unexpected sight of a strange face had affected her.

It was now two or three years since I had witnessed a similar effect produced on her; in anticipation of a quiet evening at Fox-How; and since then she had seen many and various people in London: but the physical sensations produced by shyness were still the same; and on the following day she laboured under severe headache. I had several opportunities of perceiving how this nervousness was ingrained in her constitution, and how acutely she suffered in striving to overcome it. One evening we had, among other guests, two sisters who sang Scottish ballads exquisitely. Miss Brontë had been sitting quiet and constrained till they began "The Bonnie House of Airlie," but the effect of that and "Carlisle Yetts," which followed, was as irresistible as the playing of the Piper of Hamelin. The beautiful clear light came into her eyes; her lips quivered with emotion; she forgot herself, rose, and crossed the room to the piano, where she asked eagerly for song after song. The sisters begged her to come and see them the next morning, when they would sing as long as ever she liked; and she promised gladly and thankfully. But on reaching the house her courage failed. We walked some time up and down the street; she upbraiding herself all the while for folly, and trying to dwell on the sweet echoes in her memory rather than on the thought of a third sister who would have to be faced if we went in. But it was of no use; and dreading lest this struggle with herself might bring on one of her trying headaches, I entered at last and made the best apology I could for her non-appearance. Much of this nervous dread of encountering strangers I ascribed to the idea of her personal ugliness, which had been strongly impressed upon her imagination early in life, and which she exaggerated to herself in a remarkable manner. "I notice," said she, "that after a stranger has once looked at my face, he is careful not to let his eyes wander to that part of the room again!" A more untrue idea never entered into any one's head. Two gentlemen who saw her during this visit, without knowing at the time who she was, were singularly attracted by her appearance; and this feeling of attraction towards a pleasant countenance, sweet voice, and gentle timid manners, was so strong in one as to conquer a dislike he had previously entertained to her works.

There was another circumstance that came to my knowledge at this period which told secrets about the finely-strung frame. One night I was on the point of relating some dismal ghost story, just before bed-time. She shrank from hearing it, and confessed that she was superstitious, and, prone at all times to the involuntary recurrence of any thoughts of ominous gloom which might have been suggested to her. She said that on first coming to us, she had found a letter on her dressing-table from a friend in Yorkshire, containing a story which had impressed her vividly ever since;---that it mingled with her dreams at night, and made her sleep restless and unrefreshing.

One day we asked two gentlemen to meet her at dinner; expecting that she and they would have a mutual pleasure in making each other's acquaintance. To our disappointment she drew back with timid reserve from all their advances, replying to their questions and remarks in the briefest manner possible; till at last they gave up their efforts to draw her into conversation in despair, and talked to each other and my husband on subjects of recent local interest. Among these Thackeray's Lectures (which had lately been delivered in Manchester) were spoken of and that on Fielding especially dwelt upon. One gentleman objected to it strongly, as calculated to do moral harm, and regretted that a man having so great an influence over the tone of thought of the day, as Thackeray, should not more carefully weigh his words. The other took the opposite view. He said that Thackeray described men from the inside, as it were; through his strong power of dramatic sympathy, he identified himself with certain characters, felt their temptations, entered into their pleasures, etc. This roused Miss Brontë, who threw herself warmly into the discussion; the ice of her reserve was broken, and from that time she showed her interest in all that was said, and contributed her share to any conversation that was going on in the course of the evening.

What she said, and which part she took, in the dispute about Thackeray's lecture, may be gathered from the following letter, referring to the same subject:---

"The Lectures arrived safely; I have read them through twice. They must be studied to be appreciated. I thought well of them when I heard them delivered, but now I see their real power; and it is great. The lecture on Swift was new to me; I thought it almost matchless. Not that by any means I always agree with Mr. Thackeray's opinions, but his force, his penetration, his pithy simplicity, his eloquence---his manly sonorous eloquence,---command entire admiration. . . . Against his errors I protest, were it treason to do so. I was present at the Fielding lecture: the hour spent in listening to it was a painful hour. That Thackeray was wrong in his way of treating Fielding's character and vices, my conscience told me. After reading that lecture, I trebly felt that he was wrong---dangerously wrong. Had Thackeray owned a son, grown, or growing up, and a son, brilliant but reckless---would he have spoken in that light way of courses that lead to disgrace and the grave? He speaks of it all as if he theorised; as if he had never been called on, in the course of his life, to witness the actual consequences of such failings; as if he had never stood by and seen the issue, the final result of it all. I believe, if only once the prospect of a promising life blasted on the outset by wild ways had passed close under his eyes, he never COULD have spoken with such levity of what led to its piteous destruction. Had I a brother yet living, I should tremble to let him read Thackeray's lecture on Fielding. I should hide it away from him. If, in spite of precaution, it should fall into his hands, I should earnestly pray him not to be misled by the voice of the charmer, let him charm never so wisely. Not that for a moment I would have had Thackeray to ABUSE Fielding, or even Pharisaically to condemn his life; but I do most deeply grieve that it never entered into his heart sadly and nearly to feel the peril of such a career, that he might have dedicated some of his great strength to a potent warning against its adoption by any young man. I believe temptation often assails the finest manly natures; as the pecking sparrow or destructive wasp attacks the sweetest and mellowest fruit, eschewing what is sour and crude. The true lover of his race ought to devote his vigour to guard and protect; he should sweep away every lure with a kind of rage at its treachery. You will think this far too serious, I dare say; but the subject is serious, and one cannot help feeling upon it earnestly."

CHAPTER XIII.

After her visit to Manchester, she had to return to a re-opening of the painful circumstances of the previous winter, as the time drew near for Mr. Nicholl's departure from Haworth. A testimonial of respect from the parishioners was presented, at a public meeting, to one who had faithfully served them for eight years: and he left the place, and she saw no chance of hearing a word about him in the future, unless it was some second-hand scrap of intelligence, dropped out accidentally by one of the neighbouring clergymen.

I had promised to pay her a visit on my return from London in June; but, after the day was fixed, a letter came from Mr. Brontë, saying that she was suffering from so severe an attack of influenza, accompanied with such excruciating pain in the head, that he must request me to defer my visit until she was better. While sorry for the cause, I did not regret that my going was delayed till the season when the moors would be all glorious with the purple bloom of the heather; and thus present a scene about which she had often spoken to me. So we agreed that I should not come to her before August or September. Meanwhile, I received a letter from which I am tempted to take an extract, as it shows both her conception of what fictitious writing ought to be, and her always kindly interest in what I was doing.

"July 9th, 1853.

"Thank you for your letter; it was as pleasant as a quiet chat, as welcome as spring showers, as reviving as a friend's visit; in short, it was very like a page of 'Cranford.' . . . A thought strikes me. Do you, who have so many friends,---so large a circle of acquaintance,---find it easy, when you sit down to write, to isolate yourself from all those ties, and their sweet associations, so as to be your OWN WOMAN, uninfluenced or swayed by the consciousness of how your work may affect other minds; what blame or what sympathy it may call forth? Does no luminous cloud ever come between you and the severe Truth, as you know it in your own secret and clear-seeing soul? In a word, are you never tempted to make your characters more amiable than the Life, by the inclination to assimilate your thoughts to the thoughts of those who always FEEL kindly, but sometimes fail to SEE justly? Don't answer the question; it is not intended to be answered. . . . Your account of Mrs. Stowe was stimulatingly interesting. I long to see you, to get you to say it, and many other things, all over again. My father continues better. I am better too; but to-day I have a headache again, which will hardly let me write coherently. Give my dear love to M. and M., dear happy girls as they are. You cannot now transmit my message to F. and J. I prized the little wild-flower,---not that I think the sender cares for me; she DOES not, and CANNOT, for she does not know me;---but no matter. In my reminiscences she is a person of a certain distinction. I think hers a fine little nature, frank and of genuine promise. I often see her; as she appeared, stepping supreme from the portico towards the carriage, that evening we went to see 'Twelfth Night.' I believe in J.'s future; I like what speaks in her movements, and what is written upon her face."

Towards the latter end of September I went to Haworth. At the risk of repeating something which I have previously said, I will copy out parts of a letter which I wrote at the time.

"It was a dull, drizzly Indian-inky day, all the way on the railroad to Keighley, which is a rising wool-manufacturing town, lying in a hollow between hills---not a pretty hollow, but more what the Yorkshire people call a 'bottom,' or 'botham.' I left Keighley in a car for Haworth, four miles off---four tough, steep, scrambling miles, the road winding between the wavelike hills that rose and fell on every side of the horizon, with a long illimitable sinuous look, as if they were a part of the line of the Great Serpent, which the Norse legend says girdles the world. The day was lead-coloured; the road had stone factories alongside of it,--- grey, dull-coloured rows of stone cottages belonging to these factories, and then we came to poor, hungry-looking fields;---stone fences everywhere, and trees nowhere. Haworth is a long, straggling village one steep narrow street---so steep that the flag-stones with which it is paved are placed end-ways, that the horses' feet may have something to cling to, and not slip down backwards; which if they did, they would soon reach Keighley. But if the horses had cats' feet and claws, they would do all the better. Well, we (the man, horse, car; and I) clambered up this street, and reached the church dedicated to St. Autest (who was he?); then we turned off into a lane on the left, past the curate's lodging at the Sexton's, past the school-house, up to the Parsonage yard-door. I went round the house to the front door, looking to the church;---moors everywhere beyond and above. The crowded grave-yard surrounds the house and small grass enclosure for drying clothes.

"I don't know that I ever saw a spot more exquisitely clean; the most dainty place for that I ever saw. To be sure, the life is like clock-work. No one comes to the house; nothing disturbs the deep repose; hardly a voice is heard; you catch the ticking of the clock in the kitchen, or the buzzing of a fly in the parlour, all over the house. Miss Brontë sits alone in her parlour; breakfasting with her father in his study at nine o'clock. She helps in the housework; for one of their servants, Tabby, is nearly ninety, and the other only a girl. Then I accompanied her in her walks on the sweeping moors the heather-bloom had been blighted by a thunder-storm a day or two before, and was all of a livid brown colour, instead of the blaze of purple glory it ought to have been. Oh those high, wild, desolate moors, up above the whole world, and the very realms of silence! Home to dinner at two. Mr. Brontë has his dinner sent into him. All the small table arrangements had the same dainty simplicity about them. Then we rested, and talked over the clear, bright fire; it is a cold country, and the fires were a pretty warm dancing light all over the house. The parlour had been evidently refurnished within the last few years, since Miss Brontë's success has enabled her to have a little more money to spend. Everything fits into, and is in harmony with, the idea of a country parsonage, possessed by people of very moderate means. The prevailing colour of the room is crimson, to make a warm setting for the cold grey landscape without. There is her likeness by Richmond, and an engraving from Lawrence's picture of Thackeray; and two recesses, on each side of the high, narrow, old-fashioned mantelpiece, filled with books,---books given to her; books she has bought, and which tell of her individual pursuits and tastes; NOT standard books.

"She cannot see well, and does little beside knitting. The way she weakened her eyesight was this: When she was sixteen or seventeen, she wanted much to draw; and she copied niminipimini copper-plate engravings out of annuals, ('stippling,' don't the artists call it?) every little point put in, till at the end of six months she had produced an exquisitely faithful copy of the engraving. She wanted to learn to express her ideas by drawing. After she had tried to DRAW stories, and not succeeded, she took the better mode of writing; but in so small a hand, that it is almost impossible to decipher what she wrote at this time.

"But now to return to our quiet hour of rest after dinner. I soon observed that her habits of order were such that she could not go on with the conversation, if a chair was out of its place; everything was arranged with delicate regularity. We talked over the old times of her childhood; of her elder sister's (Maria's) death,---just like that of Helen Burns in 'Jane Eyre;' of those strange, starved days at school; of the desire (almost amounting to illness) of expressing herself in some way,---writing or drawing; of her weakened eyesight, which prevented her doing anything for two years, from the age of seventeen to nineteen; of her being a governess; of her going to Brussels; whereupon I said I disliked Lucy Snowe, and we discussed M. Paul Emanuel; and I told her of ------'s admiration of 'Shirley,' which pleased her; for the character of Shirley was meant for her sister Emily, about whom she is never tired of talking, nor I of listening. Emily must have been a remnant of the Titans,---great-grand-daughter of the giants who used to inhabit earth. One day, Miss Brontë brought down a rough, common-looking oil-painting, done by her brother, of herself,---a little, rather prim-looking girl of eighteen,---and the two other sisters, girls of sixteen and fourteen, with cropped hair, and sad, dreamy-looking eyes. . . . Emily had a great dog---half mastiff, half bull-dog---so savage, etc. . . . This dog went to her funeral, walking side by side with her father; and then, to the day of its death, it slept at her room door; snuffing under it, and whining every morning.

"We have generally had another walk before tea, which is at six; at half-past eight, prayers; and by nine, all the household are in bed, except ourselves. We sit up together till ten, or past; and after I go, I hear Miss Brontë comedown and walk up and down the room for an hour or so."

Copying this letter has brought the days of that pleasant visit very clear before me,---very sad in their clearness. We were so happy together; we were so full of interest in each other's subjects. The day seemed only too short for what we had to say and to hear. I understood her life the better for seeing the place where it had been spent---where she had loved and suffered. Mr. Brontë was a most courteous host; and when he was with us,---at breakfast in his study, or at tea in Charlotte's parlour,---he had a sort of grand and stately way of describing past times, which tallied well with his striking appearance. He never seemed quite to have lost the feeling that Charlotte was a child to be guided and ruled, when she was present; and she herself submitted to this with a quiet docility that half amused, half astonished me. But when she had to leave the room, then all his pride in her genius and fame came out. He eagerly listened to everything I could tell him of the high admiration I had at any time heard expressed for her works. He would ask for certain speeches over and over again, as if he desired to impress them on his memory.

I remember two or three subjects of the conversations which she and I held in the evenings, besides those alluded to in my letter.

I asked her whether she had ever taken opium, as the description given of its effects in "Villette" was so exactly like what I had experienced,---vivid and exaggerated presence of objects, of which the outlines were indistinct, or lost in golden mist, etc. She replied, that she had never, to her knowledge, taken a grain of it in any shape, but that she had followed the process she always adopted when she had to describe anything which had not fallen within her own experience; she had thought intently on it for many and many a night before falling to sleep,---wondering what it was like, or how it would be,---till at length, sometimes after the progress of her story had been arrested at this one point for weeks, she wakened up in the morning with all clear before her, as if she had in reality gone through the experience, and then could describe it, word for word, as it had happened. I cannot account for this psychologically; I only am sure that it was so, because she said it.

She made many inquiries as to Mrs. Stowe's personal appearance; and it evidently harmonised well with some theory of hers, to hear that the author of Uncle Tom's Cabin was small and slight. It was another theory of hers, that no mixtures of blood produced such fine characters, mentally and morally, as the Scottish and English.

I recollect, too, her saying how acutely she dreaded a charge of plagiarism, when, after she had written "Jane Eyre;" she read the thrilling effect of the mysterious scream at midnight in Mrs. Marsh's story of the "Deformed." She also said that, when she read the "Neighbours," she thought every one would fancy that she must have taken her conception of Jane Eyre's character from that of "Francesca," the narrator of Miss Bremer's story. For my own part, I cannot see the slightest resemblance between the two characters, and so I told her; but she persisted in saying that Francesca was Jane Eyre married to a good-natured "Bear" of a Swedish surgeon.

We went, not purposely, but accidentally, to see various poor people in our distant walks. From one we had borrowed an umbrella; in the house of another we had taken shelter from a rough September storm. In all these cottages, her quiet presence was known. At three miles from her home, the chair was dusted for her, with a kindly "Sit ye down, Miss Brontë;" and she knew what absent or ailing members of the family to inquire after. Her quiet, gentle words, few though they might be, were evidently grateful to those Yorkshire ears. Their welcome to her, though rough and curt, was sincere and hearty.

We talked about the different courses through which life ran. She said, in her own composed manner, as if she had accepted the theory as a fact, that she believed some were appointed beforehand to sorrow and much disappointment; that it did not fall to the lot of all---as Scripture told us---to have their lines fall in pleasant places; that it was well for those who had rougher paths, to perceive that such was God's will concerning them, and try to moderate their expectations, leaving hope to those of a different doom, and seeking patience and resignation as the virtues they were to cultivate. I took a different view: I thought that human lots were more equal than she imagined; that to some happiness and sorrow came in strong patches of light and shadow, (so to speak), while in the lives of others they were pretty equally blended throughout. She smiled, and shook her head, and said she was trying to school herself against ever anticipating any pleasure; that it was better to be brave and submit faithfully; there was some good reason, which we should know in time, why sorrow and disappointment were to be the lot of some on earth. It was better to acknowledge this, and face out the truth in a religious faith.

In connection with this conversation, she named a little abortive plan which I had not heard of till then; how, in the previous July, she had been tempted to join some friends (a married couple and their child) in an excursion to Scotland. They set out joyfully; she with especial gladness, for Scotland was a land which had its roots deep down in her imaginative affections, and the glimpse of two days at Edinburgh was all she had as yet seen of it. But, at the first stage after Carlisle, the little yearling child was taken with a slight indisposition; the anxious parents fancied that strange diet disagreed with it, and hurried back to their Yorkshire home as eagerly as, two or three days before, they had set their faces northward, in hopes of a month's pleasant ramble.

We parted with many intentions, on both sides, of renewing very frequently the pleasure we had had in being together. We agreed that when she wanted bustle, or when I wanted quiet, we were to let each other know, and exchange visits as occasion required.

I was aware that she had a great anxiety on her mind at this time; and being acquainted with its nature, I could not but deeply admire the patient docility which she displayed in her conduct towards her father.

Soon after I left Haworth, she went on a visit to Miss Wooler, who was then staying at Hornsea. The time passed quietly and happily with this friend, whose society was endeared to her by every year.

To Miss WOOLER

"Dec. 12th, 1853.

"I wonder how you are spending these long winter evenings. Alone, probably, like me. The thought often crosses me, as I sit by myself, how pleasant it would be if you lived within a walking distance, and I could go to you sometimes, or have you to come and spend a day and night with me. Yes; I did enjoy that week at Hornsea, and I look forward to spring as the period when you will fulfil your promise of coming to visit me. I fear you must be very solitary at Hornsea. How hard to some people of the world it would seem to live your life! how utterly impossible to live it with a serene spirit and an unsoured disposition! It seems wonderful to me, because you are not, like Mrs. ------, phlegmatic and impenetrable, but received from nature feelings of the very finest edge. Such feelings, when they are locked up, sometimes damage the mind and temper. They don't with you. It must be partly principle, partly self-discipline, which keeps you as you are."

Of course, as I draw nearer to the years so recently closed, it becomes impossible for me to write with the same fulness of detail as I have hitherto not felt it wrong to use. Miss Brontë passed the winter of 1853-4 in a solitary and anxious manner. But the great conqueror Time was slowly achieving his victory over strong prejudice and human resolve. By degrees Mr. Brontë became reconciled to the idea of his daughter's marriage.

There is one other letter, addressed to Mr. Dobell, which developes the intellectual side of her character, before we lose all thought of the authoress in the timid and conscientious woman about to become a wife, and in the too short, almost perfect, happiness of her nine months of wedded life.

"Haworth, near Keighley,

"Feb. 3rd, 1854.

"My dear Sir,---I can hardly tell you how glad I am to have an opportunity of explaining that taciturnity to which you allude. Your letter came at a period of danger and care, when my father was very ill, and I could not leave his bedside. I answered no letters at that time, and yours was one of three or four that, when leisure returned to me, and I came to consider their purport, it seemed to me such that the time was past for answering them, and I laid them finally aside. If you remember, you asked me to go to London; it was too late either to go or to decline. I was sure you had left London. One circumstance you mentioned---your wife's illness---which I have thought of many a time, and wondered whether she is better. In your present note you do not refer to her, but I trust her health has long ere now been quite restored.

"'Balder' arrived safely. I looked at him, before cutting his leaves with singular pleasure. Remembering well his elder brother, the potent 'Roman,' it was natural to give a cordial welcome to a fresh scion of the same house and race. I have read him. He impressed me thus he teems with power; I found in him a wild wealth of life, but I thought his favourite and favoured child would bring his sire trouble---would make his heart ache. It seemed to me, that his strength and beauty were not so much those of Joseph, the pillar of Jacob's age, as of the Prodigal Son, who troubled his father, though he always kept his love.

"How is it that while the first-born of genius often brings honour, the second as almost often proves a source of depression and care? I could almost prophesy that your third will atone for any anxiety inflicted by this his immediate predecessor.

"There is power in that character of 'Balder,' and to me a certain horror. Did you mean it to embody, along with force, any of the special defects of the artistic character? It seems to me that those defects were never thrown out in stronger lines. I did not and could not think you meant to offer him as your cherished ideal of the true, great poet; I regarded him as a vividly-coloured picture of inflated self-esteem, almost frantic aspiration; of a nature that has made a Moloch of intellect---offered up; in pagan fires, the natural affections---sacrificed the heart to the brain. Do we not all know that true greatness is simple, self-oblivious, prone to unambitious, unselfish attachments? I am certain you feel this truth in your heart of hearts.

"But if the critics err now (as yet I have seen none of their lucubrations), you shall one day set them right in the second part of 'Balder.' You shall show them that you too know---better, perhaps, than they---that the truly great man is too sincere in his affections to grudge a sacrifice; too much absorbed in his work to talk loudly about it; too intent on finding the best way to accomplish what he undertakes to think great things of himself---the instrument. And if God places seeming impediments in his way---if his duties sometimes seem to hamper his powers---he feels keenly, perhaps writhes, under the slow torture of hindrance and delay; but if there be a true man's heart in his breast, he can bear, submit, wait patiently.

"Whoever speaks to me of 'Balder'---though I live too retired a life to come often in the way of comment---shall be answered according to your suggestion and my own impression. Equity demands that you should be your own interpreter. Good-bye for the present, and believe me,
"Faithfully and gratefully,

"CHARLOTTE BRONTË.

"Sydney Dobell, Esq."

A letter to her Brussels schoolfellow gives an idea of the external course of things during this winter.

"March 8th.

"I was very glad to see your handwriting again. It is, I believe, a year since I heard from you. Again and again you have recurred to my thoughts lately, and I was beginning to have some sad presages as to the cause of your silence. Your letter happily does away with all these; it brings, on the whole, glad tidings both of your papa, mama, your sisters, and, last but not least, your dear respected English self.

"My dear father has borne the severe winter very well, a circumstance for which I feel the more thankful as he had many weeks of very precarious health last summer, following an attack from which he suffered in June, and which for a few hours deprived him totally of sight, though neither his mind, speech, nor even his powers of motion were in the least affected. I can hardly tell you how thankful I was, when, after that dreary and almost despairing interval of utter darkness, some gleam of daylight became visible to him once more. I had feared that paralysis had seized the optic nerve. A sort of mist remained for a long time; and, indeed, his vision is not yet perfectly clear, but he can read, write, and walk about, and he preaches TWICE every Sunday, the curate only reading the prayers. YOU can well understand how earnestly I wish and pray that sight may be spared him to the end; he so dreads the privation of blindness. His mind is just as strong and active as ever, and politics interest him as they do YOUR papa. The Czar, the war, the alliance between France and England---into all these things he throws himself heart and soul; they seem to carry him back to his comparatively young days, and to renew the excitement of the last great European struggle. Of course my father's sympathies (and mine too) are all with Justice and Europe against Tyranny and Russia.

"Circumstanced as I have been, you will comprehend that I have had neither the leisure nor the inclination to go from home much during the past year. I spent a week with Mrs. Gaskell in the spring, and a fortnight with some other friends more recently, and that includes the whole of my visiting since I saw you last. My life is, indeed, very uniform and retired---more so than is quite healthful either for mind or body; yet I find reason for often-renewed feelings of gratitude, in the sort of support which still comes and cheers me on from time to time. My health, though not unbroken, is, I sometimes fancy, rather stronger on the whole than it was three years ago: headache and dyspepsia are my worst ailments. Whether I shall come up to town this season for a few days I do not yet know; but if I do, I shall hope to call in P. Place."

In April she communicated the fact of her engagement to Miss Wooler.

"Haworth, April 12th.

"My dear Miss Wooler,---The truly kind interest which you always taken in my affairs makes me feel that it is due to you to transmit an early communication on a subject respecting which I have already consulted you more than once. I must tell you then, that since I wrote last, papa's mind has gradually come round to a view very different to that which he once took; and that after some correspondence, and as the result of a visit Mr. Nicholls paid here about a week ago, it was agreed that he was to resume the curacy of Haworth, as soon as papa's present assistant is provided with a situation, and in due course of time he is to be received as an inmate into this house.

"It gives me unspeakable content to see that now my father has once admitted this new view of the case, he dwells on it very complacently. In all arrangements, his convenience and seclusion will be scrupulously respected. Mr. Nicholls seems deeply to feel the wish to comfort and sustain his declining years. I think from Mr. Nicholls' character I may depend on this not being a mere transitory impulsive feeling, but rather that it will be accepted steadily as a duty, and discharged tenderly as an office of affection. The destiny which Providence in His goodness and wisdom seems to offer me will not, I am aware, be generally regarded as brilliant, but I trust I see in it some germs of real happiness. I trust the demands of both feeling and duty will be in some measure reconciled by the step in contemplation. It is Mr. Nicholls' wish that the marriage should take place this summer; he urges the month of July, but that seems very soon.

"When you write to me, tell me how you are. . . . I have now decidedly declined the visit to London; the ensuing three months will bring me abundance of occupation; I could not afford to throw away a month. . . . Papa has just got a letter from the good and dear bishop, which has touched and pleased us much; it expresses so cordial an approbation of Mr. Nicholls' return to Haworth (respecting which he was consulted), and such kind gratification at the domestic arrangements which are to ensue. It seems his penetration discovered the state of things when he was here in June 1853."

She expressed herself in other letters, as thankful to One who had guided her through much difficulty and much distress and perplexity of mind; and yet she felt what most thoughtful women do, who marry when the first flush of careless youth is over, that there was a strange half-sad feeling, in making announcements of an engagement---for cares and fears came mingled inextricably with hopes. One great relief to her mind at this time was derived from the conviction that her father took a positive pleasure in all the thoughts about and preparations for her wedding. He was anxious that things should be expedited, and was much interested in every preliminary arrangement for the reception of Mr. Nicholls into the Parsonage as his daughter's husband. This step was rendered necessary by Mr. Brontë's great age, and failing sight, which made it a paramount obligation on so dutiful a daughter as Charlotte, to devote as much time and assistance as ever in attending to his wants. Mr. Nicholls, too, hoped that he might be able to add some comfort and pleasure by his ready presence, on any occasion when the old clergyman might need his services.

At the beginning of May, Miss Brontë left home to pay three visits before her marriage. The first was to us. She only remained three days, as she had to go to the neighbourhood of Leeds, there to make such purchases as were required for her marriage. Her preparations, as she said, could neither be expensive nor extensive; consisting chiefly in a modest replenishing of her wardrobe, some re-papering and re-painting in the Parsonage; and, above all, converting the small flagged passage-room, hitherto used only for stores (which was behind her sitting room), into a study for her husband. On this idea, and plans for his comfort, as well as her father's, her mind dwelt a good deal; and we talked them over with the same unwearying happiness which, I suppose, all women feel in such discussions---especially when money considerations call for that kind of contrivance which Charles Lamb speaks of in his Essay on Old China, as forming so great an addition to the pleasure of obtaining a thing at last.

"Haworth, May 22nd.

"Since I came home I have been very busy stitching; the little new room is got into order, and the green and white curtains are up; they exactly suit the papering, and look neat and clean enough. I had a letter a day or two since, announcing that Mr. Nicholls comes to-morrow. I feel anxious about him; more anxious on one point than I dare quite express to myself. It seems he has again been suffering sharply from his rheumatic affection. I hear this not from himself, but from another quarter. He was ill while I was in Manchester and B------. He uttered no complaint to me; dropped no hint on the subject. Alas he was hoping he had got the better of it, and I know how this contradiction of his hopes will sadden him. For unselfish reasons he did so earnestly wish this complaint might not become chronic. I fear---I fear; but if he is doomed to suffer, so much the more will he need care and help. Well! come what may, God help and strengthen both him and me! I look forward to to-morrow with a mixture of impatience and anxiety."

Mr. Brontë had a slight illness which alarmed her much. Besides, all the weight of care involved in the household preparations pressed on the bride in this case---not unpleasantly, only to the full occupation of her time. She was too busy to unpack her wedding dresses for several days after they arrived from Halifax; yet not too busy to think of arrangements by which Miss Wooler's journey to be present at the marriage could be facilitated.

"I write to Miss Wooler to-day. Would it not be better, dear, if you and she could arrange to come to Haworth on the same day, arrive at Keighley by the same train; then I could order the cab to meet you at the station, and bring you on with your luggage? In this hot weather walking would be quite out of the question, either for you or for her; and I know she would persist in doing it if left to herself, and arrive half killed. I thought it better to mention this arrangement to you first, and then, if you liked it, you could settle the time, etc., with Miss Wooler, and let me know. Be sure and give me timely information, that I may write to the Devonshire Arms about the cab.

"Mr. Nicholls is a kind, considerate fellow. With all his masculine faults, he enters into my wishes about having the thing done quietly, in a way that makes me grateful; and if nobody interferes and spoils his arrangements, he will manage it so that not a soul in Haworth shall be aware of the day. He is so thoughtful, too, about 'the ladies,'---that is, you and Miss Wooler. Anticipating, too, the very arrangements I was going to propose to him about providing for your departure, etc. He and Mr. S------ come to ------ the evening before; write me a note to let me know they are there; precisely at eight in the morning they will be in the church, and there we are to meet them. Mr. and Mrs. Grant are asked to the breakfast, not to the ceremony.

It was fixed that the marriage was to take place on the 29th of June. Her two friends arrived at Haworth Parsonage the day before; and the long summer afternoon and evening were spent by Charlotte in thoughtful arrangements for the morrow, and for her father's comfort during her absence from home. When all was finished---the trunk packed, the morning's breakfast arranged, the wedding-dress laid out,---just at bedtime, Mr. Brontë announced his intention of stopping at home while the others went to church. What was to be done? Who was to give the bride away? There were only to be the officiating clergyman, the bride and bridegroom, the bridesmaid, and Miss Wooler present. The Prayer-book was referred to; and there it was seen that the Rubric enjoins that the Minister shall receive "the woman from her father's or FRIEND'S hands," and that nothing is specified as to the sex of the "friend." So Miss Wooler, ever kind in emergency, volunteered to give her old pupil away.

The news of the wedding had slipt abroad before the little party came out of church, and many old and humble friends were there, seeing her look "like a snow-drop," as they say. Her dress was white embroidered muslin, with a lace mantle, and white bonnet trimmed with green leaves, which perhaps might suggest the resemblance to the pale wintry flower.

Mr. Nicholls and she went to visit his friends and relations in Ireland; and made a tour by Killarney, Glengariff, Tarbert, Tralee, and Cork, seeing scenery, of which she says, "some parts exceeded all I had ever imagined." . . . "I must say I like my new relations. My dear husband, too, appears in a new light in his own country. More than once I have had deep pleasure in hearing his praises on all sides. Some of the old servants and followers of the family tell me I am a most fortunate person; for that I have got one of the best gentlemen in the country. . . . I trust I feel thankful to God for having enabled me to make what seems a right choice; and I pray to be enabled to repay as I ought the affectionate devotion of a truthful, honourable man."

Henceforward the sacred doors of home are closed upon her married life. We, her loving friends, standing outside, caught occasional glimpses of brightness, and pleasant peaceful murmurs of sound, telling of the gladness within; and we looked at each other, and gently said, "After a hard and long struggle---after many cares and many bitter sorrows---she is tasting happiness now!" We thought of the slight astringencies of her character, and how they would turn to full ripe sweetness in that calm sunshine of domestic peace. We remembered her trials, and were glad in the idea that God had seen fit to wipe away the tears from her eyes. Those who saw her, saw an outward change in her look, telling of inward things. And we thought, and we hoped, and we prophesied, in our great love and reverence.

But God's ways are not as our ways!

Hear some of the low murmurs of happiness we, who listened, heard:---

"I really seem to have had scarcely a spare moment since that dim quiet June morning, when you, E------, and myself all walked down to Haworth Church. Not that I have been wearied or oppressed; but the fact is, my time is not my own now; somebody else wants a good portion of it, and says, 'we must do so and so.' We DO so and so, accordingly; and it generally seems the right thing. . . . We have had many callers from a distance, and latterly some little occupation in the way of preparing for a small village entertainment. Both Mr. Nicholls and myself wished much to make some response for the hearty welcome and general goodwill shown by the parishioners on his return; accordingly, the Sunday and day scholars and teachers, the church-ringers, singers, etc., to the number of five hundred, were asked to tea and supper in the School-room. They seemed to enjoy it much, and it was very pleasant to see their happiness. One of the villagers, in proposing my husband's health, described him as a 'consistent Christian and a kind gentleman.' I own the words touched me deeply, and I thought (as I know YOU would have thought had you been present) that to merit and win such a character was better than to earn either wealth, or fame, or power. I am disposed to echo that high but simple eulogium. . . . My dear father was not well when we returned from Ireland. I am, however, most thankful to say that he is better now. May God preserve him to us yet for some years! The wish for his continued life, together with a certain solicitude for his happiness and health, seems, I scarcely know why, even stronger in me now than before I was married. Papa has taken no duty since we returned; and each time I see Mr. Nicholls put on gown or surplice, I feel comforted to think that this marriage has secured papa good aid in his old age."

"September 19th.

"Yes! I am thankful to say my husband is in improved health and spirits. It makes me content and grateful to hear him from time to time avow his happiness in the brief, plain phrase of sincerity. My own life is more occupied than it used to be I have not so much time for thinking I am obliged to be more practical, for my dear Arthur is a very practical, as well as a very punctual and methodical man. Every morning he is in the National School by nine o'clock; he gives the children religious instruction till half-past ten. Almost every afternoon he pays visits amongst the poor parishioners. Of course, he often finds a little work for his wife to do, and I hope she is not sorry to help him. I believe it is not bad for me that his bent should be so wholly towards matters of life and active usefulness; so little inclined to the literary and contemplative. As to his continued affection and kind attentions it does not become me to say much of them; but they neither change nor diminish."

Her friend and bridesmaid came to pay them a visit in October. I was to have gone also, but I allowed some little obstacle to intervene, to my lasting regret.

"I say nothing about the war; but when I read of its horrors, I cannot help thinking that it is one of the greatest curses that ever fell upon mankind. I trust it may not last long, for it really seems to me that no glory to be gained can compensate for the sufferings which must be endured. This may seem a little ignoble and unpatriotic; but I think that as we advance towards middle age, nobleness and patriotism have a different signification to us to that which we accept while young."

"You kindly inquire after Papa. He is better, and seems to gain strength as the weather gets colder; indeed, of late years health has always been better in winter than in summer. We are all indeed pretty well; and, for my own part, it is long since I have known such comparative immunity from headache, etc., as during the last three months. My life is different from what it used to be. May God make me thankful for it! I have a good, kind, attached husband; and every day my own attachment to him grows stronger."

Late in the autumn, Sir James Kay Shuttleworth crossed the border-hills that separate Lancashire from Yorkshire, and spent two or three days with them.

About this time, Mr. Nicholls was offered a living of much greater value than his curacy at Haworth, and in many ways the proposal was a very advantageous one; but he felt himself bound to Haworth as long as Mr. Brontë lived. Still, this offer gave his wife great and true pleasure, as a proof of the respect in which her husband was held.

"Nov. 29.

"I intended to have written a line yesterday, but just as I was sitting down for the purpose, Arthur called to me to take a walk. We set off, not intending to go far; but, though wild and cloudy, it was fair in the morning; when we had got about half a mile on the moors, Arthur suggested the idea of the waterfall; after the melted snow, he said, it would be fine. I had often wished to see it in its winter power,---so we walked on. It was fine indeed; a perfect torrent racing over the rocks, white and beautiful! It began to rain while we were watching it, and we returned home under a streaming sky. However, I enjoyed the walk inexpressibly, and would not have missed the spectacle on any account."

She did not achieve this walk of seven or eight miles, in such weather, with impunity. She began to shiver soon after her return home, in spite of every precaution, and had a bad lingering sore throat and cold, which hung about her; and made her thin and weak.

"Did I tell you that our poor little Flossy is dead? She drooped for a single day, and died quietly in the night without pain. The loss even of a dog was very saddening; yet, perhaps, no dog ever had a happier life, or an easier death."

On Christmas-day she and her husband walked to the poor old woman (whose calf she had been set to seek in former and less happy days), carrying with them a great spice-cake to make glad her heart. On Christmas-day many a humble meal in Haworth was made more plentiful by her gifts.

Early in the new year (1855), Mr. and Mrs. Nicholls went to visit Sir James Kay Shuttleworth at Gawthorpe. They only remained two or three days, but it so fell out that she increased her lingering cold, by a long walk over damp ground in thin shoes.

Soon after her return, she was attacked by new sensations of perpetual nausea, and ever-recurring faintness. After this state of things had lasted for some time; she yielded to Mr. Nicholls' wish that a doctor should be sent for. He came, and assigned a natural cause for her miserable indisposition; a little patience, and all would go right. She, who was ever patient in illness, tried hard to bear up and bear on. But the dreadful sickness increased and increased, till the very sight of food occasioned nausea. "A wren would have starved on what she ate during those last six weeks," says one. Tabby's health had suddenly and utterly given way, and she died in this time of distress and anxiety respecting the last daughter of the house she had served so long. Martha tenderly waited on her mistress, and from time to time tried to cheer her with the thought of the baby that was coming. "I dare say I shall be glad some time," she would say; "but I am so ill---so weary---" Then she took to her bed, too weak to sit up. From that last couch she wrote two notes---in pencil. The first, which has no date, is addressed to her own "Dear Nell."

"I must write one line out of my weary bed. The news of M------'s probable recovery came like a ray of joy to me. I am not going to talk of my sufferings---it would be useless and painful. I want to give you an assurance, which I know will comfort you---and that is, that I find in my husband the tenderest nurse, the kindest support, the best earthly comfort that ever woman had. His patience never fails, and it is tried by sad days and broken nights. Write and tell me about Mrs. ------'s case; how long was she ill, and in what way? Papa---thank God!---is better. Our poor old Tabby is DEAD and BURIED. Give my kind love to Miss Wooler. May God comfort and help you.

"C. B. NICHOLLS."

The other---also in faint, faint pencil marks---was to her Brussels schoolfellow.
"Feb. 15th.
"A few lines of acknowledgment your letter SHALL have, whether well or ill. At present I am confined to my bed with illness, and have been so for three weeks. Up to this period, since my marriage, I have had excellent health. My husband and I live at home with my father; of course, I could not leave HIM. He is pretty well, better than last summer. No kinder, better husband than mine, it seems to me, there can be in the world. I do not want now for kind companionship in health and the tenderest nursing in sickness. Deeply I sympathise in all you tell me about Dr. W. and your excellent mother's anxiety. I trust he will not risk another operation. I cannot write more now; for I am much reduced and very weak. God bless you all.---Yours affectionately,

"C. B. NICHOLLS."

I do not think she ever wrote a line again. Long days and longer nights went by; still the same relentless nausea and faintness, and still borne on in patient trust. About the third week in March there was a change; a low wandering delirium came on; and in it she begged constantly for food and even for stimulants. She swallowed eagerly now; but it was too late. Wakening for an instant from this stupor of intelligence, she saw her husband's woe-worn face, and caught the sound of some murmured words of prayer that God would spare her. "Oh!" she whispered forth, "I am not going to die, am I? He will not separate us, we have been so happy."

Early on Saturday morning, March 31st, the solemn tolling of Haworth church-bell spoke forth the fact of her death to the villagers who had known her from a child, and whose hearts shivered within them as they thought of the two sitting desolate and alone in the old grey house.

CHAPTER XIV.

I have always been much struck with a passage in Mr. Forster's Life of Goldsmith. Speaking of the scene after his death, the writer says:---

"The staircase of Brick Court is said to have been filled with mourners, the reverse of domestic; women without a home, without domesticity of any kind, with no friend but him they had come to weep for; outcasts of that great, solitary, wicked city, to whom he had never forgotten to be kind and charitable."

This came into my mind when I heard of some of the circumstances attendant on Charlotte's funeral.

Few beyond that circle of hills knew that she, whom the nations praised far off, lay dead that Easter mooring. Of kith and kin she had more in the grave to which she was soon to be borne, than among the living. The two mourners, stunned with their great grief, desired not the sympathy of strangers. One member out of most of the families in the parish was bidden to the funeral; and it became an act of self-denial in many a poor household to give up to another the privilege of paying their last homage to her; and those who were excluded from the formal train of mourners thronged the churchyard and church, to see carried forth, and laid beside her own people, her whom, not many months ago, they had looked at as a pale white bride, entering on a new life with trembling happy hope.

Among those humble friends who passionately grieved over the dead, was a village girl who had been seduced some little time before, but who had found a holy sister in Charlotte. She had sheltered her with her help, her counsel, her strengthening words; had ministered to her needs in her time of trial. Bitter, bitter was the grief of this poor young woman, when she heard that her friend was sick unto death, and deep is her mourning until this day. A blind girl, living some four miles from Haworth, loved Mrs. Nicholls so dearly that, with many cries and entreaties, she implored those about her to lead her along the roads, and over the moor-paths, that she might hear the last solemn words, "Earth to earth, ashes to ashes, dust to dust; in sure and certain hope of the resurrection to eternal life, through our Lord Jesus Christ."

Such were the mourners over Charlotte Brontë's grave.

I have little more to say. If my readers find that I have not said enough, I have said too much. I cannot measure or judge of such a character as hers. I cannot map out vices, and virtues, and debatable land. One who knew her long and well,---the "Mary" of this Life---writes thus of her dead friend:---

"She thought much of her duty, and had loftier and clearer notions of it than most people, and held fast to them with more success. It was done, it seems to me, with much more difficulty than people have of stronger nerves, and better fortunes. All her life was but labour and pain; and she never threw down the burden for the sake of present pleasure. I don't know what use you can make of all I have said. I have written it with the strong desire to obtain appreciation for her. Yet, what does it matter? She herself appealed to the world's judgment for her use of some of the faculties she had,---not the best,---but still the only ones she could turn to strangers' benefit. They heartily, greedily enjoyed the fruits of her labours, and then found out she was much to be blamed for possessing such faculties. Why ask for a judgment on her from such a world?"

But I turn from the critical, unsympathetic public---inclined to judge harshly because they have only seen superficially and not thought deeply. I appeal to that larger and more solemn public, who know how to look with tender humility at faults and errors; how to admire generously extraordinary genius, and how to reverence with warm, full hearts all noble virtue. To that Public I commit the memory of Charlotte Brontë.

24242209R00087

Printed in Poland
by Amazon Fulfillment
Poland Sp. z o.o., Wrocław